THE GIRL WHO COULD FLY

Denise Okonkwo

THE GIRL WHO COULD FLY

ALSO BY DENISE OKONKWO

Beguiled

Under Lock and Key

For my little ones.

PART I

Chapter One
Meet Gwen

"Am I boring you, Guinevere?"

I looked up from my triangle and face doodling and glared at Mr. Grayfin. How I wish that I could knock his head right off his frail body. It would roll around on the floor, his eyes spinning like pinwheels until some jock got excited enough to pick it up for a quick game.

Mr. Grayfin. What a stupid name. Not that he isn't aptly named. Mr. Grayfin, with his tweed jackets, elbow pads, and tasseled loafers sans socks no matter the weather (I live in the Midwest.) is like an outdated and grossly out of place cliché.

"Nope," I replied, lying. "Everything is good."

Mr. Grayfin's lips curled at the edges as he approached my desk. He hovered over me and eyed my notebook. He stood so close that I could almost reach out and grab one of his extra-long nose hairs. Not that I would actually do that. Gross. "Your artwork aspires to mediocrity," he said. "And yet it has an almost appealing quality to it. *Almost*. Maybe your talents would have been better spent with paint and brush rather than the demands of this class."

Some of the students in the class made a low 'oooo' sound. Embarrassment dragged me down several inches in my chair. Anger pursed my lips. I refrained from making eye contact with anyone. Didn't want to reveal any emotions. Didn't want to appear vulnerable. I didn't want anyone to know how much Mr. Grayfin got to me, especially Mr. Grayfin.

"You really shouldn't waste words of kindness on her, Mr. Grayfin. She can handle the truth. Surely she has heard worse from her parents given their frequent disappointment in her. They probably wish they stopped at one child. I heard that she is the reason behind her dad leaving her mom."

Vivienne Sato. If I could have one wish in life, just one, it would be to do away with Vivienne Sato. Not just make her disappear. No, that would be too easy and she deserves so much more than that. I would first do away with her hair. She is always tossing it around and giggling as she wraps it around her index finger. She gloats that she doesn't do anything to create the shine that so many find enviable. No one has ever told her that they envy her hair; she just takes this assumption as a fact. Sometimes she chews the ends of her hair. This is a flaw, but not enough to eradicate my desire for her hair to vacate its current residence.

Next, I would give her some extra baggage. Thirty-five to forty pounds ought to do the trick. We'll see how well those short-shorts fit then. Gone will be the near constant assertions of how she needs to have her clothing tailored because American clothes don't fit her slim body type and how the rest of us are so lucky to be able to "buy off the rack."

A pimple or ten would be a wonderful asset to her face. Every time she would manage to terminate one, two more would appear, larger and redder than the one before.

Vivienne would become so hideous that no one will want to be around her. She will run off to some far away country where veils are a standard piece of attire, never to be seen or heard from again.

"Now, Vivienne," said Mr. Grayfin, "None of us knows the reason why Guinevere's father left her."

3

I clenched my teeth. My dentist has warned me about this, but since she is also my mother, I feel it is OK to ignore her never ending suggestions to better myself.

Mr. Grayfin has always had a soft spot for the pretty girls. Before coming here to teach Romantics, he taught at an elite private high school in New York. He became well known for his extra tutoring sessions that were only available to pretty girls. Whenever a student of the wrong sex or of average beauty requested help, that student was directed to the library or the internet for extra learning.

Despite Mr. Grayfin's lanky frame, he is easy on the eyes and so naturally a lot of the girls had crushes on him. Plus he had a reputation for being an easy grader. However, a few of the girls were weary of the attention that they received from him. Mr. Grayfin had the habit of sitting too close and was very hands-on. After a few stern complaints by some of the parents, Mr. Grayfin was sacked. Officially, he was made redundant due to budget cuts. Unofficially, word got around and none of the schools in the area would hire him.

I was the first one to leave the classroom when the bell rang. A month into the school year and I was kicking myself daily for taking this class. The only other option that would have fit my schedule was comic book drawing. However, those kids who talk about nothing but who would win an end of the world battle, the characters of DC Comics or Marvel, don't seem so weird anymore.

"Hey Gwen, wait up."

I turned and my heart stopped. I've known Greg Kemp since last year when I started high school. He is a senior and on the football team with my brother, Oliver. Greg is probably who Michelangelo had in mind when he sculpted *David*. Who am I kidding? David couldn't hold a candle to Greg.

Greg put a hand on my shoulder when he caught up with me. "Are you OK?"

I am now. "Mr. Grayfin doesn't bother me."

Gregg smiled. His teeth had the right amount of slight crookedness to make them cute and still render braces unnecessary. "He's an idiot." He shook his head. "But I meant Vivienne. I know you two don't get along."

Vivienne once spread a rumor that I had lice. When we were in the fifth grade, she ran a collection to help my family get off food stamps. The principal confronted her about this and she apologized. She stated that it was an honest mistake based on an assumption she made because of my unique choice of attire.

"It's fine." I bit my inner cheek to prevent from saying something obscene.

"She really isn't as bad as she seems."

I twisted my face. What the hell is that supposed to mean?

"She can be really nice sometimes," Greg continued.

"Vivienne?" I was confused.

Greg smiled. I almost reciprocated until I realized that he was looking over me and not at me. Turning around I saw that he was eyeing Vivienne who was talking to one of her friends at her locker.

"I have to go," I said as I walked away.

"Yeah, yeah. Sure," Greg said as he continued to eye Vivienne.

≈

The almighty pain in the ass Keith Jess was home when I arrived. My mother married him after a mere four months of dating. Five years later and I am still weary of him. My parents divorced when I was five years old. Oliver and I were given the usual talk. No, this has nothing to do with the two of you. Yes, we still love each other; we just can't live with each other. Even at age five I knew that they were feeding us a load of crap. Who on earth loves someone that they can't be in the room with for more than five minutes without wanting to scratch their eyes out? Words between them were always harsh. My father could not understand why my mother felt the need to wash his work shirts before she took them to the dry cleaners. My mother could not understand why my father felt the need to chew his food so noisily. Their arguments were petty and frequent. Eventually the two got together and agreed that we did not live in a happy home.

My brother and I were to live with our mother and have liberal visits with our father. We saw him the first two weekends after the separation. It then went to once a month to it being three months before we saw our dad again. There was always a reason. Our father is a very busy person and I respect this. He works hard so that we can have nice things. I only wish that we could have him.

"What are you doing here?" I asked.

Keith looked at me with annoyance. "That is the kind of unequivocal benefit one is allowed to enjoy after purchasing a house."

Always the jerk. "Don't you have something to cut up?" I said nastily.

Keith's eyes narrowed. "I'm a surgeon, not a butcher. I work with patients. I save lives. I don't prepare slabs of beef."

"Nor do butchers," I said in a low tone.

"What?"

"Nothing."

"Why don't you like me?" Keith said through his teeth.

I shrugged my shoulders. "I like you just fine."

"I'm no fool. I know when a person harbors contempt for me. I don't know why. It would do you a world of good to see me as a paragon. There is so much that you could learn from me if only you possessed the facility. Ah, well. You just keep shooting for the middle. Best not to set yourself up for three pointers when you are better off just cheering from the sideline."

I snatched a bag of Doritos from the cabinet.

"Or eating a hot dog from one of those vendors," he continued. "Maybe you have more intellect than I give you credit."

Bite me.

"Where is Oliver?"

"Practice. Where else?"

Keith grabbed his jacket off the chair and walked to the back door. "It is good to see that one of you is focused. No thanks to your father of course."

"How's Katie?"

Keith's face tightened. Red hues bled into his usual peach tone. "Your mother will be home late. Order a pizza for dinner." The door slammed behind him.

Keith was always trying to make my father seem deficient. As though he is the epitome of father of the year and my father is the poster child for wayward baby daddies on the run from child support and other parental responsibilities. My father is a great dad. He isn't perfect, but neither am I. However, I am a far cry from Katie, Keith's daughter from his first marriage.

Three stints at a rehabilitation center for excessive drug and alcohol use have not made a dent on her illicit appetite. She slept her way to a high school degree – the kind of sleep that requires condoms and not the kind that results in feeling refreshed the next morning. She then convinced her parents to pay for an expensive private university by insisting that knowing that her parents were paying so much would make her focus and try harder. She is currently on her second attempt as a freshman.

My head flung forward. "Ouch." I turned to see what happened.

Oliver was laughing.

"That's not funny. I didn't hear you come in. What was that?"

"A snowball."

"A snowball?" I strained my neck from where I was sitting to get a glimpse of outside. Brown and yellow leaves covered the still green grass.

"You are too gullible," Oliver said laughing. "It was just a small ball."

My brother – always the prankster no matter the venue. Given his good looks and quick feet on the field, his if-it-were-anyone-else-they-would-get-detention antics are laughed away and sometimes encouraged. These aren't just run of the mill pranks where the teacher merely brushes off some silly string. He and a few teammates once had a teacher's car towed. Another time the principal was tricked into believing that the football coach died and the entire team was allowed to go home for the day. Coach Barnes was actually at home with the flu.

Oliver looked around the kitchen. "Where's dinner?"

"Mom's working late so we have to order a pizza."

"Again? Agh! Can't you cook something?"

"Can't you?"

"I'm tired. I just got back from practice."

"So. I'm tired too."

"From what? Reaching for the Doritos?" He snatched the bag of chips that were sitting in front of me.

"Are you calling me fat?"

"Shut up." Oliver opened the fridge and took out a beer.

"What are you doing?" I asked.

"Baking a pie."

"Keith will be pissed if you drink his beer. And what will mom say?"

"She would have to be here to say something. Besides, I will replace it."

Before I could say anything further, Oliver was up the stairs and in his room. I heard his door close and knew that was the end of our conversation.

I woke up the next morning dreading the day ahead. Another day filled with Vivienne and Mr. Grayfin. Oh how early Christmas has come this year.

"Stop tugging at your hair."

My mother was always a morning person. Where I saw an unacceptable invasion of eye-breaking light, my mother saw the bright start of a wonderful day. Another chance.

"I will stop pulling on it when you let me get a relaxer." I pulled my hair even harder for effect.

"Why would you want to relax your beautiful hair?"

"If this type of hair is so beautiful then why do you relax yours?"

"That wasn't my choice. My mother started relaxing my hair when I was very young."

"Is she still booking your appointments?" I said smartly.

My mother gave me an expressionless look that carried a heavy meaning.

"Please, mom? I hate my hair."

"That is exactly why I'm not going to let you get it relaxed. You need to learn to love it. Embrace it."

"I will after you embrace yours."

"I do not have to time to grow out my relaxer then relearn how to do my hair. I'm a very busy woman."

"I am too," I said.

My mother gave me a look that was a cross between skepticism and annoyance.

I continued, "I will have more time to focus on my studies. This will be especially important when I start college. And think about when I graduate and start a challenging career. Do you want me to get passed over for promotions all because I wasted valuable time dealing with my hair rather than honing in on my skills?"

My mother wasn't convinced. She was determined for me to love my kinky curly hair. She said that there were too many black women who loathed their natural hair and she didn't want me to be one of them. I didn't understand why I was being forced to love my hair while she enjoyed living life with her manageable tresses that she gets relaxed every 6 to 8 weeks. Talk about a two way street.

After lassoing my hair into a ponytail and throwing on my usual jeans and t-shirt, I stomped off to school. My dad bought Oliver a car that he sometimes uses to pick up some of his teammates. Rarely do I get offered a ride. Instead I am forced to wait outside for the yellow bus which also picks up the kids that go to the nearby middle school. Besides Comic Book Billy, I am the only high school kid on that stupid bus.

I peruse the patrons of the bus as I enter. The usual suspects. I briefly make eye contact with a boy who looks to be about twelve. He misinterprets my temporary glance and tells me that the seat next to him is being reserved. I ignore him and head to the back where I plop down and set my backpack on the space next to me to discourage company.

Once I got off the bus, I took the long way into the building, crossing through the parking lot where I 'accidentally' ran into Greg. This route adds another 5-7 minutes to my trip, sometimes causing me to be late, but it is well worth it. Greg was so close to me as we walked into the building together. His smell was intoxicating. It made me want to grab him and do something vulgar to him.

"So what do you think?" Greg asked.

"What?"

"About what I just said."

Crap, I wasn't paying attention. I didn't even realize he was talking. "Oh, um. I don't know. My mom always says that we know in our hearts what to do when confronted with a difficult situation," I said, hoping that it would somehow apply.

Greg tilted his head like a confused puppy.

I continued, "You, deep inside, you know what you should do. When we ask other people for their opinion, we are really just looking for someone to agree. For confirmation."

Greg twisted his face, "Do you want to study Romantics together or not?"

My face lit up. "Oh, yeah. Sure. Of course."

"You're weird, Gwen. But in a good way."

He patted me on the shoulder and took off. I could have died a semi-happy woman at that moment. My body always feels like putty when he touches me. And I never want it to end.

The bell rang and I had yet to make it to my locker. With my destination in sight, I pushed through my fellow last minute stragglers. Before I knew it, I was frantically flapping my arms in a sad effort to prevent myself from falling. This is one area where time and experience does more harm than good. Babies have it right when they fall on their bums. Arms up, bottom to the floor. Simple and with minimal consequences.

"Will you watch where the hell you are going?"

I looked around, shocked. A few students glanced my way, but then continued on their journey. The face of contempt hovered over me.

"Are you going to at least apologize?" she said with her arms opened wide.

"I'm...I'm..." I looked around again. The hall was empty except for the two of us. "It was an accident. Why are you being so rude about it?"

She threw off her cardigan revealing a stub where her left forearm should be. "Didn't anyone tell you that people like me get to be rude about everything and that nothing is ever our fault, even when it is? You are always required to apologize to me. Even after I have just purposefully ran over your precious dog that your dad bought for your seventh birthday."

My mouth hung open.

"What? Pollyanna has never heard anyone use such words?" she teased.

"Screw you," I said as I stood up, standing a good two inches over her.

"Ouch, that hurt," she said sarcastically.

"What is your problem?"

13

"Some jack-ass ruined my life when he went hacksaw crazy and started going through town, randomly hacking away at things. When he realized that it was taking too long to get the job done, he upgraded to a machete. When he got bored with hacking away at inanimate objects, he broke into my house and went after my family." Her voice became solemn. "One by one he hunted us down in that house. I still remember the dull, emotionless look on his face as he raised that machete over his head then brought it down, tearing into my flesh, slicing through my bones like they were raw spaghetti. I was the last one. The baby in the family. They called me God's miracle."

It was only when I finally exhaled that I realized I was holding my breath. What does one say in response to such a horrific story? I didn't want to say anything stupid or seem heartless. I managed to say, "I'm so sorry for your loss. That is such a tragic thing to happen to a person."

My eyes repeatedly made contact with her stub. I tried to stop them, but they didn't seem to be under my control. She flung the stub forward and I jumped back.

She laughed hysterically.

"I'm sorry," I mumbled with my eyes to the floor.

Her laughing intensified.

"Why are you laughing?" I asked. "I don't see anything funny."

"You are! Gosh you are so gullible." Her tone mocked. "My family was hacked away by a crazed maniac with a machete." She mimicked the sound of a robot as she repeatedly raised and lowered her right arm as though she were chopping some invisible wood.

14

"That was a lie? You actually lied about something like that. What the hell is wrong with you?" I said with an expression of complete disgust.

She threw her head back. "Oh, come off it. It was a joke. Get a sense of humor already."

I stomped off to my locker. I could hear her giggling from behind.

"Don't go. I'm sorry. Please. Wait. Come back."

She continued to giggle in between her words.

I opened my locker as she forcefully leaned against the locker next to mine. The loud sound reverberated down the empty hall. She again apologized for her unique, and yet to be understood, humor. I gave in and told her that it was fine.

Her name is Marie Malone. She is new to the school and is in the same grade as me, but we don't share any classes. It was too late for me to go to class – Romantics, so it's not that much of a loss – so I hung out with Marie. Things were a little bumpy at first, but they smoothed out the more we talked. She turned out to be pretty cool. She was born in California. Her mother is a paralegal that suffers from restlessness, which is why they move every 6 months to a year. Marie has lived in more places than she can remember. Her father was left behind somewhere between Arizona and New Mexico. Her mother unilaterally decided that he was 'bringing them down' and was more of a burden than a benefit, and so it was suggested that he not tag along anymore. Marie said that it doesn't bother her so much that her father wasn't around anymore. I don't believe her.

Marie offered to take me out for breakfast as a way to apologize for her jocularity. Neither of us has a car so we were forced to dine at a nearby diner that specializes in all things greasy. My mother

15

would kill me if she knew I was eating here. In her world, if something other than a tablespoon of extra virgin olive oil was required for preparation then the food fell into the unhealthy category and should be avoided at all costs. This is precisely the reason that I stand in the drive-thru line at McDonald's (don't want to get the smell of fried food on my clothes) and scarf my fries down before heading home. I also keep a couple of other forbidden food items hidden in my room. The irony of us ordering pizzas when my mother is working late is not lost on me, but bringing such to her attention would be stupid as I would lose out on occasionally eating pizza.

The diner was of the typical variety. A stand-alone yellow brick building with large people watching windows throughout. Unclothed rectangular tables occupied the middle of the floor while brown vinyl booths lined up the walls. Each table was similarly decorated with salt and pepper, ketchup, butter and jelly packets, and a dolly of small glass pitchers of various artificially flavored corn syrup. Marie and I sat in a booth and talked over a large stack of buttermilk pancakes, Canadian bacon, hash browns, and fried eggs. My body both thanked and cursed me as the delicacies traveled down providing minimal nourishment and guilty pleasure. The normally throat clogging pancakes easily slid to their destination given the extra grease from the bacon and hash browns.

Marie, who is exactly three months older than I, is an only child. I was in awe of this. While Oliver doesn't bother me so much now, I could have done without all of the tormenting that I suffered from age four to twelve.

Neither of us has any concrete plans for our future. I revealed to Marie that I usually keep a subset of impressionable occupations at my disposal for the benefit of adults who inquire. Most adults mean well when they ask, but I know they don't want to hear anything remotely unpleasant or unworthy, and so I throw on my veil and I extract something off the list with a smile. Depending on my mood, when I grow up I want to be a pediatrician, marine biologist, veterinarian specializing in small to medium sized animals, virologist focusing on biosafety level 4 viruses, or college professor of mathematics. If the inquirer is a close relative, I will usually throw in a few specific details to give it that wow factor. When I am in hot water with my mom, I'm focused on being a dentist. Keith once asked if I meant to say dental hygienist.

It was refreshing to sit and talk to Marie. I felt free and open with her. Like there was no need to be someone other than myself. I often spend so much of my time behaving in ways that I think people want me to behave. I always fall short of this expectation. I desperately want to just be myself around people, but I have been putting on a ruse for so long that I wouldn't know where to begin. Or what people will think of me when they learn what I have been doing.

≈

"Where have you been?"

Marie and I spent four hours in the diner. Afterward, we headed to Lake Michigan and sat on the large rocks that bordered the land. Winter was on its way. The temperature was much cooler by the water. Waves splashed against the rocks, spitting water as us relentlessly. We were cold and getting wetter by the second, but we didn't leave and we didn't talk much. We sat and watched.

My mother threw her hands up to her hips. She usually did this when she meant business. Then again, she seemed to always mean

17

business. "Guinevere, don't have me repeat myself. I asked you a question."

My mother only calls me Guinevere when she is really upset. I might as well go to the basement and retrieve my old blue time-out chair, the one my mother used until I was eight. By then my knees reached up above my hips and aimed, with near certainty, at my chest. She finally decided to do away with this incongruous form of discipline when one of the legs of the chair started to buckle. Now after my lecture, I get sent to my room without television or dessert.

Chapter Two
See What Gwen Can Do

"So you can't go out tonight?"

Marie was sitting across from me wearing a cotton purple cardigan over a pair of bright green jeans and a yellow t-shirt with 'Rebel With A Smile' written across the front. Her long black hair lay flat and hung past her shoulders. It was lunch, the only hour we had together. Mary was upset that I would not be able to hang out with her. My mother put me on punishment and made it clear that I was only permitted to go from school to home with no stops in between, before or after.

"My mother was pretty pissed that I skipped school yesterday," I said before slipping a ketchup coated French fry into my mouth.

"That sucks."

"You didn't get into trouble?" I asked assuming Marie would replay her own story of getting disciplined.

"My mother appreciates life lessons that arise from, well, living life." Marie spun her water bottle around on the table as she spoke.

A small spark of jealousy erupted in me then sputtered away. "My mother feels that life lessons are to be learned when I am out of her house. In the meantime, if it's not in a book then I need not bother with it."

Marie's eyes narrowed. "Is your room on the first floor?"

I was perplexed. Marie was always two steps ahead of me and this occasionally left me feeling lost and a little dumb. "Second, why?"

"No reason. Is there a tree or some other stable structure outside of your window?"

"No," I said, finally understanding.

"Oh."

"But there is a large tree outside of our rarely used guestroom."

"Well who said Mother Nature isn't giving?" Marie chuckled.

"No one."

"Shut up. You're ruining the flow."

"Of what? Incorrect sayings?"

Marie gave me a deadpan look. "Are you open to having some fun tonight?"

"Doing what? Texting?"

The deadpan look returned.

"I don't think that it will be a good idea for me to sneak out. My mother is absolutely furious about yesterday."

Marie lowered her voice to a whisper and brought her face closer to mine. "She won't even know. Is she working late tonight?"

"Yes, but-"

"What time does she usually get home?"

I shook my head thinking that this was going to be a big mistake. "Around 11."

"I'll have you home by 10:30."

"I don't know," I said while slowly shaking my head.

"Come on. You have to. It will be an epic night. I promise." Marie raised two fingers.

"Isn't it supposed to be three fingers?"

"I don't know. I got kicked out on the first day."

I twisted my face. "How do you get kicked out of Girl Scouts?"

"By testing the theory that there is no such thing as a dumb question. I think I proved that theory right because rather than there being dumb questions, there are a lot of dumb people."

"OK. Um…OK…about tonight, what do you have in mind?"

"It's a secret."

I raised my eyebrows. "I'm not risking my freedom for the foreseeable future on a secret."

Marie exhaled forcefully. "We are going to the zoo."

"I'm sorry, what?"

"The zoo."

"What's that?"

"You don't know what the zoo is?"

"I do, but I am hoping that your zoo and my zoo are not the same."

"I've scored some booze."

"I don't drink."

"Yet," she said correcting me. "You don't drink yet."

"I'll pass."

"Noooo. You can't. You must come. You owe it to yourself."

"I owe it to myself?"

"How often do you participate in activities purely for your enjoyment?"

"I-"

Marie's look cut me off before I could even try to come up with something. "How is drinking at the zoo fun?"

"Have you done it before?"

"Uh, no."

"Then trust me."

"Sounds like a huge risk for something that doesn't even sound worth it."

Marie spent the rest of our lunch hour trying to convince me to indulge in alcoholic fare while gazing at animals in man-made habitats. I was reluctant. The risk was not proportionate to the reward, but the idea of doing something mindless and without purpose was somewhat appealing. I would not have to think about the consequences. I didn't have to care about what my mother would say. Or stupid Keith. I could partake in reckless teenage behavior and not care about its effect on my future. So what if I have a math test coming up. That book report will just have to wait. It is time for me to live. It is time for me to be a typical rebellious teenager.

"I don't think I can do it," I said with a deflated tone. I was ready to jump off a cliff with Marie during lunch, but afterward, I had time to talk myself out of it. By the end of the day I was completely against it.

"Don't bail on me now," Marie pleaded. "I can't do this by myself."

"Then don't go."

"I need to and I need you to come with me."

"Why?"

"I just do, OK?"

"I can't. I would get into so much trouble."

"You won't. I promise."

"I don't know."

"Please?"

I looked around. Kids were starting to leave the campus. The yellow buses were lined up along the side of the building. I knew it was only a matter of time before they, too, left.

"Marie, I really wish that I could, but I can't. I have to go now. If I miss the bus, I won't have a way home."

"Don't say no just yet. I will come to your house tonight. Decide then."

"I don't know."

"Decide then," she urged.

I looked back at the buses. A few of the doors closed. "Fine," I said so that I could leave. Marie smiled and waved as I ran to my bus.

"Took you long enough."

The comment startled me. It was Comic Book Billy. He was sitting four rows from the back and wore a strange expression on his face. It was a cross between excitement and dismay. He then smiled as I passed him.

"I was joking," Comic Book Billy said when I did not respond.

I flashed a quick, toothless smile and slid into my seat.

Keith was home. Again. Sometimes I am able to lounge about alone for an hour or so before Oliver comes home from practice. But mostly my afternoons were saturated with unwanted interactions with a man in my life simply because my mother doesn't want to grow old alone when my brother and I leave the nest. Simply because my mother couldn't hack it with my dad. Simply because she can. Lately it feels that it is simply just to annoy me. Keith is such a jerk. What my mother finds appealing in him is a mystery to me.

"Eating again?" Keith said. He crawled out of the home office when he heard me enter the kitchen. I was in the middle of extracting the remains of a semi-stale baguette from a bag twice the length of my arm. I had to wrestle with the bag and bunch it up just to get near the piece of bread.

"Still here? Again?" I said smartly.

Keith put on one of his more serious faces and pointed a finger two inches from my nose. "This, this here is *my house*. You are a guest here for as long as *I* allow it. Don't you forget that."

He was so close to me that I could feel his warm breath on my face. He continued to rant on about his house and how he was tired of me and my ways. Spittle flew from his hot mouth and landed on my lips. While he spoke, I watched as lines of saliva stretched from the roof of his mouth to his tongue. Four of his molars had silver filings. His breath smelled nastily of old coffee. I wanted desperately to lash out at him. To strike him somewhere, anywhere.

Inhale. Exhale.

He stopped talking and stared at me. I returned his glare, determined not to blink. My body was beginning to turn on me. I could feel the tear production initiating. My hands were trembling.

Keith stood erect. "You're luck you're your mother's daughter."

I didn't respond. I just kept breathing. *Inhale. Exhale.*

Keith's demeanor changed and he displayed his yellowing teeth. "Where's Oliver?"

Inhale. Exhale. Repeat.

"Showing off at practice I assume," Keith said without waiting for me to respond. He turned to open the fridge. "Your mother will be home late. Order a pizza. Or you can just continue to ravage the fridge until you're finally full. Or until you pass out. I'm banking on the latter."

Inhale. Exhale. Repeat.

"Who the hell keeps taking my beer?"

Inhale. Exhale. Repeat.

"Shit. I'm going to work."

After Keith left the house and I saw that his car was at the end of the driveway, I screamed at the top of my lungs for as long as my body would allow. And when I was finished, I did it again. I ran to my room, slammed and locked my door. Life was increasingly becoming unbearable. I wanted out, but I knew that I was stuck. At least for a few more years. Then I'll be off to college far, far away from here. Away from Keith and his stupid mouth. Away from my mother and her stupidity.

God, I hate this place!

Despite my attempts, my rage began to boil. Every emotion that I tried to suppress began to erupt. I screamed again. I pulled the sheets off my bed. I tossed my lamp on the floor. I threw my pillows and shoes at the wall. All the while, I screamed. I flung my stuffed animals onto the floor. I ripped up any paper that I came across.

I kept this up until my rage and erratic breathing made me dizzy. I fell to the floor. Parts of my body were held up by the plethora of stuff that I tossed there. I rolled my head around and looked at the mess that I made. The mess that I would later have to clean up.

Why am I such a pathetic idiot?

I sat up with my head tilted down in a depressed manner. *If it's not one thing, it's another. Way to go, Gwen.*

So this is my life. Keith, my mom, me, this, nothing. I thought about how great it would be to have something special about me. Something that made life worth living or at least tolerable.

I laid my head down and stared at a lamp that I threw on the floor. It was an orange, teardrop ceramic lamp with a white shade. Luckily it did not break when it made contact with the floor. I love that lamp. I picked it out last year when my mother let me redecorate my room. For years I returned to My Little Pony and Bratz. I was no longer a child and my mother agreed. She took me to the store and set me free. I picked out a new bed, sheets, duvet, curtains and anything else I deemed necessary for my grown-up quarters. I saw the lamp on my way to pick out wall décor. It was sitting alone on a shelf. The only one of its kind. It was dusty and the shade sat at a tilt. I don't know what it was, but I had to have that lamp. It was perfect. Just perfect.

I focused on the orange lamp that now lay on the floor. I put all of my energy into that lamp. Such a beautiful lamp. So perfect. Wouldn't it be nice if that perfect and beautiful lamp would return to its place on my nightstand? That would be great. I focused harder on the lamp. Harder. Harder. Harder.

The lamp began to shake. Not vigorously. A quiver. A calmness penetrated me as I continued to focus on the lamp. It hovered above the ground a few centimeters.

I jumped.

I sat up and turned to see what startled me. My doorknob jiggled then there was a knock.

"Gwen, what are you doing in there?"

I exhaled heavily. *Oliver.* I looked at the lamp. It was back on the floor lying on its side, motionless.

"Gwen!" Oliver pounded on my door.

"Stop, banging on my door," I said as I flung it open.

27

"The hell you doing? I've been calling your name for ten minutes."

Oliver's eyes took in my mess.

"What the hell happened in here? Did you get your period and lose a chocolate bar at the same time?"

I tried to close the door, but Oliver's body was in the way.

"Stop," he said. "Seriously, what's going on?"

"Nothing," I said with my eyes pointed to the floor.

"This is nothing?" Oliver waved a hand around my room as he posed the question.

"I am rearranging things."

"Is that so?"

I looked at Oliver's hand. He was clutching a can of beer. The very beer that Keith drinks.

"Should you be drinking that?"

"Drinking what?" Oliver lifted both of his hands as though he wasn't holding a beer in one.

"Your mother's husband won't be too happy that you are drinking his beer."

"I'm just rearranging the fridge. I'm sure your stepdad won't mind."

I tried to kick him, but he jumped back.

"What do you want?" I asked with irritation.

28

"Checking to see if you are home."

"I am. You can go now."

"Better not let mom see this mess."

"I will clean it up as soon as you leave."

Oliver shrugged then turned to leave. "Are you sure you are OK?" he shouted as he walked down the hall.

"I'm fine," I said as I closed my door.

I plopped down on the floor. *I'm not fine.* I didn't dare take another look around my room. The thought alone was overwhelming. I put my head down on the bed and closed my eyes. Maybe I could wish it all away. Or even better, I'll wake up and find out that past five years has been nothing but a bad nightmare.

"Gwen."

The sound was muffled, but I was certain that I heard my name.

"Gwen."

Crap, please don't tell me I've lost my mind.

"Gwen!"

The window. Marie was standing outside shouting my name.

"What are you doing down there?" I asked after lifting the window.

"Did you forget about tonight? The zoo?"

I opened my mouth, but no words came out.

Marie raised her hand. "I have beer!"

I considered my options. I could stay here in my muddled room and sulk about my pitiable life. Thoughts frequently consisting of Keith. Or I could go out, have fun and kill some brain cells. Perhaps I'll get lucky and obliterate the cells that are responsible for memory retention. The choice was simple once I put it into perspective.

I didn't want to open one of the doors downstairs. Our alarm system always announces when that occurs and I didn't want Oliver to know that I was leaving. He would just try to talk me out of going. He might even go so far as to call mom if I held fast on leaving. I didn't want to find out.

I headed to the rarely used guest room. My mother decorated it with blue and white stripes throughout. The comforter, decorative pillows, curtains, everything was in the same striped blue and white design. She thought this created a cool, comfortable atmosphere for our guests. It made me dizzy.

I opened one of the windows and removed the screen. It was old, dirty, and stiff and seemed susceptible to tearing with the wrong placement of a finger. I carefully laid it on the floor then kicked it causing a large tear near the edge.

The tree that grew outside near the guest room was not an old sturdy tree. It was more of a mature teenager. Still, I was determined. I made up my mind and I was going to follow through. With my gut sucked in, I squeezed out of the window and grabbed the closest branch. At this point I realized that I should have climbed out feet first. Too late now. I grabbed the strongest looking branch and pulled myself out until I was able to swing a leg out of the window. Now I was in business. Or so I thought. I turned my body so that I could position myself on a branch with my leg. However, the branch that I chose snapped. I tumbled to the ground hitting several branches along the way. Luckily I landed on my bum.

Marie came running when she saw me.

"What happened?" Marie asked; her eyes wide and her hand still clutching the beer.

I carefully rolled to the side to move the branch that I fell on. "In case you haven't noticed, I'm not exactly the outdoorsy type."

"Sorry, but at least your step-father didn't hear you."

"Please don't call him that. Besides, he isn't here."

"Why didn't you just leave out the front door?"

"I didn't want Oliver to hear me leave. He would try to talk me out of going."

"Good call."

I winced in pain.

Marie put the beer on the ground then reached for my arm. "Take it from me, your wounds are superficial and will heal. Let's go." Marie tugged on my arm until I stood up.

"I'm in pain," I shot back.

Marie released my arm and placed a can of beer in my hand. "Drink it."

I gave her a look that said, "Really?"

"Trust me. It will make the pain go away."

"Whatever." I cracked open the can and started downing it. It took all of my energy to keep the beer from emerging. It was nasty and smelled even worse.

31

Two beers and a bus ride later and we were at the zoo. Normally the zoo closes at 6 or 7 in the evening, but today was a special event: A Night Out at the Zoo.

Alcohol is not permitted on zoo grounds so Marie hid the beer in a bag before we entered. She handed me another beer once we were in the zoo. I declined. I was not used to drinking and was already beginning to slur my words.

"You are such a lightweight," Marie said as she chugged a beer.

Marie wanted to see the female lion. She said that it was her favorite animal. She didn't understand why the male is considered the king of the jungle when it's the female lions that do the hunting.

"It's the hair," I said. "It presents the image of…something big." I waved my hand in the air in a half circle.

"Yeah, that sounds scientific," she laughed.

The lions, one male and one female, were sleeping – the male occasionally twitching an ear.

"I thought there were supposed to be nomadic," Marie said.

"You mean nocturnal."

Marie turned toward me. "What did I say? Isn't that what I said?"

"I don't remember."

We stared at the boring, sleeping lions for about ten minutes before heading off to the bear grotto. It too was replete with inactive animals.

"It's just not right," Marie said while shaking her head.

"What?"

"Shouldn't they be up, doing something? Entertaining us? Can't someone give them a ball?"

"This isn't the circus."

"Wha-What? They can't play with balls at the zoo? What kind of place is this? What kind of place doesn't allow Winnie and Yogi to play with balls?"

I laughed and laughed. For some reason it was the funniest thing I had ever heard. I kept laughing until I heard a familiar voice.

"Have you run through your high yet?" Marie asked after I stopped laughing.

"Do you hear that?"

"What?"

"I know that voice." I spun around looking for the source of the familiar voice. My heart stopped when I found it.

"You like him?" Marie asked when her eyes met my destination.

"He is OK," I said, lying. "Don't you think?"

"I'm not really into the big, burly, muscle bound types."

"He's not that big," I said smiling.

"He is a jock and that says it all."

"He's smart. Besides, not all jocks are the same. My brother is one too."

"You just want to screw him."

I widened my mouth. "I do not."

"You want him to give it to you real good." She was thrusting her hips as she was talking.

"That's gross."

"That is because you are a vegetarian. If you had a little meat in your life, you would not think it was so gross."

I twisted my eyebrows. "I eat meat."

"Don't be so dense, Gwen."

My face was blank.

"His penis. I was talking about his penis."

"Oh, yeah. I knew that."

"Here, drink another one of these then go and talk to him," Marie said as she handed me another beer.

"No, he is with his friends."

"He'll leave them."

"What if he doesn't?"

"Then you will know."

"Know what?"

"Not to waste your time with him."

"I don't know."

"Don't over think it. Just do it."

"I don't know."

"Go."

"What about you?"

"We are at the zoo, Gwen. Did you really think that I wanted to come here to see lions, tigers, and bears, oh my?"

I held my head askew. "You knew Greg was going to be here?"

"I may have overheard him mentioning that he was coming. And I may have noticed the way that you ogle him."

"Oh god, is it that noticeable?"

"You're like a prisoner who has just laid eyes on a man after being in solitary confinement for 10 years."

I looked back at Greg. He was wearing the same jeans he had on earlier, but now they were paired with a blue and white button down that matched his eyes instead of the green and grey sweater he wore at school. He smiled as he talked with his friends. They stood about 30 yards away. Marie and I were blocked behind a stingray exhibit. His teeth were so white they almost glowed. His auburn hair had just the right amount of body to it to make him cute, but not feminine. His skin was blemish free. Goodness he was gorgeous. I'd swear it was like he was always posing for a picture. A perfect picture.

I turned to Marie. She was chugging yet another beer.

"So you are cool with me going over there?"

"Go."

"Come with me."

Marie turned up her face. "No."

"Why not?"

"I brought you here so you could spend some alone time with Greg. Not so we could have a threesome."

My eyes found Greg again. He turned toward my direction causing me to duck behind a large rubber stingray. My hand wrapped around its tail, which unfortunately was not as robust as the rubber body. It cracked and I fell to the ground. Marie found this to be terribly amusing. She laughed for about five minutes before regaining her composure or even asking if I was OK.

"Finished?" I asked after her last snort.

"Oh come off it. I'm just having a laugh. We are supposed to be having a good time tonight."

"Then why am I the one who keeps landing on her bottom?"

"You'll have to ask yourself that one. Hey, hurry up. It looks like they might be headed elsewhere."

I was going to respond to Marie's insensitive statement, but when I glanced at Greg, it did look like he was getting ready to leave. Without thinking, I jumped up and made long strides in Greg's direction. Marie and I agreed to meet up later if need be.

Greg's expression was one of confusion then happiness when he laid eyes on me.

"What are you doing here?" he asked.

"Just hanging out."

"Alone?"

"Um, no, um, a friend of mine wanted to do something else so we decided to split."

Greg squinted like he was looking for my friend in the distance. I could smell the alcohol on his breath even though I was standing about three feet away from him.

"Where's O?"

"Oliver? He is at home."

"Well I can't have the little sister of my teammate out here alone. That would not be very teammate like of me now would it?" Greg teetered as he stood. "Hey," Greg called out to his friends. "You all go ahead. I'm going to keep an eye out on O's little sister."

"Yeah, OK," laughed one of the guys before they all left.

Greg smiled as he looked at me and swayed. "How long have you been here?"

"Not long. You?"

"Yeah, me too. It's nice, yeah?"

"Yeah."

"Do you like bears?"

"Um, they are OK, I suppose."

"I like bears. They are so cool. You know, they like stand up on the back two feet like humans and they put their paws in the air and they roar," Greg imitated this as he talked. "How cool is that?"

I nodded my head, uncertain of how to respond.

"And cows! I love cows. I haven't seen any tonight though."

"I don't think they have cows here."

"Why?" Greg asked, sounding disappointed, spit flying with every word. "They're animals aren't they?"

"I don't know why."

Greg grabbed a handful of my hair. "You're pretty. And I like your hair. It's so you."

"Thanks." *I guess.*

Greg stepped closer to me. His chest was a mere inches from my nose. He released his grip on my hair and instead used his hand to caress the side of my face. His hand slid down to my jaw then to my chin. He outlined my lips. The entire time my body went through so many phases. At first I was unsure of what he was doing. Then I was unsure if I wanted it done. Finally, I gave in and welcome all the possibilities.

Greg lifted my head with a gentle nudge of his finger under my chin. He pressed his lips to mine. At this point the smell of the alcohol on him became overwhelming and I wanted to vomit. But I also didn't want him to stop. He may not try again if I rejected him in such a way. His tongue slipped out of his mouth and traced the contours of my lips leaving behind saliva that reeked of booze. I held my breath to contain any involuntary reactions. As I stood there trying to ward off anything that would give even the slightest hint of what I was really feeling, Greg's tongue entered my mouth. I opened wide and let him explore. He pulled me into him and just as I thought, *"Finally,"* my mouth was filled with a warm mushy substance. I quickly pushed Greg off me. I bent over trying to expel anything that came from Greg's stomach and entered my mouth. I tried using my salvia, my shirt; I even considered sticking my head into the stingray exhibit. That is when I spotted a water fountain. Repeatedly, I rinsed my mouth out until I felt that I did the best I could with the resources at my disposal. Greg was on the ground with his hands on his head. A pool of vomit lay next to him. Part of me wanted to leave. A larger part of me felt sorry for him and wanted to make everything better in the way that a good friend would. A good female friend. A girl friend. A girlfriend.

"Are you OK?" I asked as I stood over Greg.

"I'm sorry. I had too much to drink." He spat and I turned my head. "I need to go home."

Greg tried to stand, but fell on his first attempt.

"You're not driving are you?"

"Yeah. I'll be OK."

"I don't think that is a good idea. Give me your keys. I'll drive."

"You drive?"

"Yeah," I said as I held out a hand.

I helped Greg into the car then climbed into the driver's side. Greg laid his head back against the seat and closed his eyes. I was so happy to be here to help him through this. I was certain this would bring us closer together, especially after that kiss. Yes, it wasn't the most romantic moment ever, but it was my first kiss. *And it was with Greg.* I'd always imagined my first kiss. Who would it be with? What would it be like? Would I have food stuck in my teeth? Would he look me in my eyes as our lips met in unison?

As many times as I imagined the *he* being Greg, I never thought that it was actually possible. Really possible. My heart thumped at what lay ahead for us. In the meantime, I needed to get Greg home.

I wasn't completely honest when I told Greg that I knew how to drive. I know the process and I have seen it done a millions times, but I haven't actually driven anything larger than a go-kart. My mother keeps saying that she is going to take me out and teach me, but that day has yet to come.

Slowly, I put the key in the ignition and started the car. *Vroom!* So far so good. I put my foot on the break and the car revved. Beginner's mistake. I took my foot off the gas and moved it to the break and put the car in drive. I was nervous about encountering someone or something and hitting the wrong pedal *again* so I kept my speed under 10 mph. It was a crawl and I may have missed a few stop signs, but we finally made it to Greg's house. I didn't dare try to park the car in the garage or the driveway so I left it on the street; a good two feet from the curb. Greg would have to sort it out later.

Greg required several shoves and a rather hard kick before he woke up with a grunt. He coughed, got out, and walked in the house without a word. I stood by the car after the front door closed. I waited to see if he would return for a good-bye kiss or at least a thank you. He didn't. I eventually gave up and hiked the mile and a half home.

The house was dark and quiet. It was just after 10 pm. My mother was still at work and so was Keith. I put an ear to Oliver's door: snoring. I walked into my room and was reminded of my earlier rampage. Exhaustion and disinclination dragged me into bed while I was still wearing my clothes and traces of vomit.

My mother was in the kitchen when I came downstairs the next morning. I stood watching her move about before I made my presence known.

"Hey," she said as I entered. Her movements stopped when she caught sight of me. "Rough night?"

I shrugged.

"What happened to your room? I nearly got a concussion when I went to give you a kiss last night."

"Oh, I'm redecorating." I smiled hoping to dissuade any analytical thought.

My mother looked at me like she knew I was lying then returned to moving about, her hands going from one thing to another. "I talked to Keith. Seems as though you were a bit harsh with him."

"Is that how he described it?" I said annoyingly.

Her hands stopped. "Guinevere, you could put in an effort to be a lot nicer to Keith. He is a wonderful man and he has been nothing but accommodating to you."

"Accommodating," I said with a huff.

"I know he is not your father, but he is my husband and you will respect him." Her voice was stern.

"So I have to respect him, but he gets to say whatever he wants to me?"

"Keith respects you."

"In what world?"

"You are being sensitive. Keith wants what is best for you."

"So his criticism is just a way to give me a boost?"

"Don't get cheeky with me."

"Why do you always take his side?"

"I'm not taking his side, Guinevere. There are no sides to take. It's about time that you grow up and accept that your father and I are

41

not getting back together. It's been 10 years. That's more than enough time for you to come to terms with the demise of our relationship."

"I get that you are not getting back together with dad. What I don't get is why you are with Keith."

"That's not for you to get, now is it?"

I glared at my mother icily.

"Again?" Oliver said as he grudgingly entered the kitchen.

"Hey, hon," my mother said in a perky tone. "Sleep OK?"

"Yeah. What are you two arguing about now?"

"We are not arguing." She smiled. "Just having a chat."

"Some chat," I said as I stormed out of the house. It wasn't time for me to leave for school yet and so I was forced to wait 30 minutes in the cold for the bus. I could have walked to school since I had the extra time, but that's a two-and-a-half mile walk. Not really my cup of tea and so I waited.

Fall was comfortably settling in. The air was full with a crisp coolness that dipped further down the thermometer whenever the wind blew. I held tightly to my sweater near my chest, wishing that I had grabbed a jacket before storming out of the house.

My mood perked up as the bus approached the two story school building. Thoughts of Greg and our night together flooded my brain. I ran through so many scenarios of how today could pan out given the enormous step Greg and I took in our relationship. Would he profess his love for me? Would he take me in his arms so we could pursue our passion together? Oh the possibilities.

I entered the building with the vigor that I usually reserve for the exit. There were no signs of Greg. No worries, we both have Romantics first period.

Unusually, I was one of the first people to enter the classroom. I took my seat and stared at the door, taking note of everyone that entered. Three minutes later, the door was closed and Greg was not in his seat. I guess that means our first study session, the one where I figured we would spend most of the time making-out, has been canceled. On the plus side, neither Vivienne nor Mr. Grayfin made it to class either.

I sat dreamily throughout my classes. At lunch, Marie wanted an entire playback of my time with Greg.

"What do you mean, 'It was fine?'" Marie asked after I tried playing coy about my evening.

"It was fine, that's all."

"You need to give me more information than that. I made sacrifices so that you could be alone with him?"

"Sacrifices?"

"Yes, sacrifices. While you were in a clean vehicle with your love interest, I took the bus home. There was a homeless man who got on two stops after I did. The bus was near empty, but that didn't stop him from choosing the seat next to me." Marie's face tightened. "The smell. I couldn't begin to describe the smell. It was horrible. Ghastly. Like death curled up and died again from its' own stench. Then he started to pick his nose. Whenever he made a find, he would flick it. Of course, it never left his finger on the first, one, two, three tries. Sometimes he wouldn't even bother and just put it in his mouth. Protein I guess."

I cringed.

"Oh, it gets better. He then took off what he was passing off as shoes and began to bite his toenails which he spat out on the floor."

"I'm so sorry."

"You should be."

"Why didn't you just get up and move to another seat?"

"I tired, but he would not move and I was not going to touch him."

"How did you get off the bus?"

"I climbed over the seat in front of me. I prayed the entire time, hoping that I would not fall onto the floor. The stuff that is on that floor would send scientists into a tailspin."

"I am so, so, so sorry."

"As you should be. Details please."

For a moment I considered whether or not Marie was telling the truth. She has a gift for storytelling, which she seems to enjoy. However, rather than pursue the issue, I decided to give her want she wanted.

"He kissed me." My lips betraying my attempt to not smile.

Marie's mouth widened. "How was it?"

"It was so very sweet. We were talking at first and then he sent his friends away, just like you said. We talked a bit more about, I don't remember, and then he made his move. He leaned in so that we stood heart to heart. He slowly caressed my face while looking me in the eyes. It was amazing. And then he kissed me."

"Wow. What happened next?"

"What do you mean?"

"Did you two keep making out?"

"He isn't like that."

"All guys are like that."

"Not Greg. He is a gentleman. He is willing to wait."

"Is that what he told you?"

"He didn't have to. I know. Plus, he let me drive his car."

"You can drive?"

"Yep."

"Did you two make out in the car?"

I tapped her on the hand. "Stop being so gross, Marie."

"Greg and Gwen, sitting in a tree, K-I-S-S-"

"Stop it," I said, cutting her off.

She smirked. "When are you seeing him again?

"Soon. He'll probably call me today."

"You be careful, Gwen," Marie warned.

"No need to worry," I said slyly. "I'm O's little sister. Greg will take care of me."

≈

I spent the evening laying on a small cleared out area on my floor. My room was still a disaster. I had considered calling Greg, but I didn't want to seem desperate. I'd read a number of articles about how men love the chase. I don't mind letting Greg chase me. Of course, I don't plan to run to far or too hard. I smiled just thinking of the two of us together. What a couple we'd make.

An abrupt turn caused my elbow to land painfully on a purple stapler. *Ouch.*

I exhaled heavily, my body flat on its back. *Why did I have to make this mess?* I rotated my head and stared at the objects that lay everywhere. I thought about what happened the other night when I made the lamp move. *Was it real?* I didn't think about it much after Oliver interrupted me for fear that it was just my imagination. But now, I had to know. Just as I did last time, I focused all of my energies on the lamp. Part of me felt silly, but I didn't stop. My breathing slowed. A calm warm feeling came over me again. The lamp shook. Slowly it rose until it was about three feet off the ground. With a quick shot of my eyes, the lamp veered to the right and landed, with a slight thump, onto my nightstand.

The largest smile I have ever manufactured erupted on my face. I was ecstatic. Never before had I felt so alive, so special. *Suck it Keith*!

I turned my attention to the rest of the wayward items on the floor. Suddenly, one by one, the objects rose in the air and carefully floated to their proper place. Before I knew it, my room was tidy. More so than when I physically clean it myself. Even my socks sat in the laundry basket that my mother made me get. Rarely do they make it off the floor.

A knock at the door interrupted my tranquility. Oliver knocked once then turned the knob.

"It's about time," Oliver said noticing my room. I looked around to make sure there were no signs that I had 'help' with cleaning my room. "Mom wants you to come downstairs. Keith has something to tell us."

Chapter Three
Gwen's Dilemma

My mother feels that information that impacts at least two members of our family should be shared to all during a family meeting. She seems to think that this will be another avenue in bringing us together. Never mind that I do not and will not ever consider Keith a member of my family. Never mind that Keith is a horrible person that I despise. Never mind that Keith treats me like I'm a failure and a complete disappointment. A burden as I'm sure he would put it.

Keith's big announcement, that I had to leave my room and walk down 18 stairs to hear, was about his beloved Katie. Apparently, and these are his words, "Katie will be staying with us for a few weeks while she works to complete a school project on community service."

"Does this community service project include an ankle bracelet and surprise drug tests from a nice man named Big Pete?" I asked.

Keith's face turned a very deep mean red. He opened his mouth to expel something I'm sure would not be pleasant, but was intercepted by my mother.

"Gwen, that will be all thank you."

"I was just asking a question," I said smugly. "You said that the best way to learn is to ask."

"Evelyn," Keith said through clenched teeth.

"Gwen, please go to your room."

"Why?" I looked from my mother to Oliver who was eyeing the floor.

"Please, Gwen," my mother pressed.

"But I-"

"Go!"

"This is so unfair," I said as I stormed up the stairs. "I didn't even do anything wrong!" I yelled. "Katie obviously broke the law and is being sent home to complete her punishment, but instead of telling us the truth, we are fed some stupid lie to protect the little felon's feelings." I slammed my door shut. I could hear murmurs from downstairs, but I could not make out what they were saying. Oliver said something then left the house.

I decided to call my dad. It had been awhile since I've spoken to him. Usually I get his answering machine and am forced to leave a message. He is a partner at a law firm so I understand his limited ability to call me back.

Ring

Ring

Ring

Ring

"Hello?"

I heard the voice just as I was about to hang the phone up. "Dad?" I asked uncertain if I was hearing things.

"Hello? Who is this?"

"It's me, Gwen."

A pause. "Oh, hey, how are you, Gwen?"

"Fine. How are you?"

"Well, thank you."

Another pause.

"How's your brother?"

"He's fine."

"School?"

"Good."

"That's good to hear."

Pause.

"Well, Gwen, I hate to cut this conversation short, but-"

"Dad?"

"Yes?"

"Things are a bit difficult here."

Pause.

"It's just that Keith doesn't seem to like me much."

"I'm sure that's not true, Gwen."

"It is. Trust me. You should hear the things that he says to me."

"I know things can be difficult. It is hard for me as well with you two living there and me living here. I understand."

"I don't want to be here."

"I know sweetie. I would have loved for the two of you to have lived with me when your mother and I separated, but your mother wanted to take you two. There wasn't much that I could do about it."

Pause.

"Do you think that I could stay with you for a while? Just a little while."

Pause.

"Dad?"

"Yes?"

"Did you hear what I just said?"

"Yes, I did." He inhaled deeply. "I don't think that would be a good idea. I would love to have you, but you have school."

"Your place is only 30 minutes from my school."

"Yes, but the bus does not come out here. How would you get there? Plus your mother would not allow it. Look, Gwen, I know that things seem impossible right now, but soon enough you will be off to college and all of this will be behind you, OK? Look, I have to go. I am late for a meeting. I will speak with you later. Love you. Keep your spirits up and know that you can call me anytime, OK?"

"OK. Bye-"

Click.

"...dad."

That Saturday I was lying on my bed moving a few objects with my mind when the phone rang. It was Marie. She wanted to go and hang out. Maybe catch a movie. I jumped at the opportunity to get out of the house.

"I'm going out," I called out as I threw on my coat.

My mother appeared from the living room. "Did you forget that you are on punishment?"

I frowned. "Mom, please. It was one mistake and I said that I was sorry. Can't I go out this one time? I will do some extra chores instead."

My mother considered my proposal. I reminded her that I don't get into trouble too often and I have never skipped school before. I'm a first time offender and should be given a break.

"It was a mistake and I have learned my lesson."

"Where are you going?"

"Out with Marie. She just called."

"I didn't hear the phone ring."

I shrugged.

My mother lowered her eyebrows. "Marie, is she the new girl at school that you have been hanging out with?"

"Yep, that would be her." I stuffed a few cookies in my coat pocket.

"You should bring her by so I can meet her." I knew my mother was elated at the prospect of me going out with a friend. The last time I went out with a friend was when they were still called playdates. I hung out a few times with a girl, Wendy, from my 6th grade class, but that is because my mother made me (she is friends with the girl's mother) and so I don't count that. All Wendy wanted to do was play with Barbie dolls. My repeated protests of being too old fell on deaf ears. I gave in and was rewarded with the headless Ken doll as a mate for my Barbie.

"One day."

"Why are you keeping her away? Is there something that I should know?"

"No. It would just be nice to have something that I don't have to share with the family."

"Fine, but I would like to meet her at some point."

"You will."

I picked up an apple and pocketed it.

"What time will you be home?"

"In time for dinner."

Marie was waiting for me by the cinema. She checked all the movies and determined that none were worth sneaking into. She said that she hasn't paid for a movie since she was 8 years old. I didn't like the idea of sneaking into a movie theater - just my luck I'd get caught and I am a horrible liar - and so I was glad that none of the movies were to her liking.

Marie and I perused around the downtown area. We stopped off at a coffee shop and had lattes. I ordered a decaf. Too much caffeine makes me jittery. Afterward we went to a few stores then stopped off to eat lunch. It was then that I saw Keith through a window. He was sitting at a table across from a curly redheaded woman that I've never seen before. Not that I have ever visited Keith at his place of employment, but I am almost certain that the relationship he has with this woman is not a professional one.

The table was small and purposed for intimacy. The curly redhead sat at about 45 degrees from Keith. Her hand rested on the table within stabbing distance from Keith's right hand. Her other hand was M.I.A., as was his. She frequently ran a hand threw her hair while he spread his lips in an exaggerated hungry smile. When the food came, she used one fork to feed the both of them. A sliver of sauce dripped down her lip and onto her chin. Keith quickly whipped out a finger and saved her from the unsightly marinade that savagely trespassed on her face. The sauce's fate: in Keith's mouth. The two acted as though they were the only people around. I wished they were.

"I'm sorry you had to see that." Marie was trying to comfort me. We watched Keith and the redhead from across the street for about 15 minutes. Marie finally pulled me away.

"I can't believe he would do that to my mother," I said.

"You said he was a jerk."

I looked up at Marie. "To me." I pointed to my chest and then to the air in the direction of my house. "He is married to her." I wanted to cry, scream, do something.

"Don't allow his shortcomings to upset you."

"I'm upset for my mother."

"Are you going to tell her?"

The question took me by surprise. I hadn't thought about how my mother would learn of Keith's betrayal. I guess part of me believe that somehow the information would magically transfer from me to her. It was like she already knew. But she didn't.

"Don't I have to?"

"You don't *have* to do anything."

"How could I not tell her something like this?"

Marie shrugged.

"Wouldn't you tell?"

"I don't know. But I do know that things were not so nice between my mother and father when my mother learned that my father cheated on her."

My eyes widened at this unexpected reveal. "What happened?"

"My father slept with some woman that he met online."

"No, I mean when your mother found out? Is that why she left your father?"

"Oh, no. She left him because she got tired of him leaving the toilet seat up. Just about every morning she would groggily enter the bathroom and fall into the toilet."

I shook off the image. "What did your mother do when she learned of your father's infidelity?"

"She threatened him with a meat cleaver that she had just used to chop up some lamb. There was blood and flesh everywhere."

My eyes nearly popped out of the socket. "She cut him with it?"

Marie waved her hand nonchalantly. "One superficial wound. Most of the blood and whatnot was from the lamb. She told him that if he ever so much as looked at another woman, she would return to finish the cut and would not hold anything back."

"That's a bit extreme don't you think?"

Marie shook her head without hesitation. "Nope. With matters of the heart, all is fair. My dad understood. What do you think your mother will do?"

"I don't know. I haven't even decided how I am going to tell her.?"

"Do you think she will believe you?"

I turned up my face. "Why wouldn't she?"

"People tend to not believe unpleasant information."

"But it's the truth."

"You know it's the truth. I know it's the truth. Deep down somewhere, your mother probably knows it as well, but that doesn't mean that she is ready to accept it."

"That's ridiculous."

"Ridiculous, but true. I've seen it a number of times. Men have explained themselves out of the most obviously perfidious moments. These women know what is going on, but they are not ready to accept it because then they have to act on it, and so they cling onto any hope, belief, or lie that will allow the pieces to stay together for a little longer."

"My mother is not that pathetic."

"I don't know. What I do know is that if she is and you tell her about Keith, it could really have a negative effect on your relationship."

"Our relationship is already on the rocks."

"All the more reason to maybe keep your mouth shut."

"So you don't think that I should tell her?"

"I think you should consider all angles before making a decision. Once the cat is out of the bag, you can't put it back."

During my walk home, I alternated between revealing Keith's infidelity to my mom and maintaining silence. I saw my mother angry and crying with me there to comfort her. Then I saw her lashing out and telling me that I am an ungrateful child that is ruining her life.

By the time that I got home I had decided to merely tell my mother what I saw. I would not label it or make any assumptions no matter how obvious. If need be, I will move in with my father. Under the circumstances, he would have to take me in.

But I was preempted.

"Oh, look who's here. It's the little step sister. Where have you been? Sneaking cookies in the backyard again have you?"

Katie.

"Back in town? What happened? Did you get kicked out of all the brothels?"

"Dad!"

"Can't the two of you just quit for one afternoon?"

I eyed Keith. My ears burned with anger as images of his afternoon raced in my head.

"You two are like oil and water," my mother said as she entered the kitchen.

The sound of my mother's voice made me jump.

"I have never been anything but nice to Guinevere," Katie said. "I can't help it if she is jealous of me."

"Jealous? I would be better served being envious of a man on death row."

"That's enough you two," my mom said with her hands in the air parting the two of us. "Let's keep the words peaceful."

"Why did she come here if she doesn't like me? What's wrong with her mother's place?"

Everyone was quiet before my mother broke the silence. "Her mother has a lot on her plate right now. Everyone thought it best if she came here during this...um...break."

I looked at Katie. Her eyes dug into a wall to her left.

My mother picked up her purse. "I'm off to the store. I am planning a nice meal for tonight so don't ruin your appetites."

"I'm not that hungry," Keith said. "I had a big lunch."

"Surprised you were able to eat, you know with the fork shortage going on downtown and all." I spoke before I could think. Pure anger elicited those words. Keith responded with a quick expression of surprise before regaining his composure.

≈

"So you didn't tell her?" Marie asked during lunch on Monday.

"I wanted to, but I couldn't."

"Sap. As much as you complain about your mother, you love her like a little puppy." She made googly eyes as she spoke. I hit her on her arm.

"Stop it."

"So what are you going to do?"

"About what?"

"Keith and your mom! He is making a fool of your mother. Not to mention, what if he catches something? Or gets the other woman pregnant? That's just gross."

"You were the one who suggested that I NOT tell her."

"I merely brought it up as a possibility. I have since thought about it. If it was me, I would want to know."

"What would you do?"

"If I was your mom?"

I nodded.

Marie responded without stopping to consider an answer. She clearly already thought this through. "I would probably stab him or in the very least, I would stand over him with a really large knife while he was sleeping. When he opened his eyes, I would tell him that I know what he has done and that it would be in his best interest to never do it again."

"OK," I said slowly. "So you wouldn't leave him? After he cheated on you?"

"Why? A lot of men cheat. Leave one, you'll just have the same happen with the next."

"Are you being pessimistic?

"I'm being realistic. Your mother has a right to know. That way, should she choose to stay with him, she can better protect herself."

"I can't imagine why she would stay with him after she learns of his activities."

"Either way, it will be her choice, not Keith's."

Marie was right. I had to do something. My mother deserved better. She deserved more. Yes, we may have our differences, but she is still my mother.

That evening I decided to test the waters. First, I talked my mom into watching a Lifetime movie with me. The storyline was eerily relevant. In it, the husband cheats on the wife, also a dentist. When the wife finds out, she is initially angry, but then decides to work on the marriage and also, stupidly, herself. She changes her hair, her clothes, and whatever else she feels attributed to her husband's wayward ways. The husband still isn't able to keep it in his pants and when his wife finds out, she goes ballistic and runs him over with her car multiple times.

During the movie I snuck glances at my mother to try and get a read on her. Most of the time she was catatonic. At the end of the movie, all she said was, "Wow!" I was going to have to push further.

"What would you do?" I asked slyly.

"About what?" she said as she fluffed the pillow she was leaning on.

"If you were in that situation."

"If I found out that my husband was cheating on me?"

"Yes, if you found out that Keith was cheating on you."

My mother opened her mouth wide. "I honestly don't know. I wouldn't run him over with a car if that is what you are asking."

I ignored her second comment. "You don't know what you would do if Keith was banging some other chic? Under your roof? In your bed?"

She smiled uneasily. "It would be easy for me to sit here and tell you that I would throw him out, but it's not that simple. Real life does not work the way it does on television."

"So you would stay with him?"

"I didn't say that either."

I was getting angry. "You didn't say anything."

"Why are you getting so upset over a hypothetical?"

"I'm not upset. I'm just wondering how you could stay with a man who is cheating on you. Where is your self-esteem?"

My mother's eyes blinked in succession. "I think that is enough excitement for one day, Gwen." She got up to leave. "Thanks for yet another lovely time together."

As she left the living room, Katie entered.

"A mother daughter squabble?" Katie said as she ate barbeque potato chips from the bag.

"Shut up."

"Don't bite my head off. I'm not the one cheating on your mother."

I looked at her in amazement. "What are you talking about?"

"You two are not exactly known for your low decibels."

"We were just having a 'what-if' conversation. No big deal."

Katie gave me a 'who are you kidding' look. "I'm not an idiot. How long has my dad been cheating on your mother?"

I took too long to respond. Katie chimed in. "Don't. He is my father. How do you think he met your mother?"

"Oh." I was deflated. I never knew my mother met Keith under such circumstances. I knew he was married, but I always assumed that he and his wife were separated. Knowing that my mother was the other woman in what could have been an otherwise happy relationship made me feel differently about her. No wonder she wasn't so quick to condemn a cheating husband.

"Don't worry about it," Katie said in response to my expression. "She wasn't the first."

"Is that supposed to make me feel better?"

She popped a chip into her mouth. "Nope."

"How did your mother find out?"

"Receipts. Receipts for jewelry my mother didn't receive, flowers she never saw and dinners she never ate. And then there was the hotel room."

"I'm sorry that she had to go through that," I said sincerely.

"Karma. My mother snatched him away from a different woman."

"Oh," I said again.

"It's the cycle of life. It never keeps spinning."

"Was your mother upset when she found out?"

"A bit. She actually had feelings for him. But at least she made out well in the divorce. She specifically put an infidelity clause into their prenup. I'm sure the extra cash helped on those lonely nights."

"You don't sound too broken up about it."

"It's been five years. I've had time to recover. Besides, I like your mom. Sorry my dad is a jerk."

"Should I tell her?"

"Your mom? Why?"

"Because she has a right to know."

"She probably already does. Unless she is a complete idiot, the wife is usually the first to know when her husband is having an affair." Katie continued to munch on her chips as though we were having a simple conversation about puppies.

"There is no way my mother knows that Keith is cheating on her."

Katie shrugged.

"Is there?" I said to myself.

Katie threw her feet on the couch and flicked through the channels. She stopped when she came upon two kangaroos lasciviously working to keep the population afloat.

I left Katie and sought guidance from a different source, one more similarly situated.

A low hum emanated from Oliver's room. I knocked on his door and waited for him to answer. He didn't. I knocked again. When I still did not receive a response, I turned the knob. It was unlocked and so I left myself in. Oliver was sprawled out on his bed. His head was buried deep in his pillow. The clothes that he wore, blue jeans and a stripped purple long sleeved button down, were bunched up in every place imaginable. I called his name. No response. His right foot, partially socked, hung off the side of his queen sized bed. The room had a slight musty smell. It was as if he suffered through a mini heat wave in his room. I went to open one of his windows to let in some fresh air and tripped over a beer can.

I picked the can up. It was empty. I looked around the room and found two more empty beer cans under his bed. I chucked them in the bottom of the trash in the kitchen instead of the recycling bin so they would not get noticed.

Oliver came downstairs the next morning looking worse for wear: low shoulders, dry and pasty face, red watery eyes, and lips in desperate need of lip balm.

"What cardboard box did you roll out of?" Katie chuckled.

"Good morning to you, too," Oliver said groggily.

"Doesn't look like one for you."

"I had a rough night."

"Looks like you had a couple of rough nights."

"Lay off alright?"

Katie threw her arms up. "Hey, not trying to make any enemies, just observations."

"Are you OK?" I asked.

"I'm fine; just have a lot going on at school right now."

Mom and Keith entered the kitchen. Oliver quickly grabbed an apple and left.

"Where is he in such a rush to?" mom asked after he left.

I was still angry at her.

"Maybe the better question is: Who is he in such a rush from?" Katie said with a smug look on her face as she glared at her father.

My mother looked from Katie to Keith. "What is that supposed to mean?"

Katie continued to look at her father. Keith ignored the all the eyes burning holes into his blue work shirt and threw up his hands. "Like I'm ever privy to the happenings around here."

My mother's gaze shifted from Katie to Keith to me. "What's going on, Gwen? Is there something I should know about?"

"There is always something. Just depends on whether you are willing to open your eyes or enjoy the blissful darkness. Do you like the dark, mom? Do you like being in the dark?"

"The hell are you talking about?" my mom said as she furrowed her eyebrows.

"Of course you do," I said as I stormed out of the house. Outside the wind whirled around at a high velocity. I extracted my hat from my backpack and pulled it over my hair. I guess there is a plus to having crazy, unruly hair: you never have to worry about hat hair. As if something as simple as weaved cotton could ever tame my hair into one place.

I made my way down the street and crossed over the intersection with the intention of veering left to the bus stop. The sight of Oliver's car caught me by surprise. Parked a block down and to the right was Oliver's bright orange Mustang. It sat running with the brake lights on full display. Streams of smoke wafted from the exhaust pipe. Our father presented the car to him on his 16th birthday. Oliver wanted a brand new vehicle, but dad didn't think that would be wise at Oliver's age and so he bought a 2-year-old, used Ford Mustang with just under 2 thousand miles on it. The previous owner was an 82 year old enthusiast who waited too long to buy one. It mostly sat in his garage as his eyesight was making it more and more difficult for him to drive. His daughter finally decided that it was best for dad to spend the rest of his years at a nursing home and so she sold all of his 'toys.'

I slowly approached the Mustang thinking me might be in the car with a girl or on the phone. I went to the passenger side of the vehicle and lowered my head. Oliver sat staring at the steering wheel. He wasn't on the phone. No one else was in the car. He didn't say anything and he didn't move.

It took him a minute to register my presence. When he did, he rolled down the window and smiled his carefree, opulent grin. "Hey, what's up?"

"Nothing. What's up with you?"

"Nothing. What are you doing out here?"

"I was headed to the bus, but then I saw your car and thought I'd come over."

"Do you want a ride to school?"

"Sure."

I slid into the warmth of the car. The heated black leather bucket seat was a welcomed retreat from the cold air outside. A red leaf hit the front windshield then drifted away. Oliver's face maintained his superficial smile. Part of me wanted to call him on it, wanted to ask him why he has been acting so strange lately, but then another part of me didn't really want to deal with it.

We sat in silence for most of the trip. Oliver with his fake smile. Me with my eyebrows raised with artificial happiness.

"How's school?" I asked.

Oliver nodded his head. "Not bad. I have a few areas that I need to work on, but I have them under control?"

Like me, Oliver wasn't an 'A' student, but he wasn't at risk of failing either. "And football?"

Oliver turned his smile toward me. "Since when do you care about football?"

"I care."

Oliver frowned.

"I care about you and you care about football."

67

"It's great. Good as ever."

"Have you had any scouts come to watch you play?"

Oliver's face seemed to drop. I'm not absolutely sure because it happened so fast, but I could almost swear that an expression of anger and fear flashed on his face. "Um, yeah, sure, they've been coming around, but I'm not sure that I want to play football in college."

I snorted. "Since when?"

"Since now. It might be better for me to focus on academics. Pull my grades up."

I snorted again. "Yeah, whatever. It has been a given that you are going to play football in college. Didn't dad take out money from your college fund to buy this car in anticipation of you getting a football scholarship?"

Oliver turned to me and flashed another smile. "Football isn't everything," he said in a way that seemed more for himself than for me.

"Did something happen?"

"Like what?"

"I don't know. That is why I am asking you."

"Nothing's happened. I'm just getting older and realizing that there is more to life than football."

Once we reached school grounds, Oliver parked his car and headed inside. He avoided his teammates by keeping his head down and rushing into the building.

Greg was already in his seat when I entered the classroom. My heart jumped when I saw him. I wanted to go and talk to him, but the bell rang while I was standing in the doorway. I climbed into my seat two rows over from Greg's where I sent him occasional smiles. I'd hope to catch his eye, but he maintained his focus on Mr. Grayfin who was blabbering on about something.

"What about you, Guinevere?"

I was like a deer caught in headlights. Mr. Grayfin dug his eyes into me from his position in the front. The room was still as everyone waited for me to respond. I smiled while I tried to scan my brain in hopes that something, anything that Mr. Grayfin said in the last 2 minutes seeped in. It didn't.

"We're waiting," Mr. Grayfin said mockingly.

"I'm not," Vivienne added. "I know better than to waste my time waiting on things that are never going to come to fruition."

"That's enough, Vivienne. Everyone deserves a chance, no matter how unlikely achievement is."

I frowned. Mr. Grayfin was always expecting the worse from me. Never mind that I am a C+ to a B- student. I may not be the smartest kid in class, but I am far from the dumbest. That privilege belongs to Tim Bellows who once stood up in front of class and said that Les Misérables is about a French guy that steals a loaf of bread because French people like bread.

"I'm sorry, Mr. Grayfin. I didn't hear what you said because I was reviewing my notes from Friday's class."

"Is that so?"

I nodded in the affirmative.

"You had a sub that day."

Mr. Grayfin did not expect an answer, but I smiled and nodded anyway.

"Was it a good class?"

"Indeed it was," I said stretching out the lie. I have totally blanked out what happened in class on Friday. Our substitute teacher, I forget his name, was such a bore. His speech was so low and jejune. I wanted to stab myself with my pencil just to add some spark of excitement.

"Please forgive me as I do not have my syllabus on hand, would you mind coming up here and summarizing what you did in class on Friday?"

"Summarize?"

"Yes?"

"Me?"

He smiled and nodded vigorously.

Crap. I looked around the room. Various eyes focused on me. Most in anticipation of a laugh they were certain would come after I humiliated myself. Others gave looks of sympathy. Tim Bellows was blank as usual. "I don't think that will be a good idea," I said as I lowered my voice. "I think I have a sore throat coming on and I should preserve my voice."

Mr. Grayfin eyed me with disbelief.

"She is such a liar," Vivienne shouted.

I widened my eyes and waited for Mr. Grayfin to tell her to be quiet. He didn't.

"Are you lying, Guinevere?"

I swallowed hard, making a show that my throat hurt. "No," I said quietly and solemnly. I peeked at Greg. His focus was on his desk.

Mr. Grayfin continued, "I have to say that I am leaning toward agreeing with Vivienne on this one. However, I have no way of proving you wrong. With that said, I will like you to write a one page summary about Friday's class."

The class moaned.

"Not everyone," Mr. Grayfin added. "Just Guinevere," he said with a sly smile. Vivienne mirrored Mr. Grayfin's expression.

I wanted to object, but I didn't see the point. Mr. Grayfin was going to make me suffer one way or another.

When the bell rang, I quickly grabbed my books to leave. Vivienne was blocking my path. I saw Greg hurry out of the classroom. I tried to catch his attention, but he was soon out of sight.

"What do you want?" I said when it didn't seem as though Vivienne had any intentions of moving out of my way.

"Why do you hate me so?"

"What?"

"You heard me."

"I don't hate you."

"Then what is it that you don't like about me?"

Where do I begin? "What is this about, Vivienne? I have another class to get to."

"I asked your brother out yesterday and he totally turned me down. Stacy said that he won't date me because you are bad mouthing me to him. What are you telling him about me?"

"Did it ever occur to you that maybe he isn't interested in you? That maybe he finds your most enduring qualities grotesque?" Most guys in our school would give their right arm for the opportunity to be with Vivienne. She, however, is very selective of who she chooses to date and usually gets who she wants. Oliver, albeit a typical horny teenage boy, never mentioned her to me and so technically it is possible that he finds her grotesque.

She threw a hand on her hip and opened her mouth in a look that was a cross between being seductive and livid. "I *know* that you have been saying negative things about me to your brother."

"Why would I be talking about *you* to my brother?"

"Why wouldn't you?" Vivienne took note of my eyes crossing and softened her tone. "Look, I know that life can be a bit difficult for you here at school and it is understandable to see someone like me as a threat. But I'm not. Really. You know, maybe we can even be friends. I would like that. Wouldn't you?"

"No."

Vivienne's body jerked slightly from the unexpected retort. "I'm here should you change your mind."

"And if Oliver wasn't my brother, would you be available then, too?"

Vivienne searched for an appropriate response.

"Don't bother," I said. "I already know the answer." I started to walk away.

"You always were a conniving little shit. Even back in kindergarten when you used to show up every day with snot nastily dripping from your nose. My parents said that I should pity you, but I knew better. I knew that I had to keep my eye on you with your goodwill clothes and that wild hair of yours. What, your mother doesn't love you enough to get your hair straightened? You probably think that it is cool to wear your hair like that so you can walk around here and act like you don't care about what anyone thinks about you, but that is not true. You care. You just don't have the ability to do anything about it and so you spend your time trying to sabotage the lives of others; others that you can never dream of being like."

I waited to see if she was finished. When she didn't add anymore words to her stream of insults, I turned on my heels and left the room. I could feel her eyes tear into me as I slipped around her. I hastily made my way to my locker, digging my head inside once it was open.

Vivienne always had the ability to get to me. No matter how much I tried to ignore her and just let the words "roll off," like my mother used to say, each word she spewed seemed to become permanently affixed to my skin. Over the years, space was at a premium.

"You look like you could use a beer?"

I lifted my head out of the locker. Marie was standing beside me wearing an electric blue cardigan similar to the one she wore when I first met her.

"I need a lot more than that," I said as I buried my head back into the locker.

"I could score you something stronger if that is your preference."

I faced Marie. "It was a joke."

"I knew that, but if you ever decide to turn that joke into a reality, I can help you."

I crossed my eyes and went back into the locker.

"What's wrong?"

"The usual."

Marie sucked air into her teeth, making a loud sound. "Don't let that wench get to you," Marie said pulling me out. "You are better than this," she said while shaking me.

"Am I?"

"You just need a pick me up."

"I don't want a beer."

"No, a day out away from here."

"My mother will kill me if I miss another day of school."

"You might kill yourself if you stay. Or Vivienne." Marie squinted. "It's almost worth the risk just to see if you will off her. Ah well, let's go."

"And my mom?"

"Is she home to get the call from school?"

74

"No, but Keith probably will be."

"Tell him you were sick and spent the day in the bathroom with woman issues," Marie said matter-of-factly. "Besides, it is one day. I don't think they call until you have missed several days."

I was too worn out from frustration to analyze Marie's statement and so I lazily accepted it. Marie and I left school grounds and just bummed around for six hours. Afterward we went to my house. Luckily no one was home yet as it was a bit early for me to be home from school. Generally the bus would not drop me off for another half an hour. Keith is one of the overly nosy types who doesn't accept that sometimes we got out of school early or that the bus driver got lucky and hit all green lights. He will press on until he is satisfied with a plausible answer. Once, I had to lie to him about a grade that I received on a test. The teacher initially marked the paper with a large red D by mistake then changed it to a blue B. Keith refused to believe that the teacher made the mistake and insisted that I changed the grade myself. I finally gave up arguing with him and admitted to his version of the truth.

Marie was impressed with the décor in my room. She said that her room has never been decorated with more than her dirty clothes and a few cans of cola.

"Let's make prank calls," she said with the receiver in her hand.

I took the receiver and put it back on the base. "Let's not. Everyone has caller ID nowadays."

"Can't we just press *69 or is it *67?"

"I have something better in mind."

Marie looked at me curiously. "Like what?"

I sat down next to her on my bed and spoke in a low tone. "If I show you something, do you promise not to tell anyone?"

"You know where there's a dead body?" she asked in amazement.

"What?"

"When I was eight, there was this kid named Paul who said he knew where there was a dead body. He said that he would show me, but that it had to be a secret between the two of us. I followed him into the woods. We walked for about three miles with me constantly asking how much further. Finally, he stopped and confessed that there was no dead body. He just wanted to get me alone so he could give me a kiss without getting into trouble."

I chuckled. "That was sweet."

"No it wasn't. I got my hopes up to see a dead body. He had me walk three miles through mud in my new shoes just so he could get fresh with me. I was so pissed I wacked him across the head and left him there."

"Oh, well, um sorry I don't know of any dead bodies."

"Then what is it?"

"I'm special," I said slowly.

She stared at me blankly. "I want to laugh, but I am going to give you the benefit of the doubt here because your expression is so serious."

"Because I'm serious. I'm special."

"Yes, my teacher told me that too when I was in kindergarten."

"Not like that. I have a special ability."

"Like you can draw?"

"Like in the show, *Heroes*."

"Yeah, there was a gap of a few years where we didn't have a television. Long story, but it ends with my mother's shoe flying past my father's head and making contact with our only television. That was the last day that I saw my father."

"Where you sad?"

"Yeah. I really missed that television. I still have the remote."

"I meant about your dad leaving."

"Oh, yeah, sure. Things would have been easier if she broke a window instead. It's hard for a young girl to get through life without her electronic sustenance. Part of me wanted to throw her out for having such bad aim."

I let out a low, uncomfortable chuckle. "In the TV show *Heroes*, the main characters have special abilities. One can fly. Another can heal herself."

The look on Marie's face cut me off. Every muscle in her face hung low. It was if she was prepared for a stream of the greatest crap anyone had ever fed her. I considered taking a different course and coming up with a lie, but I was tired of keeping this to myself. I wanted to tell someone. I continued, "I can do something, too."

"Oh what the hell, I'll take the bait. What can you do?"

I looked around the room for just the right thing. My Kindle e-reader was on the floor next to my closet. My mother has repeatedly stated that she will not replace it if it breaks and has sternly suggested that I 'take better care of it." I leaned in and focused. The room grew quiet. All the background noise was reduced to a memory. The now familiar warm feeling started at my feet and rose to my chest. As I exhaled the Kindle slowly rose from the ground. I couldn't see it or hear it, but I knew Marie was aghast. The Kindle rose higher and higher until it was about three feet off the ground. It then came to a stop and spun upright on an axis. Slowly at first, then at top speed. After that, it made a figure eight in the air. I felt Marie's hand on mine. Her fingers were cold. I turned to look at her.

"You're telekinetic? How? How did you do that?" she managed to say with her mouth wide open.

I looked back at the Kindle. It was lying on the floor again. "I don't know. I just can."

"Oh my goodness! Was that real?"

"Yes."

"You are shitting me. That was a magic trick. How did you do it?" She stood up and started waving the air in search of a string.

"It wasn't a trick."

Marie's face went through a variety of stages before she spoke again. "Can you show me?"

I tried to explain to Marie that I cannot teach her my special ability. That it is a gift that was given to me. She would not accept this answer, which prompted me to spend a ridiculous amount of time coaching her as she stared at various inanimate objects in my room. Slow your breathing. Focus on the object and where you want it to go. Use your mind to reach out and grab it. Feel it with your brain. Marie, thankfully, finally gave up and decided to focus her energies on coming up with schemes for using my abilities on others.

I left her with her malevolence and went downstairs to get food. I hadn't eaten since breakfast and I was starving. Oliver was standing next to the refrigerator with a beer in his hand.

"You must have a death wish," I said as I nodded toward the beer can in his hand.

"I don't take that many. Keith will never notice. Besides, if he has, he hasn't said anything about it."

"If you say so." I opened the fridge. "You sure seem to be drinking a lot lately. Is there something on your mind?"

He cracked open the can and downed half of it. "Like what?"

"Anything. You seem a bit off lately."

"A lot going on I guess. Nothing to worry about. You'll see when it is your senior year." Oliver grabbed his book bag and started walking out of the kitchen.

"Marie is here if you want to meet her," I called after him.

"Who's Marie?"

"My friend."

He smiled. "Is she cute?"

I frowned.

"Stop the pouting, I'm only joking. Glad to see you have a friend. Was starting to worry about you."

"Since when do you care about someone other than yourself?"

"Hey, that hurts. Do you really feel that way?"

"No." *Sometimes.*

"I'm going upstairs. I'll meet your friend some other time. I'm tired."

I watched Oliver climb the stairs and walk toward his room. He came to an exaggerated stop near my door. I thought he was about to enter, but then he started walking again. I waited until I heard his door close. I went back to gathering food to carry upstairs. Marie smiled as I entered the room. She told me that she had come up with several ideas for using my ability. I repeatedly told her that I didn't want anyone to know about it. She asserted that no one would. However, my ability was a gift and I should use it to exact revenge on those who have wronged me. I asked her if she had recently watched *Carrie*.

≈

Greg has been elusive since our passionate kiss at the zoo. He has refrained from making eye contact and being within five feet of me. It is only natural that he would be embarrassed by what happened that night. I would be devastated if I puked all over the place in front of someone that I cared about. I would fear that the other person would be completely disgusted by me and would never want anything to do with me again. But I could never feel that way about Greg and it was important that I let him know this.

After the bell rang ending our first class, Greg tripped over a bent metal desk leg sending his book and pencils to the floor. I immediately rushed to help him. He thanked me while looking at the floor. I touched his hand and smiled, hoping to soothe his anxiety.

"You've been dodging me," I said.

"No, no. I've just been busy."

"We were supposed to study together for this class."

This realization lifted his head. "I forgot about that. We don't have to."

"I want to."

"OK," he said, slowly nodding his head.

"How about today? Are you free after school?"

Greg and I agreed to meet at our local library. Marie came over to help me prep for what I hoped would be a moment of reveal for me and Greg.

I perused my mother's room for some makeup since I had yet to dive into the ritual of slathering chemicals onto my face. The occasion seemed to be the perfect time to start. My mother's room was icy and dark. Thin streams of light slipped through the slits between the window and the drapes. Bodily smells from sleep and perfume circulated the air. I didn't venture into my mother's room very often since she remarried. It felt like Keith's domain and I wasn't welcomed. Even though my mother's effects encompassed most of the room, Keith's few articles held the weight that mattered most. They sucked the room of my mother's energy and left his deceit. I wanted to smash everything of his that I looked at. His tablet, the glass that he keeps on his nightstand for water, his clock, even his box of tissues.

I put aside my rage and went into the bathroom. My mother keeps her makeup in a pink train case that my grandmother bought for her a few years ago. My grandmother used to sell Mary Kay products as a way to make extra cash when my mother was young. She still owns the pink Cadillac that was initially leased to her for being a top sales consultant. When she decided to retire, the regional director gifted the car to her. My grandmother passed down her philosophy on makeup (*always* wear it) and has been unsuccessfully been trying to recruit me. Up until now, I couldn't be bothered to spend the extra time in the bathroom.

I opened the train case and was greeted by more colors than in a box of crayons. Clearly my mother had her favorites, evidenced by the dents, but she apparently stocked up on others just in case. Eye shadow, mascara, eyeliner, blush, you name it. I closed the case and took it with me. As I was about to leave the room, a wave of disgust hit me. I looked over at Keith's side of the bed. Without a thought, I swiped my hand across his nightstand sending his tablet and glass to the floor. "That's better," I said to myself.

Marie was wide-eyed at my bounty. She had never before seen so much makeup outside of a store. Like a kid at a toy store for the first time, she picked through each item then tossed it aside when she saw a 'better' one. After about fifteen minutes of this, Marie finally settled on the makeup that I should wear.

"It's a bit colorful," I said as I shifted through the items that she laid out, which included purple and green eye shadow.

"That is what's in."

I looked at her with skepticism.

"Trust me."

"I don't want it to be overdone."

Marie showed me a picture of a supermodel on her mobile phone. The woman was wearing purple and green eye shadow and looked absolutely stunning. I was sold. Marie made several attempts to get the makeup 'just right.' Finally, she was finished and she handed me a mirror. I was speechless by what I saw.

"Are you sure you did it right?" I asked while holding the mirror at different angles.

"It's not exact, but I think it is a good approximation. Do you think your mother will mind if I take a few things?"

"Probably not. Just a few and not any of the ones that she uses." I held the mirror still and turned my head from left to right trying to see my face in a different light. "I'm not sure about this."

"Well, either you go with that or you wash it off and go bare-faced. Make up your mind soon because you don't have a lot of time."

I looked at the clock. I was to meet Greg at 4 o'clock. It was 3:54 pm. "Are you sure that I look OK?" I asked one last time.

"Yes, now go."

I threw the mirror, grabbed my supplies, and headed down the stairs. I heard Marie scream out that she was taking the purple and green eye shadow before I shot through the door.

The library was only a few blocks away. I arrived with two minutes to spare. I didn't see Greg's car in the parking lot and so I headed inside. The stacks, tables, and chairs were in the same place as when I was last here. I don't visit that much. In the past year I'd probably been twice. Once was to use the restroom. Love the idea of the library, but never knew what to do when I got there. Occasionally, I would find a book or two that was of interest, but I couldn't read it there. It is too cold, the chairs are uncomfortable, and eating is not allowed. I usually read on my e-reader in the comfort of my room, which is far superior to the much used and abused books that litter the library shelves.

Greg was 10 minutes late to our study session. He apologized profusely. "No worries," I said with a smile that I hoped was enticing.

During the study session, Greg glanced at me frequently. I wanted to believe that it was because he was smitten with me, but he looked uneasy and confused. I dared not ask him about it for fear of what he might say. *Gwen, I'm not interested in you. Gwen, you're not my type.* What if that kiss was a fluke? The room was starting to spin and I was beginning to sweat.

Greg asked me a question, but I couldn't process it. I kept squinting trying to understand what he was saying. His mouth was moving. Words were coming out, but my ears weren't working. Eventually he stopped talking and just stared at me.

"I'm sorry," I said after finding my voice. "I guess that my mind is somewhere else."

"Does this have anything to do with what happened at the zoo?" he asked.

I smiled uneasily.

"I'll take that as a yes. I've been thinking about that day. I've been meaning to apologize for what happened."

"It's OK. You shouldn't feel bad for vomiting."

"That too."

"Too?"

He lowered his eyes.

"What do you mean too? What else are you sorry for?"

Greg took a deep breath and blurted it out. "The kiss. I was drunk. I never should have led you on. I'm sorry."

My heart cracked.

"You're a great girl," Greg continued, "but I'm not looking for anything right now and you deserve someone who is invested in you."

I held my breath to keep from crying. How could I not see this coming? All this time I thought he was avoiding me because he was embarrassed about his revisiting his earlier nourishment when he was actually avoiding me because he thought I would read more into the kiss than then there was. Sad part is that he was right. I feel like the clueless girl in some cheesy romcom except I don't get a happy ending. Instead I am sitting here across from the guy that I love with my heart in a thousand, irremediable pieces.

We ended the session early. I told Greg that I wasn't feeling well. After assuring him that it had nothing to do with his earlier statement, we parted ways.

I took slow, short strides home. It was sickening to know that I had spent so much time fawning over Greg. What would possess me to think that someone like Greg would like someone like me? Life was so frustrating. So maddening. I looked up admiringly at a flock of birds that flew over me. They were lucky. They lived a life that was truly free. Their past firmly behind them as flew from one destination to the next. Unencumbered by the shackles that created my agony, my discomfiture. How lovely it would be to be free like them. I spread my arms and closed my eyes and imagined myself floating in the air, high in the sky, anywhere but here.

Katie was pulling in the driveway when I arrived home. "Great," I thought to myself. I tried to quickly enter the house before she got out of the car, but I could get the stupid key to turn.

"Do you need the instructions for that?" Katie asked as she approached.

I turned to look at her and she jumped back. "Whoa! You do know that Halloween has come and gone don't you?"

A rush of emotions erupted out of me in tears. I was baffled by my display, but I couldn't stop it. I was bawling like a baby who lost her favorite rattle.

Katie stood dumfounded, uncertain of what to do or of what she started. "I'm...I'm sorry," she said as she came closer.

I wiped away a stream of snot from my nose. "I'm fine."

"You don't look it. Surely my attempt at comedy isn't the reason for your crying."

I shook my head. "I just have a lot on my mind right now."

"Does it have anything to do with all of that makeup you are wearing?"

An image of Greg flashed in my head. "Partially."

"Guy troubles I take it?"

I crossed my eyes.

"Or girl troubles. No judgments."

"It's a guy."

"In that case, we can talk about it inside. No man is worth standing out in the cold for."

Once we got inside, Katie wet a few paper towels and handed them to me.

"What are these for?" I asked.

"To scrape some of that madness off your face."

"Is it that bad?"

"You passed by bad about two layers ago. Why on earth did you think purple and green would look good on you?"

"I saw it on a model. She looked great."

"Yeah and she had a team of professional makeup artists working on her. Who did yours?"

"A friend."

"Maybe you should consider your friendship status if she allowed you out here looking like an extra for the Ringling Brothers Circus."

"That's a bit harsh."

"Not from this angle."

I exhaled heavily.

"Who is this guy?"

"No one." I was reluctant to say anything. I'd had enough heartbreak for one day. I didn't need to compound my sorrow with smart talk from Katie.

"I'm here to help."

"Since when? You are always so negative. And mean." My forehead furrowed.

"At my prom, my date, who was an hour late picking me up, passed out drunk in the bushes outside of the banquet hall. And he lost the keys so I had to hitch a ride home with the Bailey twins who went to the prom together wearing matching pale blue tuxedos. Did I mention that the Bailey twins are girls? The first boy that I ever kissed did so in order to work up the nerve to kiss a different girl that he had a crush on. The first time that I ever had sex, the man had a heart attack. He then rolled over on my clothes. I had to call the paramedics then run out of the hotel wearing a sheet and his sport coat. Do you need anymore?"

I was thunderstruck. "No, I think that was sufficient."

Katie put a beer in front of me. I told her about my crush on Greg, the kiss that we shared that night at the zoo, his avoiding me afterward, my assumption of what that meant and his correction today.

"That sucks," Katie said before taking a gulp of beer.

"Do you think the makeup had anything to do with it?"

"It didn't help, but no. Sometimes guys are jerks."

"Greg is a great guy," I protested.

"Yeah, sounds like it. His vomiting in your mouth must have sealed the deal."

I lowered my head.

"Oh stop. I'm only joking. Look, I get it. You really like him."

"So how do I get him to like me?"

"It may not be possible."

"Then why would he kiss me?"

"The same reason guys scratch their balls. It's there so why not."

"So you don't think a guy like Greg could like me?"

"I didn't say that."

"Then what are you saying?"

"Not everything means something."

"How does that help me?"

"You can't make a person like you, but you can trick them into taking notice of you."

"He already notices me."

"You want him to notice you in a different way."

"How?"

"First, don't ever wear makeup like that again. It is ghastly. Second, men like a challenge. It's innate. You could be the ugliest girl that has stepped foot on earth, but if you have confidence and you act like you are a catch that he has the smallest chance of getting then he will take notice."

"That doesn't sound difficult at all," I said sarcastically.

Katie laughed. "Have you ever watched *Memories of a Geisha*?"

"You're theory comes from a movie?"

"Do you want my help or not?"

"I'm not sure."

"Call your friend over. The two of you can finish coloring your face with rainbow shades."

"What do I have to do?" I asked quickly.

≈

The next few days continued as usual. The wind twirled the cold air, whipping it around trees and houses and smacking people across the face knocking their hats right off their heads. The halls at school were stuffed with noise and busy bodies. But somehow I felt different. Ever since my talk with Katie, I'd started walking with my head held a little higher. Katie told me to, 'fake it until you make it,' and so I did that. I no longer peered through crowds looking for Greg. In class, I kept my eyes to the front. Whenever Greg said hi, I would merely give him a cursory wave. I made sure to smile and laugh whenever he was around.

Marie thought I was wasting my time on Greg. She said that any guy that let me slide through his fingers wasn't worth my time. I tried to explain it to her, but as soon as I mentioned *Memoirs of a Geisha*, she tuned me out.

My mother was sitting solemnly at the breakfast table when I got home from school one day. I'd been avoiding her ever since our discussion on infidelity. If she wanted to stay with a cheating dog of a man, that was her business.

My mother swiped her hand across her face when I entered the kitchen. I'm not certain, but it appeared as though she had been crying. Several pictures of me and Oliver in our youth were scattered on the table in front of her. My father was in a few of them.

I tried to sneak past, but was intercepted.

"Gwen, hey. Come here. I've haven't seen much of you lately."

Reluctantly I walked over to my mother. She gathered the photos in a pile then held one of me and Oliver in her hand. I was three years old in the picture. It was my birthday and my parents had just gifted me a beautiful purple bike with training wheels and purple and white streamers hanging out of the handle bars. It had a large white basket in the front with a purple flower painted on it.

"Do you remember this bike?" my mother asked.

"Yep. I repeatedly asked you to take the training wheels off so that I could be like Oliver. You finally gave in and I ended up with three stiches on my arm."

My mother laughed. "You always were stubborn. Come and sit with me."

I pointed to the ceiling. "I have homework."

"Just a few minutes? We don't talk anymore."

"That's not my doing," I said under my breath. I pulled out a chair next to my mother and plopped down. I picked up a picture of us with my dad. "Do you sometimes miss dad," I asked.

She smiled. "It's complicated."

"I don't see how. It's either yes or no."

She let out a light snort. "Everything in your world is so simple isn't it?"

"Why did you ask me to sit down if you are just going to chide me?"

"I'm not chiding you. I just…I just miss the way things used to be between us. You used to talk to me. We used to have conversations. Lately there is all of this animosity. Why?"

"Keith for one."

"He is my husband, Gwen. He has been for five years. When are you are going to get used to it?"

"He treats me like crap and you let him."

"He does not, but you could try to respect him more."

"Of course, take his side. You always do." My anger was rising. I could feel perspiration gathering on my underarms.

"Let's not do this," my mother said sounding exhausted.

"Whatever makes you happy. Close your eyes and ignore what is before you. Like they say, ignorance is bliss. In your world, there must be a raging party going on."

"What the hell is that supposed to mean?"

"Nothing. Nothing at all." I forcefully pushed back my chair and started to leave the kitchen, but then I turned around. "Why did you and dad break up?"

My mother wrinkled her face as she tried to process what said. "Why does it matter now?"

"If it doesn't matter then why won't you tell me?"

"It just didn't work out. Sometimes things just don't work out. You'll learn this when you grow up. You will see that not everything can fit so nicely in the little boxes that you have prepared for them."

"Why didn't you let us live with dad?"

My mother's eyes widened. She opened her mouth as though she was going to say something, but then changed her mind.

"So it is true. Dad wanted us and you wouldn't let him."

"Is that what your father told you?"

"It's the truth and you have just confirmed it. My life is hell because of you. Things would have been so much better for me if you'd let him take us. But instead you had to be a selfish bitch! And if that wasn't enough, now you are dragging us along while you play the part of the perfect happy wife in this shitty, fake marriage of yours!" I stormed out of the kitchen and up the stairs before my mother could say anything. I slammed and locked my door. I was two seconds into my room before the avalanche of tears came. I don't know what came over me. I have never spoken to my mother like that before. Part of me was scared of how I acted. Another part was relieved for finally letting her know how I feel.

Ever since my mother and father divorced, Oliver and I don't get to see my father that much. Dissention between my parents continued when my father moved out of the house. My parents argued over the phone then my mother would slam the receiver down. She would go to her room and sit for a while before returning to tell us that our father has a business meeting or other pre-arranged meeting to attend and thus we would not be able to visit. *Next time.* I never believed it. I always figured she was feeding us crap because she never looked us in the eye when she was delivering these excuses. I assumed that she was keeping us from our father as a way to get back at him. I never called her on it though.

I lay down on my bed, filling my pillow with mass produced salt water. I expected my mother to come upstairs and berate me for speaking to her so disrespectfully, but after ten minutes all I heard was the front door closing. Then the phone rang. It was my dad.

"Hey, sweetie. How are you doing?"

I was still sobbing, but tried to sound as normal as possible. I didn't want him to know that I'd been crying. "I'm fine."

"Are you sure?"

I kept quiet. I feared that any word out of my mouth would be followed by a fury of tears.

He continued. "Your mother just called me. She is really concerned about you."

"I bet she is," I managed to say.

"Your mother loves you, Gwen and you need to learn to be more respectful of her. She has sacrificed a lot for you."

"Like what?" I spat.

"She has worked really hard to maintain her career and raise the two of you. She has been the main caretaker for a very long time. I, for one, am very grateful for that. She has raised two wonderful young adults. I could not ask for better kids."

I felt my disposition soften a bit. "You're just saying that."

"No, I am not. I don't think I could have done as good of a job and it pains me to hear how you are speaking to her."

"Doesn't it bother you that you were robbed of the opportunity to raise us?"

My father took a deep, exaggerated breath before he spoke again. "There were logistical issues involved. I am sorry that our family broke up. I would have loved it if we were able to stay together and live as one big happy family, but unfortunately things don't always work out that way. The fact that your mother and I no longer want to be married has nothing to do with the love that we each have for you. Your mother loves you more than you could even begin to understand. There is nothing that she wouldn't do for you."

"Then why is she still married to Keith? He is so mean to me."

"I have never been a fan of Keith's, but he doesn't hate you."

"Oh, yes, take her side."

"I'm not taking sides, Gwen."

"You should hear the things that he says to me."

"Like what?"

"He says that I am a burden and that I will never amount to anything."

"He said that?"

"YES!"

My father was quiet. I heard him put the phone down. When he returned, he told me to hang in there. He accepted that I was in a difficult situation, and suggested that I stay out of Keith's way. I was going off to college in a few years and that time would go by quickly. He ended the call with his usual reminder that he is always available should I ever need to talk about anything.

I angrily hung up the phone then sank my head into my pillow. I must have fallen asleep, because the next thing I knew the sun was down and the street lights were on full display. The phone was ringing again. I hoped it was my father calling me back telling me to pack my bags because I was going to live with him. My eyes veered toward my closet where I keep my suitcases.

"Gwen?"

It was 10:30 pm. The voice was low and harsh. Vaguely familiar.

"Hello, Gwen? Are you there?"

"Oliver?"

"I need your help."

"Speak up, I can hardly hear you."

"I NEED YOUR HELP!"

I turned my ear away from the phone to allow the flow of cacophony stream into the air. "Where are you?"

"I'm on Chestnut near Cedar."

"Why?"

"I need you to come," he said, ignoring my question.

"Oliver, it is almost 11 o'clock at night. Why do you need me to go to Chestnut and Cedar? It is only a few blocks away. Can't you just drive home?"

"I can't"

"Why?"

"Look, I just can't. Are you coming or not?"

"Not until you tell me what is going on," I said sternly.

I heard some movement on the other side of the phone. I looked out of my window. A full moon was on display. The clock read: 10:32 pm.

"I was in an accident," Oliver finally said.

"Oh, my goodness. Are you OK?"

"I'm a little banged up, but I'm OK."

"Did you call the police?"

"No."

"Call the police."

"No, I can't."

"You can't? Was anyone hurt?"

"No one was hurt. I hit a pole. I just want to go home. Please, just come and help me."

I considered asking Oliver more questions but he was becoming more and more agitated as we spoke so I figured that I would get my answers at Chestnut and Cedar.

Winter was well on its way. The nighttime temperature was already in the 20s. I wrapped myself in my blue winter coat, matching scarf and threw on a hat, but I was moving too quickly and forgot my gloves. Big mistake. The cold wind attacked my hands as soon as I stepped outside and I was forced to stuff them in my pockets for some relief.

97

I took a left when I reached the end of the driveway and walked four blocks to Chestnut then turned right. This side of Chestnut ran through Ridge Park and Forest Preserve. The street was empty except for a pair of stationary car lights about two blocks away. As I got closer, I could see that the car had jumped the curb and hit a pole that was holding up a sign warning drivers to beware of deer. The sight scared me. After pausing to process what I was seeing, I ran and called out Oliver. He was sitting on the curb a few feet from the car, his head buried in his hands.

"Oliver," I called out again.

He lifted his head. I stepped back in shock. A cut about three inches in length ran from his eyebrow down the side of his nose. Blood coated most of his face.

"You said you weren't hurt," I said trying to gage the seriousness of the wound. I took off my scarf and wiped some of the blood off his face. He winched when I touched the area around the wound. "You need to go the hospital."

"I'm fine. It looks worse than it is."

Oliver wasn't wearing a coat. His clothes were tinged with blood and dirt and there was a strong hint of alcohol coming from him.

"Have you been drinking?" I asked.

"No."

I tilted my head and gave him the 'don't lie to me' look.

"One beer," he fessed. "That hardly counts."

"Is that why you don't want to call the police?"

"I don't want you to call the police because I don't want to make a big deal out of this. I hit a pole. No one got hurt. I don't need to go to the hospital. A police officer would insist that I be seen by a doctor. Mom would have been called in unnecessarily. It would have all turned into a big production over absolutely nothing. The car isn't even that badly damaged."

I stood up and walked over to the car to survey the damage for myself. "What are you going to do about the car?" I asked.

"It should be drivable," Oliver said, still sitting on the curb.

The driver's side door was open. I peeked in and was immediately bashed in the face by the strong odor of alcohol. I counted at least six beer cans, two bottles of vodka and a bottle of whiskey. I walked around to the passenger side of the car. There was a dent near the right front headlight. Streaks in the paint ran from there to the passenger side door. Pieces of the plastic that covered the headlight and indicator and fog lights littered the grass around the pole and the street. The pole, while deeply bent, managed to not touch the ground. The damage was not as slight as Oliver suggested, but it wasn't excessive and the car should still be drivable.

I grabbed Oliver's coat from the backseat of the car and walked back to where he was sitting. He was holding the now red scarf to his head.

"How are you feeling?"

Oliver moved the scarf from his face. "My head hurts. I'm a little shaken up."

"There's a lot of alcohol in the car. A lot of empty cans and bottles." I said without making any accusations.

99

"I was out with some of the team. They left that behind and I guess some of it spilled when I hit the pole."

"Are you sure?"

"Am I sure about what?"

"Did you have too much to drink? And is that why you didn't want to call the police?"

"Gwen, I told you. I had one beer."

I nodded my head as I looked back at the car. The amber light from the street lamps was overshadowed by the incandescent full moon.

I didn't believe that Oliver only drank one beer, but I wasn't prepared to do anything about it. He was right, no one got hurt. However, if I call the police, they will very likely arrest Oliver. That could mark the end of his football career and his chance of attending any decent college.

"Come on," I said trying to lift him up. "Let's go before someone comes along and tries to be a Good Samaritan."

Oliver was unsteady when he stood up. I wasn't sure if it was because of the booze or the head wound. Slowly we walked to the car. I instinctively put him in the passenger seat. I didn't realize what I had done until I reached the back of the car. "Crap," I thought then headed back to the passenger side.

"I don't have a driver's license."

"You'll be fine," he said, still holding the scarf to his head.

I stood up then bent over again. "No, I don't think this is a good idea."

"Haven't you driven before?"

My mind went to the one time I was behind the wheel. Greg was in the passenger seat trying not to vomit. I was doing 10 M.P.H. trying not to get into an accident. I was drenched in sweat and fear by the time I reached Greg's house. After that day, I vowed never to attempt such a stunt again.

"Gwen, in case you haven't noticed, I am in no condition to drive. Now, unless you want to call mom and explain to her why *we* are out here so late at night and what happened to my car then I suggest you climb into the driver's seat and figure it out."

"You don't have to be so nasty about it. I'm doing *you* a favor."

"I'm sorry. I'm just really tired. The accident has me on edge. Please, can we just go?"

I stood up again and looked down the street. There weren't any houses on this block, but once I turned onto Evergreen, there were homes on both sides with occasional cars parked on the street. I took in a deep breath. Recently there was a news report about a nine-year-old boy who stole his father's van and went for a 20 minute joy ride. Sure he hit three cars in the process, but if you factor in the time and distance covered (10 miles), that's not bad for a nine-year-old. If he can drive, surely I can manage to drive a few blocks home. It's not like it's my first time. I'll cross my fingers on the 'not hitting any cars in the process' part.

I crept to the driver's side and fell into the seat. My heart thumped like it wanted to escape. My hands shook as I grabbed the keys which were still in the ignition. "You've done this before," I told myself as I turned the key. It's just like riding a bike. A bike you have not yet mastered. A part of me became excited, but then nothing happened.

101

"Your car isn't working," I said facing Oliver. He had his head resting on the head rest.

"You have put your foot on the brake and the clutch to turn it on then put the gear into reverse."

"I have to do what?"

Oliver turned toward me. "This is a manual transmission; you can't just start it by turning the key."

"SHIT!"

"Calm down. It's not as difficult as it seems. Put your left foot on the clutch and your right foot on the break."

My breathing intensified. "Where's the clutch?"

"On the left of the break."

I looked down. It was dark. I could barely make out three pedals. "Shit, shit, shit," I said to myself.

"You'll be fine. Just do as I say."

"OK. OK. OK."

"Stop saying OK."

I looked at him and nodded nervously while biting away another OK.

"Put your left foot on the clutch and your right foot on the break then turn the key," Oliver said calmly.

I did as I was told and the car came to life. "It worked!"

"Now put the gear in reverse and slowly press on the gas while lifting your foot off the clutch."

"So I take my foot off the break?"

"Yes."

I put the gear into reverse and slowly pressed the gas while taking my foot off the clutch. I must have done something wrong because the car jerked and shut off.

"Don't worry about it, just start it up and try again."

It took me three attempts before I finally got the car to reverse. Going forward proved to be another challenge. Twenty minutes, several shut offs and jerking later we pulled into the driveway. Once the car was put into the garage, Oliver had me put a cover over it. He didn't want to alarm mom because she would only worry. I did as I was told.

Everyone was still sleep inside. We quietly went up the stairs and into Oliver's bathroom. I helped him clean and bandage his wound. He winced a few times. I told him that was his penance for being stupid. Afterward he climbed into his bed without changing out of his clothes. I watched him for a few minutes before going to my own room.

I didn't sleep that night. I stayed up worrying about Oliver. I wondered if he was telling the truth about the alcohol and if so, what caused the accident. Oliver probably had someone who could fix the car for cheap so my mother may never see it, but what about the gash on his face. How was he going to explain that one? Was I wrong to have helped him? Would I get in trouble if someone found out? I heard something while we were out there. I wrote it off as a squirrel at the time. What if I was wrong? What if it was a person?

I tossed and turned in my bed for hours. I tried to will myself to sleep. I tried to fill my mind with innocuous thoughts, but it kept shifting back to the car against the pole and Oliver sitting on the curb, blood soaking the asphalt.

I turned to look at the clock on my nightstand. 5:43 am. 5:44 am. 5:45 am. A loud noise came blaring out of the clock. Instinctively, I hit it with a heavy hand. It was time to get up and get ready for school.

Chapter Four
Just Keep Swimming

Ring.

Ring.

Ring.

"Sorry, I'm not available at the moment. You know what to do at the beep."

"Hey, dad, It's Gwen. I've been trying to get ahold of you for some time now. I know that you are busy, but can you call me back? It's sort of important. Things are OK at school. Have you spoken to Oliver lately? I'm a little worried about him. It's probably nothing, but I'll feel better knowing that you talked to him. I-"

Beep.

If you would like to hear your message, press pound. If you would like to leave a different message, press 8. For other options, press 9.

≈

Oliver did not get up for school the next morning. He told mom through the door that he wasn't feeling well. She looked at me for an answer. I shrugged and said, "Something must be going around." When she left, I went into Oliver's room.

Sometime during the night, Oliver changed his clothes. He was now wearing a pair of green and yellow basketball shorts and a plan white t-shirt. He sat up on his bed when he saw me.

"How are you feeling?"

"Horrible," he said while pressing his forehead back with his hand. "My head is killing me."

"That would be the alcohol," said a voice from behind.

I turned to see Katie standing in the doorway.

"What?" I asked.

Katie ignored me and addressed Oliver. "I thought you knew what you were doing?"

I looked from Katie to Oliver. "What is she talking about?"

Katie smiled. "Grown up matters, dear."

"Stop patronizing me."

"It's nothing," Oliver said.

Katie faced me. "Maybe you should step out for a minute so Oliver and I can have a chat."

"Bite me," I said.

"Ouch. That hurt," Katie said with a chuckle.

"Why do you insist on being such an ass all of the time?"

"Because I'm so good at it," she said with a smirk.

"Oh yes, indulge in the spectacular talents of yours which are usually at home wallowing at the bottom of a very long, dark barrel."

"Congratulations. You have finally succeeded in your last phase of turning into my father."

I inched closer to her. "Take that back now."

The two of us angrily threw words at each other. We didn't stop until prompted by Oliver.

"Katie bought me the alcohol," Oliver confessed.

"You said that your teammates had the alcohol. You lied to me. Why?"

"Don't," Oliver said to Katie before she could say anything. "I didn't lie to you, Gwen. I said that it was for me and my teammates."

"Except they couldn't make the party," Katie joked.

"Katie, please," Oliver pleaded.

"Oh, cut the crap, Oliver. Who are you kidding here?"

"How did she manage to buy alcohol? She's not even of age?" I said to no one in particular.

"Can you please leave me alone with my sister?"

Katie threw her hands in the air. "Fine. Live your lives under blankets." She turned toward me on her way out. "My dad would be so proud."

"What is going on?" I asked after Katie left.

"She always has one foot in crazy," Oliver said nonchalantly.

I sat next to Oliver on his bed. "I mean with you. You haven't been yourself lately and now the accident and the alcohol. You're not an alcoholic are you?"

"Don't be silly, Gwen. I made a stupid mistake. A very stupid mistake and I have learned from it. I won't be doing that again."

"And there is nothing else going on?"

"No, I promise. Everything is great."

"What about your car?"

"Everything is fine. Don't worry about anything."

We chatted for a few more minutes before I had to leave. I left for school that morning feeling uneasy despite Oliver's assurances. I didn't believe him when he said, "Everything is fine." Oliver, unlike me, always looked on the brighter side of things. To him, the glass was always half full. I was always on the fence, unable to lean one way or another. Oliver did all he could to make everyone around him smile, including me. I hate to admit this, but I preferred this about him. It allowed me to think of him as blithe. Not that he is without flaws, but that he can look past them and see some ray of light. I depended on this quality about him. I counted on it. But now I'm starting to see things differently. All those beer cans are starting to add up. Were those smiles ever bright and perky? What if Oliver is crying out for help? What if he needs my help?

"Stop being ridiculous," Marie said before she stuffed a muffin in her mouth. "Is everything a Greek tragedy to you?"

"You don't know Oliver."

"I've seen him around and I know disturbed. He isn't disturbed. It was a stupid mistake. He isn't the first teenager to make one. That is what we are supposed to do at this age. Trust me. Have your fun now because it is all downhill after this. Work, babies, mortgage. Ugh!"

"You make it seem like we should all slit our wrists once we graduate high school."

"No, I hear the college years are a blast. You might want to consider the wrist splitting thing once the college years are over though."

"I can always count on you to look on the brighter side."

"I'm here to speak the truth not to make it look pretty." Marie drowned a French fry in ketchup and put it in her mouth. "What do you have planned after school?"

"I have a study session with Greg today."

"Ugh. Blow him off. Come out with me."

"I can't do that."

"Why? He's a jerk."

"He is not."

"He totally blew you off."

I hated having this discussion with Marie. In her opinion, Greg was not worthy of my time. She felt that he used me that night in a fit of horniness. I told her that wasn't true. Greg would have to be a jerk to do that and he is far from a jerk. He was always nice to me and I believe that he just doesn't want to ruin what we have. It is difficult for guys to find a good female friend and when they do, they are reluctant to change the relationship for fear of what might happen.

"Fine, go to your prince charming, but don't say I didn't warn you."

"Must you be so negative?"

"Must you be so dense?"

I spent the rest of the day debating with myself on whether Katie or Marie was right about Greg. Katie believes that Greg just needs a little nudge. Most men, she said, will not pass up the chance to be with a decent looking girl. In her opinion, women have a power over men and can pretty much get their pick once she learns how to use it.

Marie agrees with her to an extent. She feels that a woman's power is between her legs and as long as she doesn't mind being used up and tossed out like yesterday's leftovers, she can get any man she wants. For the night that is. The deal is off once the sun rises. Or if there is a football game on the television. Or if, God forbid, you expect to snuggle afterward.

I didn't want to believe Marie's version. I wasn't going to believe Marie's version. Greg is a great guy. He would never treat me so harshly. Yes, he kissed me without the intention of a relationship, but that doesn't make him a bad person. Actually, it is evidence of just the opposite. Greg was so concerned about my feelings that he avoided me. Only the most worthy of suitors would ever consider the woman's feelings.

Greg walked into the small private room that I reserved for the two of us just as I was contemplating a plan to win him over. The world always takes a break when Greg enters the room. He has the most amazing blue eyes that I have ever seen. They are so pure that they don't even look real. Greg put a hand through his auburn hair and flashed his knee quivering smile.

"Hey, you," he said.

"Hey. You." I wanted to reach across the table and kiss him. My lips were stuck in a wide stretch.

Greg sat down and took a pen and some paper from his backpack. "Man, I so regret taking Romantics. I didn't think it would be so much work."

"Yeah," I said, still smiling like a star struck fan.

"You are so funny."

Was than an insult or a compliment? I ran Katie's advice through my head. *Be elusive. Seem unattached. Don't smile too hard. Eye contact should be deep and short. Always be the one to pull away.*

Quickly I pulled my lips together. This was no easy feat. Greg always made me smile. He once told me that I had a very pretty smile. This made me smile more. "Think of the greater good," I told myself.

I took a deep breath to gather myself.

Elusive.

"If you say so," I said with a sly smirk. "I can't study too late. I have plans later."

"That's cool. We can reschedule if you need to leave now."

"No," I said a little too eagerly. I then tried to recompose myself. "Can I ask you your opinion on something? I need a male perspective."

"Shoot."

"Comic Book Billy is always staring at me. Do you have any idea why?"

Greg laughed. "Don't ask me. He is a weird one. His whole crew is weird. Any chick that would want to get with him needs her head examined." Greg's expression went from relaxed to worried. "Unless you are interested in him. Hey, far be it from me to get in the way of young love. The heart is a fickle thing, but it wants what it wants."

"No...no...I...no. I'm not interested in him."

Greg threw his hands up. "Hey, some chicks like the geeky type." He stopped and smiled at me then resumed. "I can see it. You two might make a cute couple."

"No. No! NO!" I said, my voice rising with every word. "I'm not interested in him. I'm interested in you." I lowered my eyes as soon as the words came out.

Silence took over the room. It pushed out all unsaid words about Comic Book Billy and replaced it with regret and uncertainty about me and Greg.

After what seemed like an eternity, Greg spoke. "Maybe I should go."

I looked up at him. "That's it?" I said incredulously. "I open myself to you and all you can say is that you have to go?"

"Look, I don't want to get into to this."

"You don't want to get into this?" My voice was now well above what is acceptable in a library.

"Can you please lower your voice?"

"Am I embarrassing you?"

"No." He put a hand on mine. I instinctively pulled back.

"I thought you were cool with this?"

"Cool with what?"

"Gwen, I like you. I really do. You are a great girl, but I am not looking to be with anyone right now."

"You can say that you don't like me. I won't break."

"Then I would be lying. It would be a privilege for any guy to be with you."

"But you don't want to be with me?"

"I don't want to be with anyone right now. I have college to think about and the scouts are out looking at me. I need to do well if I am going to get recruited to a good school. I can't get sidetracked by a relationship right now."

I looked into his eyes to try and discern if he was telling the truth or feeding me a bunch of bull. I got nothing. "Really?" I asked.

Greg stood closer to me. I could smell the cologne that he wore. It was mixed with a bit of perspiration, but it still smelled good. I imagined him walking out of a hot shower wearing nothing but a towel. The fragrance that emanated off him was probably intoxicating.

Greg ran a finger along the side of my cheek and stared deep into my eyes, enough to make me tremble, and said, "You are amazing. Don't ever let anyone tell you otherwise." He then looked down at my breast and licked his lips.

"I gotta get going," he said as he picked up his belongings; a backpack, book, cell phone and keys. "I'll catch you later."

He was out the door before I could bring up the fact that we never actually studied. Seven minutes. That is how long we were together. That is how long it took me to fail miserably in my attempt to win him over. I am such a loser.

I slid into my chair and sat motionless for the remainder of the 30 minutes that I had left in my reservation for a room meant for two, but was now being used by one. I didn't do anything or think about anything. All that I could manage to do was to sit and listen to my breathing. It was both a soothing and pathetic experience.

The door opened and the library assistant asked if I still needed the room. I don't know what I told him, must have been no because the next think I remember, I was walking outside in the cold. My books and coat were stuffed in my backpack, which was hanging precariously on my left shoulder. Each foot defiantly dragged me toward home. The steps becoming more difficult as I walked. A rock got in my way and I hit the ground - hard. I rolled on my back and stared at the sky. Blood dripped from my forehead. I let it roll down my right temple, slide across my ear and hit the ground. Drip. Drip. Drip. My forehead hurt, but I didn't do anything to contain the pain or the flow of blood.

A flock of small black birds flew over me. They were uncharacteristically quiet as they soared through the air, circling above. I felt free watching them, freer than I have ever felt. At that moment my worries were gone. Greg didn't matter. Keith didn't matter. Nothing mattered. At that moment, nothing could bother me. I closed my eyes and envisioned myself floating in the air. Higher and higher I went until I reached the birds. The circle transformed into an arrow with me making up the left most point. Together, the birds and I traveled the earth. We flew up north to Canada. We flew

114

over Niagara Falls then headed to the Appalachian Mountains. Afterward, we went east and crossed the Atlantic to Europe. We passed by the London Eye and Big Ben before making our way to the Eiffel Tower and Neuschwanstein. Next were the deserts of the Middle East complete with camels, the smog in Beijing, and the bright lights in Tokyo. We turned around and passed through India on our way to Nigeria where we saw Farin Ruwa Falls. A slight left and we were traveling along the beautiful beaches in South America. I ditched the flock and decided to hang out at Praia do Sancho, a bay on the archipelago Fernando de Noronha in Brazil.

Slowly I made a twirling descend toward the crisp blue water. My shadow, easily viewable through the pellucid water, grew larger with every passing second. I held my breath in the moments before my fingers broke through the warm, turquoise liquid. In the moments before, I closed my eyes and prepared to fully immerse myself.

But instead of feeling the water penetrate my clothes, I felt repeated shaking. I opened my eyes.

"Oh, thank God. Thank God. You're OK."

I blinked a few times to adjust my eyes. My mother was sitting next to me on my bed. Oliver and Katie were standing side-by-side along a wall.

"How are you feeling?" my mother asked when I looked back at her.

I tried to lift my head, but was met with excruciating pain.

"Don't get up," My mother said as she pressed me back down.

"What happened?" I asked.

"I don't know," my mother said while shaking her head. "I was hoping you could tell us. Oliver found you sprawled out on a sidewalk. You weren't wearing a coat and you were bleeding from your head. We assumed that you tripped on a nearby rock."

"Yea, I remember now," I said, cutting her off. "I wasn't paying attention to where I was going. Sorry." I turned to Oliver. "Thanks."

My mother's face became confused. "But that doesn't explain why you weren't wearing your coat."

I opened my mouth in hopes that a plausible excuse would spill out. "I guess I was hot."

"It is 11 degrees outside."

I nodded my head. "Yea."

The room was quiet for a while. Everyone moved their eyes around, questions swirling, but no one said what was on their mind.

"Well," my mother began, "I was going to take you to the emergency room, but Keith looked you over and said that you should be fine. He suggested that you get some rest and so we are all," she looked at Oliver and Katie, "going to leave you so that you can rest." She rubbed my arm, but didn't move. "You know sweetie," she said in a lowered voice, "I'm here if you ever need to talk about anything. I know that Keith said that you need to rest, but if have anything that you would like to talk about, I can stay here and talk with you. Or if you want to talk later, that would be fine too." She smiled nervously.

"Um, OK," I said. "I don't really have much to talk about. Sorry about scaring you all, but maybe you'd be better off going after that rock." I forced a laugh, but no one joined in.

"Sweetie, should I be worried about you?"

116

"No, mom. I'm sorry about what happened today, but really there is nothing to be worried about. I'm fine. Really."

"Get some rest." She kissed me on the forehead and stood up while still holding my hand.

Katie gave me a sorrowful look before following my mother out the door. Olive took a step toward the door, but then turned to me. "You really scared us. Seeing you laid out on the ground like that, it really freaked me out, Gwen."

"I'm sorry."

"I know you and mom don't exactly have the best relationship, but if there is something that you need to talk about…"

"Don't lecture me, Oliver. I told you that everything was fine. By the way, how are you doing?"

"Really, Gwen? That's how you plan to handle this?"

"No, Oliver. I'm just trying to point out that sometimes people do dumb things for no other reason than doing something dumb. Not everything has a reason. Unless, of course, you want me to call mom back in here so we can have a group chat?"

"I'm just worried all right? I'm allowed to be worried."

"Thank you, but I'm fine. Really, I'm fine. I was just having a really weird day that is all. There is nothing else."

"Sure?"

"Positive."

My mother took off work the next few days so that she could monitor me. After about a day and a half of this, I was eager to get back to school. My mother resisted this decision until I reminded her about the number of days that I'd already missed from school - some of which she was not privy to thanks to my deleting certain messages from the answering machine - and the negative impact they could have on my future. She relented.

I was standing in my usual spot waiting for the same bus that I wait for each school day, but nothing about this day felt normal. Comic Book Billy was sitting in a middle row seat. He smiled at me as I walked passed. I flashed a smiled with questioning eyebrows. He cornered me as soon as we got off the bus.

"Hey, Gwen."

"Hey, Comi- Billy."

"Uh, the name's William. My friends call me Will or Retch."

"Retch?"

"It's a video game thing."

Of course.

"How have you been?" he asked.

"Fine. Thanks."

He continuously nodded his head as he searched for his next words.

"*The Royal Tenenbaums* came on this weekend. Did you happen to catch it?"

"Nope."

"Have you seen it before? It's a classic."

"Yeah, I've watched it before."

"Cool huh?"

I looked around trying to prepare to break away from this boring conversation. "If you say so."

"You didn't like it?" he asked.

"No."

"It is a great movie. It takes you on a journey. Maybe you just didn't like where it took you."

"However you want to define it. It was almost two hours of my life that I can never recoup. I would prefer to not extend that time by talking about it."

"OK, um, did you finish your report for Social Studies?"

"I'm putting the final touches on it." *I hadn't even started.*

"That's cool. I'm almost finished as well. If you like, we can get together and review each other's work."

"Yeah, sure," I said unenthusiastically.

William was surprised. "Oh, great. How about today after school?"

I took a few steps toward the building. "Today won't work, but I'll be in touch."

He reached into his pocket and I took this as my opportunity to leave. "I'll talk to you later," I said as I quickly walked away. When I turned to wave bye, I saw him standing pitifully with a mobile in his hand.

Back to school and to the miserable existence that has become my life. I walked down the halls noting the smiling faces and laughter. I wondered if it was all just a ruse. Were they actually quarries rich with despair and bleakness? Do they, too, feel the uncertainty that greets each day? Or was I alone on this island?

I contemplated this as I sloughed off to Romantics. Greg was standing over Vivienne who was half ignoring him. He was trying to retell some joke that he heard on television. Either he isn't a very gifted raconteur or he was watching crap.

Vivienne perked up when she saw me. She immediately acted immensely interested in whatever Greg was saying. She started flipping her hair. Her teeth were no longer confined by her lips, which now needed a new coat of slowly applied lip gloss. Noticing the change, Greg looked up. I quickly averted my eyes when ours made contact. I mindlessly sat through class, only focusing on my desire to not look at Greg.

Marie was waiting for me at my locker. She immediately wanted to know why I haven't been in school the past two days. I tried to explain to her that I fell and hit my head, but she kept pressuring me for a different explanation.

"Do you want the truth or do you want a lie?" I said exasperatedly.

"I just want my friend back," Marie said with a downcast look.

"You say that as though I went somewhere."

"You haven't been the same lately."

"I just have a lot on my mind."

"I know. How about we go to my house and watch some bad movies?"

I smiled. "I wish I could, but I am supposed to meet my dad for dinner tonight."

Marie's face turned sullen.

"I'm not lying. How about tomorrow?"

"I guess."

I avoided another run in with Comic Book Billy by leaving the school building a few minutes early and ducking into the back of the bus. I avoided eye contact as he gave me a puzzled look when I got off at my stop.

Chapter Five
Clear Skies

A clean, Estoril Blue Audi R8 was parked in the driveway when I got home. My hand grazed the immaculate car as I walked by. Still warm.

I caught a glimpse of my mother and father through the door and had a small flash of how my life could have been. *If…*

My mother smiled a little uneasily when I entered the kitchen. She was sitting at the breakfast table. My father was standing opposite her.

Never one to be caught in anything less than the best, my father was dressed in blue pinstriped pants and a tailored red and yellow button-down with gleaming silver and yellow cuff links.

"Hey, sweetie," my dad said when he caught sight of me.

I smiled. My dad gave me a hug; or rather he stood somewhat erect as I stood on the tip of my toes and hugged him. Our hugs have always been awkward. Move in the wrong direction and you risk brushing your lips inappropriately on the other person. My dad is also 6 feet 2 inches to my 5 feet 4 inches – the height difference only complicates matters.

"How's school?"

"Fine."

"I hear that you've missed a few days."

"Richard," my mother said through her teeth. "Now is not the time."

"What? I can't talk to my daughter."

My mother didn't look too happy. She never was when my father came around. In spite of my well calculated and seemingly fool proof attempts, my parents never did more than tolerate each other. I used to pray at night that God would bring my parents back together. When I was in first grade, a classmate of mine told me that God answers all prayers, you just have to tell him what you want while kneeling down beside your bed at night with your hands pressed together.

When that didn't work, I started finding reasons for my mother and father to come together. I told my mom that I had an assignment that I needed to work on with the *entire* family. Instead of scheduling a time for us to be together – I figured they would see how wonderful it is to be a family and immediately get married – she gave me the phone and told me to call my dad and work with him over the phone on his contribution.

By second grade I was slighted by my unsuccessful attempts at my parents' reconciliation, but not yet deterred. The stakes needed to be raised. I coaxed my mother into having a movie night, just the two of us. Once the lights were out and the popcorn buttered, I lit a few candles around the house on the premise that it created a better atmosphere for the movie. I then called my dad and, being as ambiguous as possible, led him to believe that there was an emergency at the house and he needed to come over a.s.a.p. I opened the front door just a bit and headed upstairs for a bathroom break when I saw his headlights.

My father rushed into the house. "Eve. Gwen. Oliver."

123

I watched from upstairs as my mother rushed to the front door. "Richard, what are you doing here? What is going on?" She looked at the open door. "How did you get in?"

"Is everything OK," my dad said, his breathing heavy.

"Everything is fine," my mother said slowly. "Why are you dressed like that?"

My father looked down at his white undershirt, heavily wrinkled pants, and untied gym shoes. "I got a call from Gwen," he said anxiously.

At that moment, sirens could be heard wailing in the background. They quickly grew louder.

"She said that there was an accident. Blood everywhere. Or something. I threw on some clothes and called the police from the car."

My mother's face went from astonishment to concerned to angry faster than I could make it to my room. "GUINEVERE! GET DOWN HERE NOW!"

Steam seemed to be emanating from my mother's head as I slowly made my way down the stairs. But before my mother could tear into me, a police officer appeared at the door followed by two EMTs. My parents stepped outside to discuss what happened. My mother apologized profusely for the misunderstanding and thanked them for their service. She promised that it would not happen again. As soon as the door closed, my punishment began. Both of my parents tore into me. They yelled at me about how serious such an accusation was and how I wasted tax payers' money and precious resources with my antics. My assertion that I never actually said anything concrete nor was I the one to call 911 didn't hold much water. It only seemed to anger them more.

124

I fessed up and told them that I was hoping to get them back together. This shut them up momentarily as they eyed each other silently. My mother wanted to know where on earth I came up with such a ridiculous idea.

"On TV."

I was put on punishment and my television privileges were revoked for two weeks. That was the last time I tried to get my parents together. I thought I would let the universe have a go. Surely there was some magical force out there that would eventually bring my parents together.

"It's fine mom. It is nothing, dad. Really. School is great."

"That is what I want to hear. How about some we put some food in your tummy?"

"OK. Where are we eating?"

"Where would you like to go?"

"Well, there is a new Cuban restaurant on 55th that I was thinking of trying."

"Cuban? You don't want to go to Mancino's?"

"We always go to Mancino's."

"Because it is our thing. It is what we do. You don't have to go if you don't want to. I just thought you liked it. You always liked it before."

I was 12 years old the last time I went to Mancino's Steakhouse. It is the only place that my dad ever takes me when we go out to eat; the occurrence of which has been in sharp decline. Mancino's is one of the few steakhouses left in the area that still has a buffet option that you can order along with your get-it-yourself fountain drink (no free refills). I used to love going there when I was about six or seven years old. The sirloin steak tips drowned in A1 sauce and a side of French fries was my meal du jour. I thought I was in heaven. Now that I have gotten older, the place doesn't hold the same special place that it used to. Now when I go there, I can't help but to notice the cracks in the table, the tears in the vinyl booths, the food caked on the menu.

We pulled into a parking spot near the door, one of many. I struggled to get out of the Nugget Brown bucket seat. My knees were situated higher than my bottom which made for a tricky entry and exit. Once outside of the car, we were immediately seated. My dad ordered for the both of us, without even bothering to ask what I wanted.

"It's nice being here," my dad said after the waitress took our menus. "With all of those fancy, expensive restaurants that I go to every day, it is nice to be able to go to a comfortable family restaurant where we have so many memories."

I smiled and nodded even though I didn't really agree with him.

"Can you get me a Diet Coke on your way up?"

I turned to look at the fountain drink dispenser. Several stacks of brown plastic cups were lined up next to it. "I-um-OK." I reluctantly got up to get my dad his Diet Coke. I got myself a drink as well so as to not to make him uncomfortable at the fact that I wasn't going to get anything to drink.

My dad and I sat opposite each other, 24 inches apart, avoiding eye contact. Our food finally arrived and we dived into it like we hadn't eaten in days. My steak was dry and bland, but a casual spectator would not have suspected this given the vigor with which I ate. I chewed each piece well past the time it should have taken, gave up on breaking it down any further and just swallowed. I gulped the carbonated flavored syrup to make sure that it stayed down. When there was nothing left on my plate, I headed to the buffet table. I decided to take a risk on a salad and fruit.

"It is good to see you eating healthy," my dad said when I sat down. "I've been trying to eat better myself."

"That's good."

He patted his belly. "I'm not getting any younger. Gotta stay fit for the ladies."

I smiled an uncomfortable smile and looked to the side, wishing that I was somewhere else.

"Your mother is concerned about you."

My eyes quickly found his face.

He continued, "But I told her that she is overreacting. You are fine, right." He plowed on without pausing for me to answer. "You are a Kemp, we are a strong bunch. We can take just about anything. You and your brother both, strong stock. There are no weak links in our family. No way. Not at all."

"Did you get my message about Oliver awhile back?" I asked slowly. "You never returned my call."

"Oh, uh, yeah, yeah. Busy. You know. I got your message. What was it again?"

"It was about Oli-"

"Oh, yeah, Oliver. You said something…" His face was twisted as he tried to find the words. "He is fine, right? Of course he is. How is football coming along? I need to get to one of those games." My dad redirected his focus when he saw the waitress. "Hey, can I get an apple pie? Thanks." He smiled affectionately at the waitress.

"When is the last time you spoke to Oliver?" I asked.

"Why do you ask?"

"Just wondering."

"I talk to him all the time. He texted me the other day. Or when was that? He just texted me about practice. Said that it was going well. I texted him back."

"Is that it?"

"Is there supposed to be more?" My dad looked at me with wide eyes.

I took a deep breath. "I just think it would be good if you two talked."

"We talk all the time." He was beginning to sound irritated.

"I'm not saying that you don't," I said treading carefully. "I'm just saying that I am concerned about him."

"About what, Gwen? What are you concerned about?"

I though carefully of my next words. I did not want to throw Oliver under the bus, but I don't think I will be doing him any favors by staying quiet. "He has been drinking. A lot."

My dad waved away my words as though they were a cloud of smoke invading his air space. "That is nothing to worry about. I drank too when I was his age. Heck I did a lot worse when I was his age. It is what boys do. He will be fine."

"But-"

"He will be fine, Gwen. You don't need to worry, OK?"

I nodded my head, but no, it was not OK.

"If there was any problem, I would know. I'm the parent, trust me to do my job."

I produced another meaningless smile.

"You are still young so I will not fault you for being overly eager. You love your brother. That is a good thing, but he has been raised well. You both have. I owe your mother a lot. She has done a superb job with the two of you. Really, she has. I don't think that I could have done as good of a job. Your mother always knew how to deal with the two of you. When you were two, you used to be so scared of hair. We had a dog at the time. Do you remember that dog we used to have?"

I shook my head.

"Ah, you were too young. His name was Colt. I got him from the Humane Society not long after you were born. Your mother was livid. She did not want a dog in her house especially with a newborn baby around. She complained and complained. You know how she does, but she eventually gave in. The thing was, Colt shed a lot. You hated hair and used to freak out whenever you saw his hair lying around. I mean, you would scream at the top of your lungs like someone was ripping your leg off. I told your mom that all she had to do was vacuum more often. She complained that I should be the one to vacuum since I got the dog. The hair didn't bother me so much. And I did vacuum. Anyway, I guess one day she had enough. She took the dog to a shelter. She wouldn't tell me which one. I'll never forget what she did. Truly horrible. He was a great dog. Everything made him happy. I used to smile every day when I got

129

home and he would greet me at the door. It didn't matter how bad my day was. And then she had to get up and go and do something as shellfish as that."

"You could have always gotten a dog after you two separated."

"It wouldn't be the same. Can't replace him. I don't have the time anyway. Just hate that you two did not grow up with a pet. Every kid should have that. But then your mother wanted out and that was that."

I squinted. "I thought you were the one who left her."

"No, I wanted things to work out between us, but she was the one who told me to leave. Don't get me wrong, I'm not saying that we didn't have our problems, but I was willing to stay. She said go and so I left. We had some good times though. When it was good, it was good." He looked up and smiled to himself. "I'll never forget the first time that I watched you all by myself. I didn't know what to do. Your mother had to take Oliver to the doctor's office for a checkup and she didn't want to bring you because you were sick. I asked her, "What better place to bring a sick kid than a doctor's office?" She threw some nasty words at me, you know how she can, and left. Boy, you had a set of lungs on you. As soon as your mother left, you cried and cried. I didn't know what was wrong. You were like that when she got home. She tried to get on me about it, but I told her that she is just better with the kids and that is why she should have taken you with her. How is that my fault? Anyway, we had our fun, too. You used to like it when I pushed you on the swings. Do you remember that? You used to say, "Daddy, again, again." "

"OK," I said, unsure of how to respond. My dad frequently spent our conversations 'remembering when.' Sometimes I wonder if he has even noticed that Oliver and I are no longer the little kids we were when he and my mother divorced.

130

My dad continued on down memory lane for about another half an hour before we finally left. He dropped me off at the house, gave me a kiss on the forehead and told me to be good. He was out of the driveway and down the street before I could even get to the door. My mother was still in the kitchen.

"You're back," My mother said while closing her kindle e-reader. "How was it?"

"It was Mancino's."

My mother briefly raised her eyebrows. "Your father and that restaurant. We could be living on the Mars and he would still make his way back here so that he can go to that restaurant."

I laughed.

"What did you two talk about?"

"It's dad. What do we ever talk about?"

"Did you talk about anything besides the past?"

"Do we ever?"

My mother shook her head. "Idiot."

"He did mention one fascinating fact."

My mother looked intrigued.

"You never told me that you were the reason for the divorce."

"What?"

"You told dad to leave."

"Is that what he told you?"

"It is the truth isn't it?"

"Let's not do this, Gwen."

"Why? You don't feel like talking about how you broke up our family?" I was beginning to raise my voice. I could feel the anger growing from within me.

"I didn't break up our family."

"So how is telling my dad to leave keeping us together?"

"There is a lot that you don't know about, Gwen."

"Right, mom. Hide behind that same old tired phrase."

"Gwen, I think you need to go to your room and calm down."

"I don't want to. I want to know why you kicked my father out of our house. Was it because you were cheating on him?"

"What?"

"Don't act like you don't have it in you. I know all about how you met Keith and how he was still married. How could you live with yourself?"

My mother was flabbergasted. "I don't…I'm not sure…You don't…"

"Please tell me you are not about to try and lie about how you met Keith?"

"No."

"Good. So you were with a married man?"

"It's complicated."

"There is nothing complicated about sleeping with a married man. He is supposed to be off limits! Or don't vows mean anything to you?"

"Watch your tone when you are speaking to me," my mother said sternly.

"Why? Why should I respect you when you don't even respect yourself?"

"Gwen, I am saying this in a calm tone, but I warn you that I will not be calm much longer-"

"Save it mom. You are a home wrecker. You wreaked our home and you wrecked Katie's!"

"*I* wrecked our home? *I* wrecked it?" My mother's tone increased with each word. "Your father, my dear daughter, is the one who deserves that award. And here I was keeping that information from you thinking that I was protecting you. But you know what? I think it is time you learned the truth. Your father got bored with playing house. He no longer wanted to be a husband and a father. It was cramping his style and he wanted the ability to come and go as he pleased without the weight of a family holding him back. So yes, while *I* was the one who told him to leave, he is the one who wanted to go!"

My mother's expression changed as soon as the words stopped gushing out of her mouth. We stood looking at each other. Both exasperated and keenly aware of what we had done. I turned and ran up the stairs, tripping on a few on my way up. I slammed my bedroom door behind me and buried myself in my bed. A fury of tears began to soak my pillow. I was so angry I wanted to burst.

"Gwen."

I jumped when I heard my name. Katie was standing beside my bed. She startled me. I did not expect anyone to be in my room, especially not her. I wiped my face, hoping to wipe the tears and pain from my face, but knowing that I was accomplishing nothing remotely near this expectation.

"Are you OK?" she asked.

"I'm fine." I did not look at her. I felt embarrassed that she was seeing me in such as state. Katie always looked immaculate. So put together. Even when she woke up.

"I heard what happened downstairs."

I raised my battered eyes.

"I wasn't eavesdropping or anything like that. You two are just really loud."

"Well. That's us. Hope you enjoyed the show."

"Cut the crap, Gwen. I'm not here to make fun of you. I just wanted to make sure that you are OK."

"I'm fine."

"Yeah, you look great."

"Well, what the hell do you expect?"

"I expect you to use your brain and lay off your mother a bit."

"You've done her bidding, now go."

"Stop being a jerk."

"Why?"

"Because you are hurting your mother and she does not deserve it."

"You heard what she said."

"Yes, I did. It may hurt, but the person you should be angry with is your father. He is the one who left you."

"She told him to leave."

"So, if he was so interested in being a father, how often did you see him after your parents separated? How many school programs of yours did he attend? Field trips? Who was there for you all those years?"

I knew what Katie was saying was right, but I was still angry. It hurt to hear out loud what I'd already suspected: that my father only tolerated me. That there exists a parent out there who does not possess the innate ability to love and care for his child and this parent happens to be mine. My body ached. Not actually hearing it allowed me to hold onto the minute chance that he really does love me and that one day he will show me and make up for all of these years. One day. But the expiration on that day has arrived and I didn't receive the outcome I hoped.

Katie sat next to me on the bed and put an arm around me. "I know this is hard to hear, but it is for the best. It will prevent you from following my path in life."

I cut my eyes at her inquisitively.

"Don't act like you don't know my dad is a jerk," she said, noticing my expression.

"Why do you do the things you do?"

Katie breathed out hard. "Who knows? At first I think I did it to be cool. And then it just became routine. And now it is just kind of pathetic. But hey, that's Katie." She released a snort-like laugh. "For me, I've screwed up for so long that I am scared to play it straight. What if I can't hack it? What if I waited too long and now it is too late? Too many questions without answers. But being here and seeing you and Oliver," Katie shook her head, "I don't know. It's weird. Somehow it has had an effect on me. I can't continue to throw away my life like this. I have been given so many chances and opportunities. I have been such a fool."

"So you are done with all things Katie?"

"I don't know."

We both laughed.

"I'm being honest. I hope that I am able to change. I am committed to changing, but words are easy to say."

"At least you are willing to try."

"You should apologize to your mother. You were quite harsh with her."

"She drives me mad."

"Don't they all? But she loves you and she is trying her best."

"I don't know."

"You only get one mother."

"And one father, but not everything works out does it?"

"We can't all win the family lottery. I'm sure my parents aren't too thrilled with me, but I am who they got." Katie stood up. "Come on. Let's drown our sorrows over some ice cream."

"I ate it already," I said bashfully.

"What? No, I just bought some yesterday."

"The Mint Pistachio and Almond?"

"Yes."

"Sorry."

≈

I didn't speak to my mother over the next few days. I know Katie was right, what she said about my mother, but part of me was still angry at her. I wanted to blame her. I wanted her to suffer.

My dad called to see how things were going after we had dinner. Surely, my mother called him sometime after our heated exchange of words. 'Dad' appeared on my phone and remained even after the ringing stopped. I slid my thumb across the phone. The screen switched to my missed call log. 'Dad' sat at the top of the list. He was also in the two spaces below. I pushed the button on the right side of my phone and the screen went black.

I laid my head on my pillow waiting for sleep. I wasn't tired and it was only 7 pm, but I was feeling exhausted and deflated. I wanted my mind to shut down and squash every thought with it. I wanted to wake up feeling refreshed and unencumbered. Free from everything that has been going on in my life in the past few months.

It was 7:23 pm. I was still up. Sleep was dodging my every attempt to catch it. Closing my eyes and just praying it would come did not work. Nor did counting sheep. It was a stupid idea, but I was getting desperate. I sat up. My room was partially lit by the full moon. When I was a little girl, my mother bought me a telescope sometime after I told her that I wanted to be an astronaut – to this day I've have never been able to find anything interesting other than the moon. She was determined to keep things as normal as possible after my dad left. She did not want things to fall by the wayside merely because we were now a one parent household – headed by a single mother no less.

My mother also refused to fall short on her career aspirations. Two years after my dad left, she opened her own dental practice. At the time I didn't understand how much of an accomplishment this was. I was always used to my mother going to work. Now it was just in a different building.

My mother managed to do all this and never miss a single activity that Oliver and I participated in: pee-wee football, tennis, ballet (I lasted two weeks), gymnastics, swimming. If we voiced the slightest interest in something, my mother went after it with full force. Nothing was deemed worthless. Not even a class on bird watching that I just had to join.

When I was in third grade, there was a father-daughter dance at my school. All of my friends were going with their fathers. I worked up the nerve to timidly ask my dad to take me. He stuttered for a bit, but then agreed to go. I spent all week looking for the perfect dress to wear: a purple crinkle chiffon rosette dress with matching shimmer ballet flats. On the day of the dance, my mother took me to the salon to have my hair straightened with her favorite beautician. I'd never felt so beautiful in my life. My hair, dress, shoes, and even a little lip gloss, everything was perfect. The dance was at 6 pm. I was ready by five. Sitting by the door by 5:15. At 5:30 pm I started to get excited by every passing headlight. At 5:35 pm, I started to get nervous.

"Relax, Gwen," my mom said. "He will be here. The school is only ten minutes away."

At 5:40 pm, my mom was tapping away on her phone. *Ring. Ring. Ring. "Richard, where are you? Gwen is here waiting for you to take her to the dance. Call me back."*

5:42 pm. "Sometimes people are late," I told myself. "Perhaps he got stuck in traffic." 5:47 pm. "The school is not that far away. We can still get there on time. Eight minutes if we make all the lights." 5:52 pm. The doorbell rang. I almost fell down when I tripped over my own foot trying to get to the door. My mother appeared just as my hand gripped the door knob. Her face was lit up. The breadth of her smile only second to mine. I quickly flung the door open. Oliver was standing there. Alone. And laughing.

"Oliver, go to your room now!" my mother yelled.

I sat back in my chair, deflated. "He isn't coming."

At 6:12 pm, the doorbell rang again. It was Mrs. Kouch from next door. She was marveled at how pretty I was, having gotten used to seeing me only in jeans and gym shoes, it was an unexpected sight. Very different from her time when girls dressed like girls, she noted.

My mother gave Mrs. Kouch some instructions and told her that we would be home before 9 pm.

"I don't understand," I said as my mother ushered me out of the door and into the car. "Is dad going to meet us there?"

"No. There has been a change of plans. I am taking you."

"No! You can't, mom. It is a father-daughter dance. It will be embarrassing if I go with you."

"It will be fine, Gwen. You are wearing a lovely dress and you got your hair done, even though it hurt like mad and you cried 80 % of the time – hmm, I hope Marcus doesn't start ignoring my calls after that – anyway, you look great and you are going to that dance."

139

I protested the entire ride over. None of it mattered. My mother was resolute. I held my breath and kept my eyes to the floor as we entered the building. We signed in and headed to the gym. My heart thumped as the music grew closer. I began to sweat. That is when I remembered that I forgot to put deodorant on. I gave my mom a desperate look, hoping that she would say that we could go home. Instead, she smiled and said, "Everything will be fine." I stiffened as the doors opened. My eyes refused to explore anything other than my feet.

"See, I told you," my mother said.

I looked up, confused. While the place was filled mostly with fathers and daughters, there were about 10 mothers with their daughters – single moms, moms standing in because dad couldn't get away from work or just didn't want to come.

I was ecstatic.

"There is no way that I was going to let you miss this, even if that meant me standing in as your father."

I gave my mother a really big hug.

It was my mother who gave me the talk about boys. My dad would occasionally add a few words here and there – make sure he treats his mother right and never try to make a boy stay that doesn't want to – but it was my mother who told me to never sell myself short. I am perfect just the way I am. Any boy that tells me to change isn't the boy for me. These words came in handy when Roy, a boy I had a crush on in fourth grade told me that I needed bigger boobs if I was going to date him. Never mind that none of the girls in my class except for Lisa, who was about 70 lbs. overweight, had developed anything remotely close to breasts.

My mother was always a constant force in my life. Someone who I could always rely on even when I didn't know that I needed her. It is a shame things would not remain that way.

When I was in fifth grade, my mother met and married Keith. Instead of continuing her role as my stand-in father, she signed Keith up for the role. It wasn't a role he was happy to play, but he did it because he was expected to. I rebuffed his role because I refused to fall into character in my mother's family that she had fabricated in her head since a little girl and now wanted to come to fruition - first time didn't work, try, try, try again. Keith was a poor choice and I wasn't going to pretend otherwise.

Despite my mother being a career driven woman, she held sternly to the belief that she is meant to be a mother *and* a wife. Her life purpose could not be fulfilled otherwise. In her world, a man is the head of the household. King of the castle. And before she met Keith, she was Queen of a home in need of a King.

In my opinion, Keith is more akin to the court jester. A king should be honorable and respectable. He presents himself in a manner that should set an example for those in his demesne. A jester is a paid ass. He acts on impulse and couldn't care less about the consequences of his actions, if he even bothers to consider them.

I was forced to go to a father-daughter dance with Keith. I spent the entire time standing against the wall and ignoring Keith, not that he noticed. After about fifteen minutes on his cell phone, he left and sat in his car until it was time to leave. When I got in the car, he asked if I enjoyed myself then proceeded to drive off before I could even answer – albeit my response would have been a smart one.

When Keith first introduced Katie, he tried to pass her off as a well-rounded, smart, talented young lady. He didn't mention that all of her skills were focused in the field of drugs, drug paraphernalia, and truancy.

During the occasions that Keith and I had to be in the same room for periods longer than required for passing through, Keith frequently let me know how he felt about me. From my 'near constant eating' to my style of clothing, nothing was off limits to him. It is a miracle that I haven't yet developed an eating disorder because of him.

When I first told my dad about Keith, he insisted that I was overreacted and told me to give Keith a chance. When Keith started including my dad in his tirades, Keith became a jerk that mom my chose to be with and there was nothing that my dad could do about it. It was suggested that I stay away from him and speak to him only when necessary. This was easier said than done.

My mother started working longer hours at her practice. She was facing stiff competition from other dentists in the area. She had to increase the hours her office was open in order to keep clients who required a more flexible schedule. Keith shifted his schedule around at my mother's request. She wanted someone to be around when Oliver and I got home from school, even if it was only for a half an hour or so. Oliver usually had practice after school and so I was the one who got to enjoy Keith's warm company after a long, tiring day at school.

My mother wasn't too receptive to my repeated complaints about Keith. Initially she said that I didn't like him because he isn't my dad. Then she said that I didn't want her to by happy. That I'd prefer it if she died old and alone. After a while, she didn't care what I said. I could have told her that Keith tortured puppies in his spare time or was a pedophile. My mother had decided that she was going to stand by her man no matter what.

Since Keith had been recruited to attend school functions, a job my mother believed he did well, my mother viewed her presence as not vital. Her appearances dipped to 'not showing up at all.' This allowed a sequence of events to occur that none of us could have foreseen.

Entering high school was both thrilling and frightening. I was happy to be putting middle school behind me. I was not very popular there and was ready for a fresh start. I was also secretly hoping that the recently announced school redistricting would result in Vivienne attending a different school.

The school year started off bumpy. I developed acne two weeks before school started, not many people wanted to befriend me, and I had three classes with Vivienne who somehow grew taller and thinner. I wasn't deterred. Tryout season was nearing and it was going to be my time to evolve from a seedling into a beautiful flower. However, things didn't exactly go as planned. I wasn't coordinated enough for cheerleading; same for majorettes; the chess team really wanted to win a trophy this year – the fact that the only piece I could accurately name was the knight meant I was not chess team material; I had to stop five times while trying to swim the length of the pool during swim team tryouts, I didn't even bother trying to swim back, I just got out and walked; I have bad aim so golf, tennis, and softball were out of the question; I am only 5'4" so no volleyball or basketball, and I don't like to run so that ruled out track, cross country, and soccer. The only club that got close to having me was the Comic Book Club, but then I asked them why Batman is considered a superhero when he doesn't have any powers; he is basically just a grown man who likes to dress up like a bat.

Oliver was a junior when I started high school. Making friends was never an issue for him. The fact that he was on the football team was like icing on the cake. Any hopes that I had for any friends acquired through the trickle-down effect from being his sister were eliminated when Vivienne announced that I had meningitis. She was later hauled to the principal's office and made to apologize, but a one-on-one apology, where I would like to point out she was insincere, does nothing to quell the murmurs from the dozens of people that she told her lie to.

A few months into my freshman year and my life was already mirroring middle school. I knew that I had set my sights at bit high and that there was minimal chance that I was going to achieve it all. But I assumed that I would have achieved *at least one* goal. Oh well. It was probably for the best. I am an introvert and having a gang of friends would be daunting. This doesn't mean I don't want *any* friends. Meeting Marie has been my saving grace. Having someone to talk to about whatever has helped me keep my sanity and prevent me from being that weird girl in school who chews her hair and wears mismatched shoes. Jill has already filled that position.

5:45 am. I turned the alarm off as soon as it started to scream. I felt sluggish as I rolled out of bed and hopped into the shower.

Marie was standing impatiently by my locker when I got to school.

"What took you so long?" she said while tapping her foot.

"Good morning to you, too," I said groggily.

"There is a *Murder She Wrote* marathon today. We should blow off school and go watch it."

I shook my head. "No. I can't miss anymore school. Besides, *Murder She Wrote?*"

"Clearly you've never watched it because anyone that has would not say what you just did."

"Uh huh. Well, as great as that show sounds, I'm going to have to take a pass."

"Come on, you owe me."

"How do you figure that?"

"You have been m.i.a. lately. Also, Mr. Preston has been busting my chomps in geometry. I need a break. Angela Lansbury will help me get my minds off things. It is not healthy to let stress linger. It can lead to high blood pressure, heart attack, or a stroke. And you look like you could use a release too so actually this would be necessary for you. Medically necessary."

As I was giving Marie the 'stop feeding me this crap look,' Comic Book Billy appeared in the corner of my eye. We made eye contact. He smiled and headed toward me.

"Hey Gwen."

Both he and Marie ignored each other. She once described him as a nerd that spends his time with comic books because he has absolutely no chance with a girl with a pulse. Or a boy. He must not think much of her either.

"Hey Com-Will…am. I can't talk. I'm on my way to class."

"Oh, no problem, I just wanted to say that I heard about what happened to your brother. It sucks. He is really the best player out there. Tell him that we are all rooting for him."

My mouth was still open when Comic Book Billy left.

"What was that about?" Marie asked.

"I don't know, but I'm going to find out."

Oliver and I don't share a lunch hour so I was not able to talk to him until after school. At 2:59 pm, I rushed out of biology, threw my stuff in my locker, grabbed my unzipped backpack – things started falling out, but I didn't care - and raced outside. Marie was on my heels as I peeled through the doors, the sun momentarily blinding me.

"He is over there," Marie said. She was pointing at the bleachers.

Oliver was sitting near the top. Rays of light beamed from every direction of his body. His head hung low like it weighed a ton. I could not see his face, but I knew he was sad. Football was everything to him. Whatever happened had to be serious.

Behind me, students were filling up the buses. I knew that if I didn't get on the bus now, it would leave and I would be out of a ride home. Not sure if Oliver is in the mood to give me a ride. I guess I could see if whoever takes Marie wouldn't mind making a detour to my house. One by one, the doors of the buses closed. I shrugged it off and proceed to walk toward Oliver. This was more important. The motorcade prepared its departure just as I was nearing the parking lot that abutted the bleachers.

"I'll wait here," Marie said standing back. "Seems personal and it is probably better if you go alone."

I glanced back at Oliver. I haven't seen him this forlorn since he sprained his ankle when he was 9 and wasn't able to play with his team during the championship game. "You are probably right. Thanks."

I trotted across the parking lot, dodging a few cars in reverse, and through the chain-linked fence that held fast to a wayward plastic grocery bag. Oliver looked up when I was a few benches

146

below. His face immediately reacted with a superficial smile. His teeth were beaming white. His lips spread from one ear to the next. But his eyes were hallow and downcast; the edges pulled down the top part of his face defying his attempted façade.

"Hey, Gwen."

"Hey." I sat down on the bleacher immediately below him. "What's going on?"

"Not much. Just needed a little fresh air."

"It's cold out here."

"I'm wearing layers."

"Good. So, what's up?"

"Nothing. Everything is good. What's up with you?"

"Nothing."

"Aren't you going to miss your bus?"

"I'll get a ride home with a friend. I saw you up here and thought I would see how you are doing. How are you doing?"

Oliver looked at me suspiciously. "Who told you?"

"Comic Book Billy. Although he didn't get into specifics. What happened?"

"It's nothing that you need to worry about, Gwen. I've got it under control."

"Oh, so it is OK for you to worry about me, but I can't be concerned about you?"

"I don't write the rules, I just live by them."

147

"Stop being a jerk, Oliver. What happened?"

His eyes left mine and found the football field. "Do mom and dad know?"

"Not yet, but they will soon I'm sure."

"I wouldn't be so sure about that. When was the last time either of them went to one of my games?"

"It has been awhile. They both have to work. It's hard. It doesn't mean that they don't love you."

"Cut the crap, Gwen. It doesn't bother me that they can't make it. I'm just making a point. This conversation need not continue to have life once we leave school grounds."

I sat up erect. "What the hell is going on, Oliver?"

Oliver took a deep breath and released it through his nose. He clenched his jaws before he started talking again. "I got kicked off the team."

My eyes widened with disbelief. "YOU WHAT? How?"

"Lower your voice."

A few students looked our way. "Sorry. I just…What? How?"

"Coach was overreacting. He decided to set an example and I was the unlucky soul."

"Any example for what?" I asked.

"Nothing that everyone else on the team isn't doing."

"An example for what?"

"Normal teenage behavior."

148

Images of Oliver at home with a beer can and the night he got into an accident flashed in my head. "You were kicked off for drinking weren't you?"

He nodded his head once.

"And it wasn't the first time you were caught drinking was it?"

No answer.

"Coach is not a whore to the rulebook. He wouldn't kick you off for one offense. That time that I saw you sitting in your car and you were ranting off about football not being important, that was because you were benched weren't you? Coach caught you drinking and he benched you."

"Yeah."

"And now you've been caught again, but this time he kicked you off the team?"

Oliver's silence told me that I was right.

"Any exactly how is this information not going to make its way to mom and dad?"

"They don't go to the games so how will they find out?"

"Won't the school notify them?"

"Nah. Coach doesn't want to mess up my chances of getting into college. He knows how much football means to me and so he figures that kicking me off will persuade me to straighten up."

"Does he know about the accident?"

"No reason for him to."

"I don't think it is a good idea for you to keep this from mom and dad. What if you are an alcoholic? Won't you need to go to AA meetings?"

"I'm not an alcoholic, Gwen."

"How do you know?"

"I'm only seventeen."

"So, Drew Barrymore was an alcoholic when she was like thirteen."

"Drew Barrymore was a cokehead. Besides, do I look like an alcoholic? Do I spend all day drinking, stumbling around and slurring my words?"

"No, but-"

"But nothing, Gwen. Think before you talk. Have some common sense. I wouldn't let myself become a drunk. Do you think that little of me?"

I thought hard about my response. I've never known any alcoholics and so I don't know what the requirements for the title are. But Oliver has been drinking a lot lately. And that is when *I* see him. Who knows what he is doing when I'm not around. Then there is the accident. Alcohol was involved. A lot of alcohol. *Katie*. She would know.

"I'm just worried that is all. What are you going to do?"

"I'm not worried. You shouldn't be either. It will all work itself out. I don't need football."

Ever since Oliver was a little kid, there has only been one thing in his life that he wants to do when he grows up: Play in the NFL.

150

He continued, "It's all good. I have other talents. I'll just focus more on my academics."

Oliver has less than four months left in his senior year. Like most athletes, his scholastic career was more focused on honing in on his on field talents rather than those off field. Not that his grades aren't decent enough to get into a college somewhere, I'm just not sure what he would do once he got there.

"I've always liked math and science. Remember when I was in that science fair?"

"In the third grade?"

"Nah, I had to have at least been in the fifth grade."

"You were in the third. I remember because I could not submit my project, which was a really cool diagram explaining the plausibility of Bigfoot being real, because it was only open the those in third grade and above."

"Whatever. Point is. I received an honorable mention for my project. And I enjoyed doing it. Maybe science is my true calling."

"Doing what exactly? Experiments. Figuring out things. Stuff like that."

I hate to say this, but Oliver would never succeed in the science field. It is meant for people who visit the astronomy center because it is fun or put up posters of the periodic table on their bedroom wall. It is not for people who use their frog carcass as marionette in biology class or who once quipped, "Why do we have to repeat the same experiments, year after year, that other people have done? I'm sure that the results are well documented by now."

"Maybe," I said. "Still, I think that you might want to do something about your drinking."

"You're back on that again?"

"I'm concerned."

Oliver stood up. "I'm fine. That is all that you need to know. Do you need a ride home?"

I looked back at where I left Marie. She was gone. I decided not to say anything more on the alcohol subject for now since doing so would risk my ride home.

Katie was just returning from performing her community service duties when we got home. Upon noticing Oliver's glum expression, she asked if anything was wrong. He flashed his usual smile and told her no. She looked at me for reassurance. I wanted to until Oliver left the room.

"You were an alcoholic right? Or are you still? I'm not sure how that works."

Katie's eyes narrowed. "I was never an alcoholic. I dabbled in some recreational drugs from time to time and I drank socially, but I was not an alcoholic."

"Then why did you go to rehab?"

"It was court ordered."

"You went to rehab, but you weren't an alcoholic?"

"I enjoyed the drugs too much. Why all the questions?"

"I'm worried about Oliver. He got kicked off the football team."

"Yeah, he told me."

"He told you? Why?" I was shocked.

"Because he wanted to."

"Why didn't he tell me?"

"I don't know."

My stomach dipped.

"Maybe he didn't want you to worry. Especially after the accident. Maybe he wanted to talk to someone who would understand what he is going through."

"Do you think he is an alcoholic?"

Katie lifted one side of her mouth. "He drinks a lot, but so do a lot of people. Is a person an alcoholic just because he or she enjoys a few drinks?"

"Where is the cut off?"

"Should there be one?"

"Don't give me that crap, Katie. Do you care about Oliver?"

"Of course I do."

"And knowing what you know about addiction, all that you learned at rehab on your frequent visits there, would you say he has a problem?"

"If he doesn't already, then he is on the right track."

"Why haven't you said anything? How can you stand idly by and let it go on without trying to do something? You of all people should know better."

"It is because I know. That is how I am able to stand by and *watch him*. Everyone has their own path. They have to make their own mistakes. No amount of talk from you, me, your mother, or anyone can take Oliver off his path. He is the only one that can effect change in his life. The more you try to interrupt that, the more you risk sending ripples through his life which can cause more damage. Right now, Oliver does not believe there is a problem and without that, there can be no road to recovery."

"So that's it. Just sit here and do nothing?" My eyes began to tear up. "Just watch him dive head first to his demise? That is what you are suggesting?"

She put a hand on my arm and slowly rubbed it. "I'm sorry that you have to go through this."

I shrugged her hand off of me. "Are you? You gave him alcohol. Lots of it. You are telling me to leave him alone and let him continue on this destructive path. Hell, you did the same thing. Repeatedly. How do I know that you don't want him to follow your path? Misery loves company. Perhaps you just want someone to join you at the table of despair and self-loathing." Tears were pouring out of my eyes before I could finish talking. I was so upset and frustrated.

"You are angry. I get that. It must be hard to stand by and watch someone make so many mistakes. To risk so much of what they have, but don't seem to appreciate."

My tears stopped abruptly. "If you understand it then why not do something about it?"

"I only get it because I am watching Oliver go through it. I've always lived my life on the other side. The seemingly destructive side. I care about Oliver and watching him go through this and

154

knowing that the best thing that I can do for him is to not doing anything at all is painful. But it doesn't change anything. He has to hit rock bottom first."

"And where exactly is his bottom?"

"It is different for everyone."

"Have you hit yours?"

"I believe so. For me, I was just tired of the cycle. It was the same thing just a different day. It has gotten to the point that I am ready to move forward. I no longer feel that life has to be crazy and spontaneous at every second. That the next party is going to be the greatest event of the year. My problem wasn't so much the booze and the drugs. It was the chaos. I was addicted to it. I was addicted to the idea of it. The mere mention of schedules and continuity freaked me out. I didn't want to be lame because that meant that I wasn't living and a life not inundated with experiences is a life not worth living."

"So Oliver wants more experiences?" I asked, confused.

"No, that was my path. Oliver has his own. He doesn't have a problem with repetition or he would have never succeeded in football. Hell, there isn't much divergence in his day-to-day routine. He gets up, showers, goes to school, goes to practice, comes home, eats dinner, goes to bed then gets up again to repeat."

"This isn't helping me."

Katie took a deep breath. "Since you are so hell bent on doing something, maybe you should talk to him. See what is behind his drinking."

"Will you come with me?"

Katie gave me an 'I'm not so sure' look.

"He talks to you. He keeps me in the dark like I'm a little girl that still watches *My Little Pony*."

"It was on last week when I got home. You were on the couch watching it."

"I fell asleep and it must have come on after the program that I was watching. I woke up when you got home."

Katie lowered her eyes brows and we both started laughing. Once we composed ourselves, we headed up the stairs to Oliver's room. My heart began to pound as we neared his door. I was nervous about what to say to him and how he would respond. I never thought I would have to deal with something so serious especially not with my own brother.

Katie knocked on the door. Oliver didn't respond, but I heard movement on the other side of the door. Katie knocked again. This time harder.

"One second," Oliver said.

Katie didn't wait. She turned the knob and opened the door.

"Hey," Oliver said, his hand slowly moving away from the side of his bed which abutted the wall.

"Busy?" I asked.

"Just resting. Trying to get my mind straight." His eyes were red and his speech slightly slurred.

Katie sat down on his bed, leaned back and grabbed something from between his bed and the wall. "Having a little assistance?"

Oliver looked perplexed, but then his expression changed when Katie held up a bottle of vodka.

"You're drinking?" I said, astonished.

"Gwen, don't come in here with that."

"Oh, so I should just go while you throw your life away. Would you like me to go and score some pills for you too?"

"Gwen," Katie urged. "That is not helping."

"So, what is this? My intervention?" Oliver dug his eyes into me. "I *told* you that I don't have a drinking problem. Now get the hell out of my room!"

I felt the tears making their way to my eyes. I looked at Katie and she subtly shook her head and gave me a look that told me to get it together. I swallowed hard and push my emotions and tears down as far as I could.

"This is not an intervention," Katie said. "And no one is going anywhere. Gwen is just concerned, as your sister, that you may have things going on that you need to talk about. We are here to give you the ability to talk about those things. We are here to listen and not judge you."

Oliver eyed me again after Katie mentioned that we would not judge him. "Really, Oliver? Since when have I ever judged you? Not to mention, who am I to judge anyone? Last week I ate a Cheeto that I found under the couch."

Katie turned her face up in disgust.

I continued, "And mom hasn't bought Cheetos in about four months."

"That's gross," Katie declared.

"Hey," I said, "no judging. Remember?"

Oliver chuckled as he shook his head. "Look, I appreciate your concern, but I'm good."

"Are you?" I asked.

"I won't lie and say that I'm not upset about getting kicked off the football team, but I'll survive."

"How is everything else in your life?" Katie asked.

"Like what?"

"Surely you have other things going on besides football."

Oliver opened his mouth, but for a while, nothing came out. "School's fine. And um…"

"Are you dating anyone?" I asked.

"Ah, you know. I hang out with a couple of girls, but I'm not looking for anything serious."

"Then what is it? What has you so worked up that you feel the need to subdue it with alcohol?"

"It relaxes me. You know."

"From what?"

"Everything. You know. It's a lot sometimes."

"What is?"

Oliver looked down. "The pressure. Sometimes it is just too much."

"The pressure to play football?"

"The pressure of college. The unknown. Here, I know what to expect. I know what I am capable of and I know who I am up against. In college." He forcefully pushed air out of his nose. "Man, that is a different ball game."

"I'm sure you went through a similar experience when you started high school," I said, hoping that I made a meaningful analogy.

Oliver looked doubtful. "Playing up against a bunch of high school students is nothing like coming up against a defensive line decked out with 300-plus linebackers."

"You are not so small yourself," I assured him.

"I'm tall, but I'm lean. I'm built for speed. Not to be pounded by a wall of blubber. Do you know each year I play, I have a 50% chance of getting injured? And playing against the guys at the college level, we are not talking about your everyday sprain or bruise. We are talking about potentially career ending injuries. Each year. Add that up over four years and it almost becomes a guarantee."

"It is a risk that you take when you play the game. It is a risk that all the players take. Surely you knew this going in. I mean, it is not like you are playing ping pong."

"Yes, football is a rough sport. I get that. But," Oliver started talking with his hands like he usually does when he means business, "couch invited a few players from State to come in and talk to the seniors about playing at the college level. Man, when these guys came in, I felt like a little punk. They were massive. I mean, *massive*."

"How does their size make you feel like a punk?" Katie chimed in. "I get how it will make you feel small. But a punk?"

"They just seem like they can take anything you throw at them. Nothing was too much for them."

"What about the other players?" I asked. "The running back, quarterback, corner, they couldn't be *that* big."

"Naw, they weren't anything like the linemen. But they seemed better in their abilities. I'd have to play against guys like them. What if they are stronger, faster, smarter? What if I can't hack it? What if I go out there and just bomb?"

"I don't care where you go or what field you get into, but there will always be someone who is stronger and faster and smarter," Katie said. "That is just the way it is. Doesn't mean that you can't be successful at what you do and it certainly doesn't mean that you should give up on what you love."

"I am sure that other guys feel the same way that you do," I said. "Have you talked to any of them? Or your coach?"

Oliver waved away my words. "You can't talk about stuff like that. You'll be seen as weak and you can't be weak and play football. Only pansies talk about their feelings."

"Yeah, well, in case you forgot, you don't play football anymore."

"Maybe it is for the best," Oliver said as he leaned back on his bed. "Maybe I am just not cut out for it. If I feel like this about college, how the hell am I going to make it to the NFL? Never mind the chances of even being drafted."

"So you drink?"

"It calms me. My mind gets so overwhelmed with all of this and I can't push it out so I drink."

I slipped out of the room just as Katie started talking again. I quickly ran to my room and rummaged around until I found what I was looking for. Katie stopped talking when I huffed and puffed my way back into Oliver's room.

"What are you doing?" Katie asked.

I walked over to Oliver, grabbed his hand and dropped what I had in mine. He looked down at what was in his hand then looked up at me.

"Do you remember that?" I asked.

"You kept this? All these years?"

"It was important to me. I will never forget the day you gave me that."

Oliver and I were supposed to be getting ready for the new school year. Oliver was entering third grade and I was entering 1st. I was so scared. I was no longer going to be in the small annex building where the kindergarten classes were. I was going to be in the main building with all of the big kids. The thought horrified me. I was scared that the kids would terrorize me, that my teacher wouldn't like me, and that I might pee on myself – I had a few accidents in kindergarten.

I sat on my bed frozen with fear. My mother didn't know this because she was busy getting ready in her room. Oliver came to my room to see if I was ready. When he saw me, he immediately knew that something was wrong. He sat down next to me and I poured out my fears to him. He took my hand and place in it a small red and yellow diamond shaped pendant with a large 'S' in the middle. My eyes lit up the minute I saw it. He saved up several cereal box lids in order to get it. When it finally came in the mail, he was never without it.

"Do you remember what you told me when you gave it to me?" I asked Oliver.

He smiled and said, "I told you that I would always be there to protect you whenever you needed me and to keep the pendant with you for when I am not around. It will give you the strength to get through anything."

"And so I took the pendant, put it in my pocket and I went to school. Whenever I felt even the slightest bit anxious, I would put my hand on the pendant. It gave me the strength that I needed."

"And you are giving it to me because?"

"Because now you need it to give you the strength to get through all of your insecurities. You have always been there for me, Oliver. Let me be there for you. Let me help protect you. And for when I am not around-"

"I have the pendant." Oliver's eyes watered, but he stopped short of letting a tear escape. "Why is it so dirty?"

I laughed. "Hey, it's been through a lot."

"Is there jelly stuck on here?"

We all enjoyed a good laugh. It was therapeutic. Especially for Oliver who I haven't seen laugh in weeks. Nothing was resolved during our talk with Oliver, but at least we talked. Now I know what is bothering him. Oliver said that he will start trying to work through his issues without the alcohol. Katie warned me about how difficult this is going to be for him and so we both made it a point to keep an eye on him.

However, I felt that more needed to be done. Oliver needed to free himself from all that was encumbering him. And I knew the perfect way for him to do this. But first I needed to perfect it myself.

I stood on the old blue plastic time-out chair of mine that I dragged up from the basement. With my arms spread wide, I closed my eyes and jumped. I hit the floor in less than two seconds. After doing this for over 30 minutes, I was no better than when I started and I was becoming frustrated.

I got back on the chair and threw my arms back into the air. This time, I thrust my head up and imagined myself flying high in the air with the birds, free from all of the difficulties that weighed me down. I imagined Oliver holding my hand and flying with me, his face beaming with excitement and the lack of pain. Up there, there is no such thing as sorrow. There are no expectations. No disappointments. Only unobstructed, unimpeded open space that is waiting for someone to experience it. Up there, the air is fresh and pure. It enters your nostrils and fills your body filtering everything negative in its path. As it leaves, it takes away all of those negative thoughts, feelings, and experiences and leaves only the good. Gone are all of those days I spent being chided by Mr. Grayfin and Vivienne. Gone are all of my memories that have anything to do with Keith. Gone are Oliver's fears of getting injured and of him getting kicked off the team.

I took in a deep breath and prepared myself.
One…Two…Three…

Bam!

Crap. That time I landed wrong and hurt my ankle. Two hours later, the results were the same and so I finally gave up.

I went to Marie's house the next day.

"So you can fly?" she asked.

"I don't see why not," I said while standing on a chair in her room.

"But you haven't been able to fly yet?"

"Look, you know that I have special abilities right?"

"Abilities that you won't pass on to me."

"For the millionth time, it is not something that I can teach you. You are either born with them or you are not. And unfortunately you're not."

"It's not fair."

"Let's not even go down that road because I might be on it all day."

"Fine."

"Thank you. Now, where was I? Oh, right. Since I have the ability to make objects move, wouldn't that infer that I should also possess the ability to make myself move?"

"Not necessarily," she said while picking at her fingernails.

"What do you mean?"

"Maybe there is a weight restriction on your ability."

"I hadn't thought about that. Wait, are you trying to say that I'm fat?"

"Cut it out, Gwen. Come on, there is an old broken down car out back. Let's see if you can move it."

Marie lived in a part of town that was run down and so it wasn't unusual to have a nonfunctioning car sitting on the premises. Some of the neighbors even put them on cinder blocks. This didn't seem to bother Marie and so I didn't let it bother me either.

"All right," Marie said. "Lift the car up a few inches."

The car she was referring to was a late model blue Chevrolet Cavalier. Rust had taken over the entire bottom half of the car and was spreading up along the sides near the wheels.

I stood about ten feet from the car. I relaxed my body and focused all of my energy on the car. It took longer than usual, but soon I was drenched in a warm, calm feeling. The car shook then slowly began to rise. Marie touched my arm when it was about six inches off the ground. I closed my eyes and it hit the dirt with a loud *thump*.

"We don't want anyone to see what you can do, but at least now you know that you don't have any weight restrictions. There must be another reason that we are missing."

"So you agree that I should be able to fly?"

"Unless of course your abilities restrict you from being able to lift yourself, then yes, you should be able to fly."

"Now we just need to be able to figure out how."

Marie and I ran so many theories through our heads, but we still could not figure out why I could not fly. Marie suggested that I jump off from a higher place. I stood on top of the car, closed my eyes and went for it. I hit the ground and ended up with a bruise.

"Are you trying hard enough?" Marie asked.

"Yes," I said while brushing off the dirt from my clothes.

"Is it this hard for you to move objects?"

"No."

"Then you are doing something wrong. Flying should not be so hard to do. If it is an ability that you have, it should be easy."

Marie was right, but I could not figure out what I was doing wrong. Or worse, if I just didn't have the ability. I gave up trying for the day.

My mother and Keith were in the driveway talking when I got home.

"Hey sweetie," my mother said as I walked up the driveway. "Have fun at your friend's house?"

I looked at Keith before answering my mother. He had a cold glare. His face was beginning to show his age. His skin was blotchy and hardened and had an almost scaly look to it. The area around his cheeks was sunken in. His brunette hair was dull and thinning.

Then his eyes flashed white. I jumped.

"Is there something wrong?" Keith slithered.

Did I just see his eyes turn white? I peered at his eyes again. They were brown, as usual. *I know what I saw. I can't explain it, but I know what I saw.*

"Gwen?" my mother said when I had yet to answer either of them.

"No, everything is fine," I fluttered. "Everything is…" I took another look at Keith's eyes. Still brown. "great."

"Keith and I feel that we should all sit down and have a calm discussion. We can air out our frustrations and talk about what is bothering us and how best to move forward."

I kept stealing glances at Keith's eyes while my mother was talking. While not very friendly looking, they remained brown.

"I'm kind of tired," I said, not wanting to hang around with Keith and his eyes.

My mother walked toward me. She lifted a hand like she was going to put it on my arm, but then changed her mind. "You only have a few years left before heading off to college. I don't want the rest of your stay here to be difficult. And I want you to feel that you can come back. This is your home."

"So you are already planning for my departure?"

"Gwen, this is not-"

"Can't wait to get me out of here so that you can live your life with your husband without any interference from me?"

"Here we go again," Keith said as he threw his hands in the air. "I told you not to waste your time."

"That's enough Keith," My mother said through clenched teeth. "Gwen, that is not what I said so stop trying to twist my words around."

"I'm not twisting anything around. I'm just saying what you are too scared to say. You want Oliver, Katie, and me out of here so that you can go on to live this lie of a marriage with that cheating bastard over there."

167

My mother slapped me. She put her hands over her mouth as soon as her hand left my face.

"You are such a bitch. I hate this place and I hate you! I can't wait to move out of here!"

I ran inside and into my room crying the entire time. My face stung, but I wasn't going to acknowledge it. Doing so would give her the power she wants and there was no way that I was giving into her or her stupid husband.

I was so angry, I was shaking. I paced the room trying to determine my next move while waiting for my mother to storm in here. She will probably kick me out. Tell me that I had to get my things and move in with my father. Or that he was already downstairs, I was to leave immediately and she will send my things later. I looked around. Maybe I should pack. I would hate to be without some of my things. Knowing her, she might just trash them the minute I was out of the door. What if she can't get ahold of my father? Will she throw me out anyway and tell me to wait outside for him. Perhaps I should call Marie just in case. I can take the bus back to her house if my dad doesn't get here in time. I picked up the phone to call her, but my mind went blank. I couldn't remember her number. I stood there for what felt like five minutes with the phone in my hand. A loud beeping sound from the phone snapped me out of a daze.

I hung the phone up then looked outside to see why my mother hadn't come upstairs yet. I could only see part of the driveway and so I left my room and slowly walked downstairs to the back door. I didn't hear any voices nor did I see any cars. Apparently my mother and Keith left. A wave a relief washed over me. Although I knew it was temporary. It was only a matter of time before I had to deal with this. Best to stay one step ahead.

I raced upstairs and took out a suitcase from my closet. I threw in whatever clothes I thought I might need for the next few weeks and anything else that I absolutely could not live without. My kindle, for example. After tossing in two pairs of shoes, my e-reader, my tablet, my favorite pillow and some toothpaste, I zipped up the suitcase and placed it by the door. I then searched my room for about ten minutes for the plastic Superman pendant before I remembered that I gave it Oliver.

Oliver. Should I tell him about what happened and why I was getting kicked out? Should I tell him to come with me now or wait until she kicks him out too?

I looked at the phone wondering why my dad hasn't called yet. I picked up the receiver and turned it on. The familiar dial tone blared through. I dialed my dad's number. *Ring. Ring. Ring.* I hung up when the voicemail came on.

Neither Oliver or Katie were home and so I was on my own for now. A heavy wave of exhaustion hit me. I widened my eyes in an attempt to fight it. This was useless. I needed to sleep. I would have to sort all of this out later. For now, I'll just take a quick nap.

I woke up the next morning to the sound of my alarm going off. Startled, I sat up and put my head in my hands while I tried to figure out what was going on. The events of the previous day came flooding in. My suitcase was still next to the door. I was still wearing the same clothes I had on yesterday. Including my shoes.

Voices emanated from downstairs and drifted to my room. I couldn't make out who they belonged to and I didn't want to take the risk by going down to find out. I sat on my bed trying to ascertain my next move.

My mother must not have told my dad about what happened. It's possible that she is embarrassed because she hit me. Or maybe Keith is still in the process of convincing her to send me away. Maybe they are looking into a place that can accommodate all three of their children.

"Oh, I can't believe this is happening to me," I said to myself. "Why does life have to be so damn difficult all of the time? Why can't things just work out for me? Argh!"

I needed to shower, but I didn't want to risk running into my mother in the hallway or her walking in on me while I was in the shower. The lock is a simple push-down lock and can be breached with something as simple as a bobby pin. Being caught in such a vulnerable state wasn't a very appealing thought and so I decided to skip the shower and just change my clothes.

It was time for me to leave and catch the bus. That is, if I decide to go to school. If I stay here, I am almost guaranteed to have to deal with her, which I don't want to do. At school, I could at least talk to Marie and get her opinion. See if I can stay with her for a few days if I my dad is unavailable. I haven't met her mother yet, but Marie makes it seem as though her mother is cool with just about anything.

The voices were still in conversation and it didn't seem like it was going to end anytime soon. I had to make a move if I was going to catch the bus. I grabbed my backpack and coat and ran downstairs. I made a beeline for the door and didn't stop when my mother called my name. She came outside and called my name again. I walked faster and faster until I broke out into a run. I made it to the bus stop just as the bus was approaching. Comic Book Billy smiled and said something to me, but I was too lost in thought to pay attention.

Marie wasn't at her locker when I got to school and so I was forced to delay this important conversation until later. I trudged to my first class and plopped in my seat. Mr. Grayfin commenced the class as usually with a boring review of what happened in our last class. Mr. Grayfin was in the middle of praising Vivienne on something that she said yesterday when I rolled my eyes.

"Is there a problem, Guinevere?" Mr. Grayfin asked.

"Not that I know of. Do you know of one?"

"Don't get smart."

"I'm not. Just stating that I don't know of any problems. Unless you want to count your incessant praising of Vivienne. Some might see that as a problem, but I'm guessing that you don't."

"Leave me out of this," Vivienne said.

"I could, but Mr. Grayfin enjoys you being in it."

"Shut up!" Vivienne said as she stood up."

"Guinevere, that is enough."

"You know, Mr. Grayfin, I don't think Vivienne is your type. You are a bit old for her. What will her parents say? You should set your sights a little lower and look for someone your own age. Someone more attainable and appropriate."

"Shut up, you idiot! Shut up!" Vivienne screamed before running out of the classroom.

"You have crossed the line. That was unacceptable."

"Yeah, yeah, yeah," I said as I stood up and gathered my things.

"Your mother will hear about this."

171

"I'm sure she will enjoy the call."

"Where are you going?"

I turned before opening the door. "Surely you want me to go to the principal's office. I'm saving you the trouble of having to tell me."

I had no intention of going to the principal's office, but I needed to get out of there and I didn't want anyone coming after me. Lunch wasn't for several hours and I didn't know Marie's schedule. I headed to the bathroom.

As soon as I opened the door, I wished I hadn't. Vivienne was standing near the wall crying.

"Does this make you happy?" she asked. Her hands full of damp tissue.

"Does seeing you cry make me happy?" *Yes, yes, it does.* "No. why would it?"

"Because you have never liked me."

"Right. Because I was the one who did and said all those horrible things to you all those years. I'm the one that told people that you have lice. I'm the one who told people that you were adopted at birth because your birth mother was a crack head and your father is in prison."

Vivienne's mouth opened and close.

"You don't have anything to say?"

Her crying intensified. "I've been a horrible person and now I am paying for it. Is that it? Is that why this is happening to me?"

"Is this about Mr. Grayfin? You don't actually like him do you?" My face turned up in disgust.

"Ew. Gross. Never. He is a prick. He thinks that he is coming off as some cool teacher when he is really just creepy. I smile because he likes me and I know he will give me an 'A' for the class."

"You are pimping yourself out for a good grade?"

"I have never done anything with him. People don't think that I like him do they?" Vivienne said with worry in her voice. "You can't let people think that there is something going on between me and him."

"I don't know what people think and I can't control it either, but I can say that it wouldn't be a stretch so say that some of the other kids think that. Heck, I did."

Vivienne's face contorted through a variety of expressions before she made a b-line for the toilet. She immediately bent over and started puking.

I turned around and covered my ears hoping to block out the sound of her semi-processed food backtracking and splashing into the water. After a few minutes, she came out of the stall and rinsed her mouth out under the sink.

"Does the thought of him sicken you that much?"

She fell to the floor and started crying. "My life is over. How could I have been so stupid?"

I looked around feeling uncomfortable and wondering if I should leave as she continued her self-depreciating monologue.

"Stupid, stupid, stupid. Just had to be the winner. I just couldn't let it go. I guess you won. I've lost. I'm the pathetic loser."

"Are you talking to me?"

She looked at me like I was an idiot.

"I take that as a yes," I said in a low voice.

"Doesn't matter anyway," she continued. "The whole thing was so absurd."

"What did I win? And how? I didn't even know we were in competition."

"Stop acting like a dunce."

"I'm trying to be nice to you because you are crying, but my level of tolerance is diminishing fast."

Vivienne pressed her palms into her face and screamed. When the screaming stopped, the shaking began. "I don't know what I am going to do. My life is over. What am I going to do?" The tears were rolling uncontrollably down her face.

Shock froze me in place. I've never seen Vivienne in such an unglued state. Part of me wanted to help her. To make her pain, whatever the source, go away. Another part of me wanted to revel in her suffering. She made my life hell for so many years merely for her own pleasure. Never once had I done anything to her to remotely deserve the horrible things that she has said and done to me. There were days where the thought of going to school was enough to make my stomach ache. Surely my reduced drive to go to school and the dismal grades I receive can, at least in part, be directly attributed to Vivienne. And she is not a dumb girl. She knew what she was doing and the potential effect it could have on me. And just in case she was

174

born without the ability to piece those two together, there were scores of television programs, advertisements, special bulletins, seminars at school - you name it – that she could have learned from. So in the end, she just didn't care.

The universe has shifted and I was no longer part of the underbelly. For once I was standing tall while she was whimpering on a dirty bathroom floor. A floor where scores of female students trampled with their filthy shoes soiled with dog poo, human urine and feces that splashed to the floor when the toilet flushed, dead bugs, and countless other cringe inducing substances. A smile erupted on my face.

Vivienne jumped up and ran back into the stall. Before long she was heaving over the toilet again. I threw my hands over my face and ears.

She started crying again and asking, no one in particular, what she was going to do.

"I can go and get the nurse if you want?" I said when she came out of the stall. "You probably have some stomach bug."

"I'm not sick," she said morosely.

"Are you sure about that? You've already puked twice and you look awful."

"I'm pregnant you twit."

The words came at me like a bulldozer sent to knock down the school building: unexpected and with full force. Vivienne pregnant? I wanted to ask her if I heard her right, but the look on her face said that I had. I immediately began to feel sorry for her. Pregnant at 16. There goes her life. And what will her parents say about it? Their little pride and joy is about to have a pride and joy of her own. Guess she has been doing a little more than studying lately. And what about the father? How will he handle this? *Wait.* The father. Who is the father?

I eyed Vivienne. She has had a huge crush on Oliver for some time now. Vivienne is used to getting what she wants. Oliver never showed any interest in her, but what if that was a ruse. Or what if this was the result of a weak moment on his part. He has been drinking. People are known to do really dumb things while intoxicated. *Wait.* What if he already knows about the pregnancy and it is the cause of his drinking? It would explain a lot. He drank because such an impending responsibility was too much for him to handle. He knew that he would have to get a job sooner rather than later. Football was such a long shot – hence the talk about looking at other avenues. What if he is thinking of not going to school at all? A lot of people do that when they have babies at such a young age. It never ends well though. What are my parents going to say? Poor Oliver. If it is Oliver.

"Does the father know?" I asked cautiously.

"No."

"Is it someone from school?"

She nodded her head.

"Someone I know?"

She flashed a smile. "I was trying to hurt you and ended up hurting myself. It was dumb really. I don't even really like him. I took advantage of an opportunity, I guess."

I lowered my eye brows. "I thought you like Oliver? You were going on and on about how you were trying to go out with him."

Vivienne raised her eyebrows. "Oliver?" She blew air out of her nose. "Oliver. You know I actually thought I had a chance with him. We were all hanging out a few months ago. I spent all night flirting with him. Stacy drove, but she got wasted so I asked one of the guys to drive us home. Oliver rode with Greg and so I thought for sure that it would be him. I was even willing to ditch Stacy if it meant that I could be alone with Oliver. Anyway they agreed to drive us home in Stacy's car. On the way to the parking lot, I realized that Oliver wasn't going to drive me home. Oliver hopped into Greg's car and Greg trailed me to Stacy's car. I felt a little stung at first, but then I thought, "Screw him. I'm tired of chasing him around. If he doesn't know a good thing when he sees one, then he isn't worth my time." Greg and I talked. I wasn't into him, but I knew he was into me. Has been for some time. Everyone drove off, but we stayed and kept talking. Eventually Stacy passed out and before long, Greg and I were making out. I wasn't really into him, but I thought, "What the hell. He'll tell Oliver and then Oliver will see what he is missing out on. Plus, I thought I would get to stick it to you as well since you have that ridiculous school girl crush on Greg. Knock out two birds with one stone. I actually thought I was doing you a bit of a favor. You spend all day looking at him with those googly eyes, but you don't get that he doesn't like you that way. You are making yourself look like a fool." Her eyes followed the floor. "Doesn't matter much now though does it?"

My heart sank sometime during her narrative when I first heard her mention Greg's name. It is as though I knew what she was going to say before she said it. I didn't want to believe it. I wanted to run out of the bathroom before she could release the words and turn a thought into reality. How could this be true? How could he touch her let alone make a baby with her? He said that he wasn't in the place for a relationship. That he does like me, that any guy would be lucky to have me. But then he ran to this trash.

177

I suddenly became angry. Angrier than I have ever felt before. I wanted to lash out at Vivienne, Greg, the world. My head began to spin and everything felt uneven. I reached out for the wall for support.

"No," I said. "No."

I looked around the room, but my eyes would not focus. Everything was blurry and unbalanced. I could see Vivienne's outline on the floor, but I could not make out her features. She was a blob. The blob stood up and started making some noises. Then it approached me. I yelled for it to leave me alone.

"This can't be," I said before storming out of the bathroom. I ran down the hall, falling occasionally. There were a few blobs in the hall. They said something, but I couldn't understand what. I just kept running.

Outside the sun was peeking out behind a grey cloud. I slipped on the concrete stairs and rolled down to the sidewalk. Thankfully I wasn't hurt. I stood up and started running again. My eyesight was still blurry, but I knew my way home and so I kept running and tripping until I got there.

I turned the door knob. It was locked. Crap. I left my keys at school. I ran around the house and tried the front door. It was locked as well. Frustrated, I sat down on the front porch. I was tired and deflated. My head was filled with too much pain and I needed to release it. Now. I needed to feel the freedom that I felt when I imagined myself flying with the birds. That is when it occurred to me. Baby birds learn to fly because they have no choice. Once they are of age, they are kicked out of the nest. And those nests are not nestled a few inches off the ground so that they will be OK should they fall. No, nests are put high up in trees such that the only option is to fly. Because if you don't, your life might end.

178

I stood up and walked to the side of my house. My old tree buddy, the one I used to climb out of the window that night I went out with Marie, stood there as if it knew my idea and was persuading me to get on with it. From the bottom of the tree, I surveyed the branches to see which one was the sturdiest. When I found it, I jumped, reached as high as I could and grabbed the branch with both hands. I then pressed my feet against the trunk of the tree and lifted myself up to the next branch. One hand slipped. Nervously, I dangled from the tree as I looked down. I was about six feet from the ground. I swung my other arm over and grabbed the branch. With my legs curled around the branch, I hoisted myself around to the top of the branch. I still needed to go up further. I grabbed a higher branch and again curled my legs up for extra support. I continued doing this until I was near the stop of the tree, but not so far that the branches were too thin to provide sufficient support. Once I selected a suitable spot. I stood up tall with my back to the tree. A few birds were flying free in the air. I closed my eyes and imagined myself flying with them.

I opened my eyes and looked down again. The grass was far away. Enough such that when I jump, I was either going to fly or possibly die. I don't want to die, but this is necessary. I was going to be like the baby birds. Now is my time to fly. It is all or nothing. I took a deep breath, looked up at the sky and let go. At first I started plunging toward the ground. Fast. I didn't let this worry me. I'd seen plenty of baby birds head to the ground first before taking off in flight. To worry now would be akin to committing suicide. No, I needed to stay focused. I can do this. The ground was getting closer and closer. I closed my eyes. Then…

A wave of calmness came over me. Was I dead? Was I not able to fly? I opened my eyes to a sea of blue. My heart jumped with excitement. I did it! The houses were far down below and were getting smaller and smaller along with my worries. I did a summersault in the sky and soared higher until I flew through a cloud.

"This is wonderful," I shouted with another summersault. "I'm flying!"

I couldn't decide where I wanted to go to and so I just flew around for a while. Marie had to see this, but I knew that she was still at school so that would have to wait. In the meantime, I could check out the lake. It has always been a relaxing place for me and now I will be able to view it from a different angle.

Anxiously, I pushed forward toward the lake. I stayed high so as to not alarm any of the non-flying humans on the ground.

I was so excited that something was finally going my way. After hearing about Greg, I don't think I could have taken much more. My life has been such a roller coaster lately and I was ready to get off. But now, I think I will be able to get over it. All of it. My life was going to be considerably different from now on.

The number of birds in the air increased as I neared the lake. They flew around me and treated me as their equal instead of a weird non-bird flying creature.

I flew by the large rocks intending to fly out to sea, but was shocked by what I saw. Is that? It couldn't be. But is looks like it. I flew a little lower so that I could get a closer look. It is. It's Marie. I thought she was at school. Always the truant.

I lowered my head and dove straight toward her with a spin. She turned so that her back was no longer facing me. I stopped my antics and slowed my pace. There was something wrong with her face. I could not make out her features. It was blurry and dark. Almost as if someone wiped it clean off her head and left a dark hole in its place. I was startled. I tried to stop flying toward her, but I couldn't. My body flew on auto pilot and I was the reluctant passenger. Try as I might to stop, nothing seemed to work. Then, just before reaching Marie, my body veered right and sped up. However, I was still descending. I closed my eyes as I made contact with the water. *Splash!*

PART II

Chapter Six
That's Not What I Had In Mind

"Please, is she going to be OK?"

The doctor's open mouth did not release any words. He looked down at the chart he was holding.

"Ravi, be straight with us," Keith said.

Ravi's face carried an immense burden that he seemed reluctant to share. His face went through a series of expressions as he debated his words. "She has multiple bone fractures: her left fibula and two left ribs. Also there is some swelling in her brain and so she has been placed in an induced coma until the swelling subsides."

Tears poured out of Evelyn's eyes as she wiped her nose in an unsuccessful attempt to keep her composure.

"What is her prognosis?" Keith asked.

"It's a little early to tell." Evelyn whimpered when she heard this. Ravi continued, "But the odds are in her favor. There is a good chance that she can come out of this and heal completely."

"And the other chance?" Keith asked.

Ravi's face turned solemn. "The bones will heal, but there is a chance," he looked at Evelyn, "a small chance, that there might be some brain damage. We won't know until the swelling subsides."

Keith nodded as he examined Ravi's face. "OK. Those injuries are consistent with a fall, but that can't be the reason for your caution. What are you not telling us?"

"We can discuss it later."

"Doctor Gupta, please," Evelyn pleaded. "She is my daughter. I have a right to know about everything that concerns her."

Ravi inhaled a room's worth of air. "Someone from Child Protective Services is on her way here to talk to the two of you."

"What? Why?"

"The neighbor who called 911 told the police that he saw your daughter jump from the tree."

Evelyn shook her head frantically. "That can't be right. My daughter is not suicidal."

Ravi continued, his words chosen carefully, "The neighbor said that he saw Gwen running around the house in a hysterical state."

"Hysterical state? What is that supposed to mean?" Evelyn asked.

"She was darting around, seemingly without purpose, and not wearing a coat in 20 degree weather."

"Seemingly without purpose? How is running around your own house considered hysterical? So, she forgot her coat. Did he ever think that that is why she was running around? And that does not make her suicidal."

"Mrs. Jess, please. I know this is difficult to hear, but I'm just relaying to you what your neighbor said he witnessed. This is what he told the police."

184

Evelyn slowly nodded her head.

"After she ran around the house, sans coat, she sat on the front porch for about 15 minutes. Then she stood up and started to climb a tree on the side of your house. The neighbor initially thought that she was looking for a different way into the house because she was locked out, but then she stood with her arms out and jumped."

Evelyn shook her head. "None of that makes sense. There has to be a different explanation."

"He also said that he frequently hears arguing coming from your house and that he recently witnessed an argument between your daughter and Keith in the driveway."

Evelyn looked from Doctor Gupta to Keith and back again. "That has nothing to do with this. What the…Which neighbor said this anyway?"

"The police will not release his information. The neighbor has requested to remain anonymous."

"It's Mr. Fletcher," Keith said. "He lives across the street from us. Retired accountant. Spends most of his days staring out of a window for excitement. Of course *he* would make more of the situation. A story like that is probably the highlight of his decade."

"Either way, a rep from CPS will be here to interview you. She will likely want to speak to Gwen's biological father as well. Is he in the picture?"

"Oh my goodness," Evelyn said with her hands to her face. "In all the chaos, I forgot to call Richard."

"Don't worry," Keith said. "I'll take care of it."

Ravi continued, "When Gwen wakes up, she will be on suicide watch. She will have to speak with a psychologist. We have one here on staff, but you are more than welcomed to use one of your own if you have someone else in mind."

"But my daughter is not suicidal," Evelyn repeated. "I don't understand why this is happening."

"We have to follow certain procedures when something like this happens. If she is not suicidal then it will come out during her consultation and the psychologist will release her to your care. After clearing it with CPS, of course."

"Why does it need to be cleared with CPS first?"

"The representative from CPS will be better positioned to answer your questions. I know that you are frustrated and eager to know what is going on, but I do not want to give you inaccurate information."

Evelyn shook her head again. "I can't believe this is happening. As if it isn't enough that my daughter is in a coma. I have to deal with this too? Why are they trying to make me out to be a bad mother? I am not a bad mother? I love my daughter." Evelyn started crying again.

Ravi put a hand on Evelyn's shoulder. "Mrs. Jess, please keep it together. Do not take this as a personal affront. We are all just doing our jobs. I'm sure you are a wonderful mother. Right now, you just need to focus on Gwen. Stay strong for her. Don't worry about the other stuff at the moment."

Evelyn looked up at Ravi. Her eyes were puffy and red. The strong light from the hospital only made worse the wear and tear that years of hard work necessary to earn a D.D.S., open a practice, and raise two kids have put on her once taut face. She was exhausted and it showed.

The call came in at exactly 10:36 am. She was working on Mrs. Gibson's teeth: Two new cavities. The woman refused to give up her daily dose of highly sweetened coffee. Evelyn suggested that Mrs. Gibson at least cut back on the amount of sweetener the barista put in each cup. Mrs. Gibson said that life was too short to not enjoy every minute of it. Evelyn threw up her hands and went to work on Mrs. Gibson's teeth.

Joyce, a newly hired assistant at Evelyn's dental practice, Everyday Teeth, came into the room to report an important phone call. One that required Evelyn's immediate attention. Evelyn put Mrs. Gibson on hold, thinking that it must be the school calling about Gwen again. She had skipped a few days of school. Evelyn was worried, but didn't know how to deal with it. She feared that scolding Gwen would only push her further away. On the other side, ignoring it might make Gwen believe that this type of behavior is acceptable. Richard was, of course, of no help. His response was always along the lines of: teenagers will be teenagers; well, you raised her; and her favorite, "What do you want me to do Eve? Quit work so that I can sit around and babysit her?"

Evelyn closed her eyes as she prepared herself for yet another phone call about Gwen. There was something in the woman's voice that usually called about Gwen. Ms. Patch always seemed judgmental. Like she was blaming Evelyn for Gwen's behavior. It was as if just beneath the surface of her words lived the true message: that Evelyn is a bad mother and Gwen's behavior is all her fault. No truly devoted mother would ever have a daughter that behaves this way. Only inept mothers, crack heads, alcoholics and the like have children such as yours. You should really be ashamed of yourself. Evelyn opened her eyes and put the receiver to her ear.

187

Ms. Patch was not on the other end. It was a nurse from the hospital where Keith works. It took a minute for the nurse to explain that the call was not about Keith, but her daughter Gwen. There has been an accident and Evelyn needed to get to the hospital as soon as possible. The nurse would not go into detail, but again urged Evelyn to make her way to the emergency room immediately.

Evelyn stared at her hands once the call was over. Usually calm in tense situations, Evelyn was showing signs of deteriorating. Her hands were shaking. Her body felt numb and sweaty.

Evelyn passed the remaining work on Mrs. Gibson's teeth onto Dr. Kovalenko. The trip to the hospital was a blur. When Evelyn arrived, she couldn't remember if she stopped at red lights and stop signs. Keith was waiting for her when she entered the doors to the ER.

"Can I see my daughter now?" Evelyn asked.

Doctor Gupta smiled assuredly. "Yes, but prepare yourself. It may be difficult to see her this way."

The three turned toward the I.C.U. Doctor Gupta grabbed Evelyn's arm and held her back as Keith continued.

Doctor Ravi spoke in a low, rushed tone, "Keith is an excellent surgeon, but he is also known for his short temper and less than kind words. This is a very serious matter. Some women risk losing their children because they chose the wrong man. Don't let that happen to you."

Evelyn's face turned angry as she snatched her arm away and caught up with Keith.

Evelyn gasped when she entered Gwen's room and laid eyes on her daughter for the first time since arriving at the hospital. Nothing could have prepared Evelyn for what she saw. Tubes seemed to be coming out of every part of Gwen's body. Her left leg was encased in a white cast. A brace was wrapped around her neck. Despite a few minor scratches, her face was the only part of her body that appeared normal. Her eyes were closed giving the impression that she was merely sleeping. Evelyn walked up to Gwen and put a hand on Gwen's hair. She rubbed her head then slid her hand down the side of Gwen's face. She was so peaceful and innocent looking. Evelyn tried to imagine Gwen attempting suicide, but threw the thought out as soon as it entered her brain. "It's not possible," she told herself. "Not Gwen. Not my baby."

"Mrs. Jess."

Evelyn turned to see a woman standing in the doorway. She wore a plain brown pantsuit with a white button-down top.

"Yes."

"I'm Phyllis Herman, from Child Protective Services. Can I speak with you for a moment?"

"I just got here. Do you have to do this now?"

"I'm afraid that I do."

Evelyn clenched her teeth.

"I understand that you have been briefed on why I am here," Phyllis said once the two were in the hall, a few feet from Gwen's room.

"Someone has erroneously suggested that my daughter is suicidal and that somehow my husband and I are at fault."

"I am not here to make the call on whether or not Gwen is suicidal. Nor am I here to lay blame. My purpose in all of this is to access the home situation to ensure that Gwen is in the proper environment."

"She is."

Phyllis flashed a smile. She was used to defensive parents and Evelyn was not going to be any different.

"How has her behavior been lately?"

Evelyn's eyes searched the walls and ceiling. She shrugged. "Same as any other teenager."

"Can you be a little more specific?"

Evelyn pursed her lips. "Sometimes she got a little mouthy. And rebellious."

"I understand how trying this must be for you. It is not easy having a stranger question you about what happens in your home. I don't enjoy having to do this, but it is necessary and it will be done. I am here as an advocate for Gwen."

"I am her advocate," Evelyn cut in while pointing to her chest.

"Good. Since we are on the same page, this should be easy. Now, specifically, in what way was Gwen rebellious and what did you or anyone else do in response?"

Evelyn spent about an hour talking to Phyllis about the frequency of Gwen's outbursts and her recent skipping of school. They discussed the breakdown of the mother-daughter relationship and how Evelyn no longer felt close to her daughter. By the time the meeting was over, Evelyn felt like a clueless, idiotic mother who had lost all control of her daughter.

"It can be hard sometimes," Phyllis said as she put her notepad away, her various remarks memorialized for later use. "I have a teenage daughter. You are not always their best friend, but they eventually come around."

"And if they don't?"

"Pray." Phyllis put the strap of her bag around her shoulder and reached out a hand to which Evelyn instinctively grabbed. "I'll be in touch. I hope Gwen gets better. You have my sympathies."

Back in Gwen's room, Keith told Evelyn that he'd called Richard and left a message with his secretary.

"Thank you," Evelyn said while looking at Gwen.

"Oliver will be arriving home soon. I will pick him up and bring him here. I don't think he should hear about this over the phone. Katie should be home soon as well."

Evelyn's heart cracked at the sound of Oliver's name. Even though Gwen and Oliver could fight like mortal enemies, they had a bond that no one could break. One minute they would be at each other's throat and the next it was if nothing ever happened. Gwen loved playing the distressed damsel in need of saving by Oliver's knight in shiny armor. Oliver never balked at his duties.

Ever since Gwen was born, Oliver took on a role as Gwen's personal protector. In Oliver's eyes, Evelyn never held Gwen right, sang to her the way he said she liked, nor fed her properly. At the tender age of two, Oliver would step in and show his mother how Gwen liked it done. When Gwen started walking, he would follow her all throughout the house to make sure that she didn't fall and hurt herself. Whenever she cried for a bottle or a diaper change, Oliver was right there ready to help tend to her needs. At reading time,

Oliver would sit beside Gwen and go through various books with her. The fact that he wasn't able to read yet did not deter him.

The two had a connection. It was almost like their personal, unspoken language. One would only have to look at the other to express a thought. Unfortunately, this talent of theirs was not always used for virtuous reasons.

Oliver walked through the door. His eyes found Gwen. Sadly, he looked at his mother as if asking "Why? How?" Evelyn walked over to her son and embraced him tightly. She held him the same as she did when she took him to his first day at Kindergarten. He was so young and yet getting to be so old. He wasn't nervous since he'd went to Pre-K the previous year, but now his classroom was in the main building with all of the older kids. She squeezed him as she fought back any tears. "You are my big boy, my favorite boy" she said before leaving. "I love you."

"Is she going to be OK?" Oliver asked.

"Yes. She is going to be fine."

"I don't understand. What happened?"

"I don't know. They think she tried to commit suicide, but I don't believe it."

Oliver was noticeably quiet before he spoke again. "Keith said that she jumped from a tree?"

"Apparently."

"Does anyone know why?"

"I've been asking myself that all morning. It just doesn't add up. I know that things haven't been exactly civil at home, but…but…"

"Don't blame yourself, mom."

"Is it my fault? Did I miss something? Did I do something wrong?"

"Stop it, Evelyn," Keith said. "You are a wonderful mother."

Evelyn looked unconvinced.

"He's right," Katie added. "You are a great mother and Gwen knew this, even though she didn't always show it."

"So you don't think she tried to commit suicide?" Evelyn asked.

"I don't know. But if she did, it wasn't your fault."

"Did she say anything to you?"

"No. I mean, she was upset-"

"Because of the argument," Evelyn interrupted.

"Yes, but I think she was getting over it." Katie and Oliver's eyes briefly made contact.

"Is there something that you two are not telling me?" Evelyn asked.

Katie and Oliver looked at each other suspiciously. "No," they said in unison.

"Now is not the time to keep secrets," Keith interjected. "If either of you knows something, now is the time to talk."

"It's nothing," Oliver said.

"Then say it," Evelyn pleaded. "You are worrying me."

Oliver contemplated his options. "I got kicked off the football team."

"You what?" Evelyn said louder than she expected.

"It happened about a week or two ago. It's no big deal."

"Then why I am just now hearing about this?"

"I didn't want you to worry."

"What does this have to do with Gwen?"

"Nothing. I don't think. She found out about it and was concerned, but it couldn't have anything to do with this. Right?"

Evelyn examined her son's face hoping to be able to read past his words and find out what was really going on. "No, that wouldn't have anything to do with this. Why did you get kicked off the team?"

"It was over some stupid prank. Coach didn't want to, but the principal wanted to make an example out of me. Said that it would be setting a precedent. Would help keep the other players in line. I wouldn't worry about it though. Coach said that he will work with me for when the scouts come."

"Does your dad know?"

"No."

"We'll talk about this later," Evelyn said. She didn't want to deal with Oliver getting kicked off the team right now. She was never really excited about him playing football in the first place because of the risks. But he seemed to really like it and he was good at it so she didn't stress the point. "Don't mention it to your father when he gets here."

Oliver nodded.

The four of them stood in silence staring at Gwen until Richard arrived. Evelyn filled him in on the details and he went through the same stages of shock and disbelief that she went through. She answered the questions that she could and referred him to Doctor Gupta for those that she couldn't.

"Why is CPS investigating this?"

"Standard procedure is what I was told."

"They ignore scores of abused kids, let them get beaten to death with pipes, bring guns to school, and have meth in their bottles, but we manage to make it on their list?"

"Richard, not now."

"You're right. I'm sorry. I'm just upset right now. My daughter is in the hospital fighting for her life and CPS...I'll let it go."

Doctor Gupta walked into the room. "Have you decided if you are going to go with the psychologist on staff or chose one of your own?"

"Will it be with Dr. Withers?" Keith asked.

"Yes."

"She's good," Keith said to Evelyn. "Professional. Competent."

"Do we have to do this now?" Richard asked. "In case no one has noticed, my daughter is in a coma."

"It is not something that will be done today. However, in situations like this, Dr. Withers prefers to talk to immediate family members before talking to the patient whenever possible. You will

195

have to speak with her if you would like a more in depth explanation of her process. Dr. Withers will have to perform a full psychiatric evaluation as soon as Gwen is stable and able to communicate. This could happen in as soon as three or four days or it could take longer. Dr. Withers is being optimistic, and I agree – Gwen is young, healthy and already showing signs of improvement – and so she would like for you all to schedule an appointment with her within the next few days. Whether or not Gwen can go home after she gets better or if she will have to go to another facility for further treatment will be Dr. Wither's decision."

"The children have to meet with the psychologist as well?" Evelyn asked.

"Yes. Kids tend to have a different perspective of things and they also tell each other stuff they don't tell adults."

≈

"You seem uncomfortable."

Evelyn shifted in her chair, unable to find a comfortable position. The room was chilly. The walls bare. It was not what she expected.

"I'm just worried about my daughter. She has been in a coma for three days now. I feel like I should be with her and not in here…"

"I understand your concern. No mother should ever have to experience what you are experiencing. Dr. Gupta has stated that she is doing quite well and they expect to take her out of the coma any day now, correct?"

"Yes. The swelling has gone down considerably and he is optimistic that there won't be any permanent damage."

"That is wonderful."

Evelyn shifted again.

"What happens after she wakes up and all the bones and bruises heal?"

"She comes home and goes back to living her life."

"She just jumps right back into the flow of things like nothing ever happened?"

Evelyn turned to the side. "No, we are not going to act like this never happened. We will talk about it."

"And what do you think she will say?"

Evelyn shrugged. "That she is sorry. That it was an accident."

"What would she be sorry for?"

"Scaring me I suppose."

"Do you know why she jumped?"

Evelyn shook her head.

"Has anything like this happened before?"

"No. Well there was an incident where Oliver, her brother, found her laid out and bleeding on a sidewalk. She wasn't wearing a coat. We were all very concerned about her, but she insisted that it was an accident. She tripped and fell. I watched her closely after that day, but she seemed fine. Moody, but that wasn't unusual at that point."

"You said that she might say that this incident was an accident. Do you believe that?"

"I don't believe that she was trying to commit suicide."

"Why is that?"

"She has a happy home. A happy life. It's not perfect, but she never expressed the desire to kill herself."

"Do you think she would have told you if she wanted to kill herself?"

Evelyn thought about it then shook her head.

"Why do you suppose she climbed up the tree and jumped?"

Evelyn's eyes filled with tears.

"Tell me what you are feeling right now, Evelyn," Dr. Wither's said in a soothing voice.

"I'm scared. Scared that I overlooked something. Scared that I don't really know my own daughter. Scared that somehow I am responsible."

"Responsibility is a very strong connotation. I am not here to assign blame."

"It feels like it," Evenly snorted. "It feels like I am being looked at under a microscope. Examined for all of my imperfections."

Dr. Withers laughed. "If that were true then we would all be doomed. No one is perfect. You should not beat yourself up for making mistakes every now and then."

"What if my mistakes are to blame?"

"Did you do anything that you feel caused her actions?"

"No, not intentionally. But what if I unintentionally did something?"

"Do you think that I am here to tally up all of your flaws so that I can determine if you are an unfit mother?"

"I know that sounds crazy, especially when you phrase it that way, but part of me feels that way."

"I'm not. We are both here for the same reason: to help Gwen. I'm not here to point fingers or to label you. In order for this to work, I need you to understand that and to trust me."

It took some time, but Evelyn finally started to relax. She talked about how excited she was when she took the pregnancy test and it was positive, how she enjoyed being pregnant with Gwen, how Gwen was such an easy baby, her first word ('dada'), how Gwen preferred carrots over potatoes. Dr. Withers finally stepped in and asked Evelyn to talk about events in Gwen's life that were not filled with happiness.

Evelyn began with Gwen's relationship with her father. Gwen was obsessed with him. She always had to know what he was doing, where he was going. Bedtime was stressful. Richard frequently worked late. Gwen refused to go to bed until her dad got home. Evelyn tried everything. She bribed her, she threatened her, she even spanked her a few times. Gwen would not yield. Eventually Evelyn gave up and let Gwen stay up in her room until her father came home from work. She tried talking to Richard about her dilemma, hoping that he would help out by coming home earlier – at least a few days a week. He told her that his work was too important to leave just so that he could watch a toddler go to sleep.

"How did that make you feel?" Dr. Withers asked.

"It was painful to hear. It was as if he was saying that his work was more important than his family."

"Did you ever ask him that?"

"Yes. And he said that what I was saying was ridiculous and so he wasn't even going to entertain the subject any further."

Evelyn began to slowly back away from her husband, but Gwen pushed forward. She did everything possible to get her father's attention. Most of the time he was too busy to notice her. Whenever he did look at her, he replied with the same dry response, "Wonderful."

One day Richard caught a really nasty bug. He was spewing things from every orifice. Obviously he couldn't go to work that day and would need someone to take care of him. He asked Evelyn get him some medicine and something clicked inside of her. She got the kids ready and left the house. They stayed out all day shopping, go kart racing, playing miniature golf, went out to eat. Richard was left home alone with no one to take care of him and she didn't care. He was furious when she returned. She calmly told him that evening that she wanted a divorce.

"How did the kids take it?"

"They were understandably sad, but they took it in stride. I never interfered with their relationship with their dad. Not that it mattered. He seemed happy when I was pregnant with Oliver, but not long after I gave birth to Gwen, Richard confessed to me that he didn't think he was ready for a family. That he still wanted to live his life without all of the responsibilities that come with being a parent. I should have divorced him then, but we had two kids together and I thought he would come around. Not my finest moment."

"How often did Gwen see her father after he moved out of the house?"

"Initially it was every other weekend. Before long, two, three months would pass without her seeing him."

"How did this affect her?"

"We never talked much about it. I felt that doing so would be akin to disparaging him. I didn't want to come off as the spiteful ex-wife who tried to turn the kids against their father. But I knew it had to hurt. Sometimes you could see the emptiness in her eyes. I tried to fill in the holes that he created with extra love and attention. I pretty much gave the two of them whatever they wanted. In my mind I was making up for his shortcomings."

"How was Gwen at school during this time?"

"Her grades didn't change. She was never a straight-A student, but she did her best. I never received any complaints from her teachers aside from them wanting her to participate more."

"Did she mix well with the other students?"

"Gwen never had a lot of friends. She isn't an outcast or anything like that, but it takes time for her to find her place. There was this one girl at school, I think she was in the sixth grade at the time, who used to bother her. I can't remember her name. Vanessa or something like that. Anyway, I was going to go to the school and talk to her teacher about it, but Richard insisted that I didn't. It was one of the few times that he was actually passionate about something that concerned the kids. He felt that Gwen needed to learn to stand up for herself else she would be a target for the rest of her life. There was some logic in what he said so I let it be."

"What exactly was this girl doing to Gwen?"

"She would spread lies about her. Say really nasty things to her."

"Did it ever stop?"

"Must have. Gwen didn't talk about it anymore and she seemed fine."

Dr. Withers slowly nodded her head. "How has Gwen adjusted to high school?"

"Fine. She tried out for a few clubs in her freshman year. She didn't get into any of them. I think that bummed her out for a while, but she got over it. This year, things seem to be looking up. She has a friend that she hangs out with a lot."

"What is her name?"

"Marie."

"Same grade?"

"Yes."

"And what is your take on Marie?"

"I haven't met her yet. Gwen has brought her to the house a few times, but I was at work."

"You opened your own practice sometime after your divorce?"

"Yes," Evelyn said, her face beaming. "It was a lot of work, but I did it."

"You should be proud. I take it that you've since had to put in more hours?"

"Yes, and I know what you are going to say next. No, this did not have a negative impact on the kids. Keith and I arranged our schedules so that one of us, usually him, is home when the kids get home."

"Keith, Dr. Jess, is your current husband, correct?"

Evelyn nodded.

"I know him professionally. Excellent surgeon. How long have the two of you been married?

"Ten years."

"And how is his relationship with Gwen?"

"Bumpy. Keith is a good man, but I think that Gwen still feels that he is trying to replace her father and she is against that. We talked about it and I repeatedly told her that no one could ever replace her father. None of it seemed to matter. She already decided that she hated him."

"Has he ever done anything to justify or give meaning to her feelings toward him?"

Evelyn looked away and bit her lip.

"Evelyn?"

Evelyn spoke as she fiddled with her nails. "A few months ago, Keith had an affair. I don't know if it was his first. I didn't ask. Gwen saw him eating lunch with her. Gwen was furious. She didn't understand why I stayed with him after that. I told her that it's complicated. Marriage is not as simple as it seems it should be when you are fifteen years old. You end up doing things, accepting things, that you never would have imagined possible. Things are so simple when they are hypotheticals. Keith has apologized and I have chosen to forgive him. I did not meet him under the best circumstances and so I can't turn around and expect the universe to forget. Things happen. That's life. It's what you chose to do next that matters. I figured that Gwen would just have to get over it." A tear fell from the corner of her eye.

"Is this why you feel responsible for what happened?"

Evelyn nodded. "Gwen just would not let it go. It was like a seed that was planted in the dirt and was given an abundance of water, sunlight, and fertilizer. No matter how many times I tried to make things go back to normal, she held fast to her anger. She screamed at me and called me names. And then one day I got so frustrated, so fed up that I blurted out that her father left us because he didn't want a family anymore. I didn't mean to, but she was always putting her father on a pedestal. It was like he couldn't do anything wrong. Never mind the fact that he is never around. Or that he constantly lets her down. She still sees him as the better parent and that hurts. It hurts to know that someone you love so much and that you put in so much time and effort into can look at you and basically say, "Screw you." No matter how much I tried, it's not easy fighting against someone who isn't around. Eventually I started to pull back a bit."

"How did Gwen behave after what you said about her father?"

"She didn't talk to me. Avoided me whenever possible. When I tried to talk to her, she twisted my words around and started screaming again. Every day is just so hard with her. I don't understand why she fights me on everything. We had another argument over nothing the day before the incident. She was screaming and I don't know why. Somehow, somewhere she came up with the notion that I want her out of my house. She ranted on about Keith being evil and…and…I don't remember all that was

204

said, but I slapped her. I hit my daughter. The next day she was in the ER. I can't ignore the correlation."

Dr. Withers waited a few minutes before speaking again. "Does anything in particular set her off or…"

"Everything. We could be talking about puppies and she would find something to complain about."

"Has she mentioned her father since the incident?"

"No."

"Has she spoken to him since?"

"Not that I know of, no. I'm sure she called him, but his phone frequently goes to voicemail."

Dr. Withers asked a few more questions about Gwen that she felt were pertinent before letting Evelyn go.

Katie was sitting with Gwen when Evelyn returned to the room.

"Has your father been around?" Evelyn asked as she sat in the semi comfortable chair next to Katie.

"Briefly. He left when I told him that you were meeting with the psychologist. Can I ask how it went?"

Evelyn grabbed Katie's hand and squeezed, but did not answer her question. The two sat in silence and listened to the cacophony of the machines.

"How are you doing?" Evelyn eventually asked.

"I hate seeing Gwen like this but I'm fine."

Evelyn smiled. "I meant in your life, but you were right to think that I was talking about this situation. I know you and Gwen were not always on the best of terms."

"It took a while, but lately we were getting along. I dare even say that we have developed a friendship."

Evelyn scooted a little closer to Katie. "How close?"

"I had no idea about this if that is what you are wondering."

"Was there anything bothering her? Something that I should know about?"

"I don't think so."

"Anything, Katie, please."

Katie sat in thought wondering just how much she should divulge. "There was this guy she was interested in. I don't know if he was interested in her much, but I gave her some pointers about getting a guy to notice you."

"Do you know who he is?"

Katie twisted her face as she tried to remember his name. "Greg I think. He plays football. Oliver should know him."

"Have you ever met her friend, Marie?"

"No, but I think Oliver did. He was home when she came over once."

Evelyn glanced at the clock on the wall. "How is Oliver doing? I haven't had the opportunity to talk to him much in the past few days."

"He is managing. This is really hard on him and I don't think he knows how to express his feelings."

"He is meeting with the psychologist later today. Maybe that will help."

"Maybe. I am meeting with her in a few minutes."

"I know that you and Oliver weren't being completely truthful when I asked the two of you what was going on," Evelyn said cautiously.

"Why are you bringing this up now?" Katie asked nervously.

"Because I need to know if it has anything to do with Gwen."

Katie looked Evelyn in the eye. "No, it doesn't. I would have told you if it did. Trust me."

Evelyn smiled a little. "What about Oliver. I don't believe that his coach kicked him off the team because of a prank. Do you know what happened?"

"No," Katie lied.

"I guess that I will just have to call the coach again. I left him a message, but he has not called back yet."

Katie flashed a grin.

Evelyn decided to try a different avenue. Katie and Oliver instantly hit it off when they met several years ago. Unlike with Gwen, Katie found an ally in Oliver. He seemed to understand her tortured soul better than anyone else. To him, she wasn't a rebellious teenager; she was a young girl who was lost and confused. She was in need of someone to listen to her and not judge, ridicule, or force scenarios of 'how her future will look if she doesn't change' down her throat.

In turn, Katie provided assurances for Oliver that life will be OK if you make mistakes. It wasn't easy, but she helped him to understand that life doesn't carve out a perfect path for you. You will make mistakes. You will fall flat on your face. What matters most is not what you did before you fell; it's what you do right after you have fallen.

Evelyn was concerned with how close Oliver and Katie had become. She liked Katie, but Katie was a free spirit that caused a lot of trouble. While Oliver was far from perfect, he never crossed the line. Evelyn didn't want that to change.

"I know that you care about Oliver and you do not want to betray his trust," Evelyn said, "but I if there is something going on that could put Oliver in danger, I need to know." Evelyn spoke in a solemn tone. "It's possible that I am to blame for what has happened to Gwen if even only by omission. There was obviously something going on in her life and I was too busy to notice. I wasn't the mother she needed. Please don't let me continue to live in the dark when it comes to Oliver."

"You really shouldn't blame yourself for what has happened. I understand that it is difficult for a parent to stand idly by while their child suffers. But I don't think that there is anything you could have done to prevent this."

"I appreciate your view, but, and don't take this the wrong way, unless I am dead, there is always something that I can do. Where it concerns my kids, I will fight to the end. You included."

Katie's eyes became misty. "It feels good to have so much support. I don't know why I didn't understand this before. For

208

whatever reason, I saw my parents' support as an intrusion. Like they were telling me: my opinions and my choices were derisory. I felt that everything I did was wrong, even when I didn't do anything. I've been slowly finding my way back. I see things differently now. Strange part is, I don't regret my path. It was mine and it was necessary in order for me to get to where I am now. My parents, teachers, psychiatrists, they all tried to explain it to me, but I wasn't ready to hear it."

"Whether you listened or not, they still had the chance to tell you. They still had the chance to fight for you. Don't deny me that. Please."

Katie took a deep breath and considered her options. Oliver would not be the least bit pleased if she betrayed his trust. In fact, He would probably stop speaking to her. But Evelyn had a point. And Katie did not want things to get any worse than they already had. Oliver maintained an outwardly appearance that he was handling Gwen's suicide attempt well, but Katie suspected that internally, it was a different story.

When Oliver and Katie arrived home after visiting Gwen in the hospital on the first day, Oliver made a jolting comment. He worried that he might be at fault for Gwen's actions. Katie tried to assure him that such a thing couldn't be further from the truth. Not to mention that it made absolutely no sense at all. But Oliver was so far down his hole that he'd started beating himself up over everything. Everything somehow was his fault. The next day, Oliver snapped out of his overindulgence on pity. He apologized for what he said. He blamed his unusual state on lack of sleep and worry.

"I should get going," Katie said as she stood up. "I don't want to be late for my meeting."

≈

"You seem bothered by something," said Dr. Withers. It was more of a statement than a question.

"Evelyn doesn't think that Gwen tried to commit suicide," Katie said. "What do you think?"

"I don't know. That is why I am speaking to all of you."

"Do you think that someone can commit suicide for reasons that have nothing to do with them? Like if something is happening to someone you really care about?"

"Anything is possible."

"But is it likely? How often does something like that happen?"

"Not often."

"But how many times?"

"I don't know of any statistics. Personally, I have never come across such a case."

"So not very likely."

"What is it, Katie?"

"Will you discuss any of this with Evelyn?"

"I'm here to help Gwen in the best way that I can. If you know something that will help me with this task, then I will appreciate it if you tell me."

"I'm just trying not to hurt anyone, but it seems as though even not doing anything is still hurting someone."

"The joy of life. Makes even inaction a difficult decision. Unfortunately, I can't make that decision for you, but you need to weigh the consequences on both sides. What is more important? Where are the greater risks?"

Katie did not respond.

Dr. Withers' continued. "I understand that you have had a rather colorful childhood. Numerous suspensions from school, stints at rehabilitation facilities."

"I enjoyed life."

"And now?"

"I have a different definition of what it means to have fun."

"So you have turned your life around for the better."

"I think so."

"Did you go at it alone?"

"What do you mean?"

"Your parents, did they abandon you? Leave you to your own devices? Or did they fight for you every step of the way?"

Katie let out a light chuckle. "You sound like Evelyn."

"Maybe she is right."

"She is a good mom, you know. Whatever happened to Gwen, it isn't her fault."

"You have a good relationship with her don't you?"

"Yeah. I didn't think that I would like her at first. She was my dad's new wife. You are not supposed to like the stepmother. She's supposed to be evil." Katie laughed at her own joke. Dr. Withers returned a polite smile. "But she was cool from the start. She became someone that I could talk to. I didn't feel like I could trust my parents at the time. I felt that they were trying to control me. Mold me into the person that they wanted me to be. Evelyn didn't have an ulterior motive. She was genuine. She also listened to me. My parents were always yelling and complaining."

"And yet you feel like you are betraying her somehow?"

"She asked me if I knew something about Oliver that she should know about. She could tell that something was going on, but didn't know what. I lied and told her that Oliver got kicked off the team because of a prank just like he told her."

"What really happened?"

"He was kicked off because he had been drinking. Gwen found out about his drinking not long after he got into a car accident. His parents never found out about it. He started coming to practice drunk. He was initially suspended, but then his coach kicked him off when he wouldn't lay off the booze."

"Why weren't his parents notified?"

Katie lifted her shoulders. "I don't know. Oliver said the coach didn't want to make it official because that could affect his chances of playing football in college. Also, the coach just thought Oliver was under a lot of stress and needed some time off to sort himself out."

"And what do you think?"

Katie looked surprised at the question. "I'm not a specialist."

"But you have experience in this area. Do you think he has a problem?"

"Yes," Katie said confidently. "I feel that he won't stop until he hits rock bottom and unfortunately he hasn't reached that point yet."

"You are right in that an addict will not begin to heal until he first determines that there is a problem. However, each person has a different route to get to that determination. Rarely does anyone make it there alone. To not give an addict the love and support that he needs can be akin to giving him a death sentence. Oliver has been kicked off the team. He can no longer play a game that he loves and has put in years of effort and dedication. His sister is in a coma and he thinks that he is to blame. Either one of those is an easy recipe for depression. Alcohol is always there promising to make it all go away."

"Except that it doesn't. Once the headache is gone and the numbness has worn off, the problem is still there and is usually compounded with more problems."

"That's right."

"Are you going to tell Evelyn?"

"No. No one's life is in immediate danger and the information does not directly affect Gwen, but I urge you to do so. Think about the worst case scenario then imagine how you will feel knowing that you didn't even try. How Evelyn will feel if she finds out that you knew and didn't say anything or try to help him."

After a moment of silence, Dr. Withers asked about Gwen. "How well did the two of you get along?"

"What did Evelyn tell you?"

"Doesn't matter. I am asking you."

"We didn't at first. We used to butt heads. She saw me as a troublemaker. I saw her as a whiny brat. We were both wrong. Or maybe we were both right and we just accepted each other's flaws. Either way, we started to talk."

"About what?"

"Stuff. She was upset with her mother a lot. I felt sorry for her."

"Why?"

"Because I think that a lot of their problems were because of my dad. Have you met him?"

"I know him professionally."

"It would be in your best interest to keep it that way. He likes the ladies and you aren't so bad looking."

"I'm not sure if that is a compliment."

"It wasn't. You don't want to be party to anything that has to do with my father."

"So you and Gwen possess a common dislike for your father?"

"You can say that. Mine has more history, but the source is the same."

"Would you classify Gwen as an angry person?"

"No, more like moody. She is easily set off."

"Reasonably so?"

"No," Katie said quickly and without much thought. "My dad can be an ass, don't get me wrong, but she gave as much as she took.

Also, she frequently took things the wrong way. Any comment you made to her was somehow, in her mind, a negative comment. She saw hidden messages in everything you said."

"You said that recently your relationship with Gwen has changed. In what way?"

"We don't fight so much anymore. We will still get smart with each other, but in a more friendly way now. We talk. She confides in me. I give her advice."

"What has she confided to you?"

"Nothing related to this. Some guy she likes. We talked about her mother and my dad cheating on her."

"She was upset about the infidelity?"

"Yes. She wondered if she should tell her mother."

"What did you tell her?"

"I told her that her mother probably already knows. The wife usually does. My mother did." Katie lowered her eyes.

"You know, not all men cheat."

"I know," Katie said, her eyes still roaming the floor. "Just kind of crappy that my father does."

≈

"Do you have somewhere to be?" Dr. Withers asked.

Keith looked up from his watch. "I don't know why I'm here.

"For Gwen."

215

Keith pressed his lips together. "She is an unstable young lady and I am not surprised that she tried something like this. She never came to terms with her parents getting divorced. She held onto this fantasy that her parents would one day get back together. My arrival only complicated things further."

"It is your opinion that Gwen didn't like you because you interfered with her parents getting back together?"

"Yes."

"How is your relationship with her?"

Keith looked at his watch again.

"Dr. Jess?" Dr. Withers craned her neck trying to get Keith's attention.

"Strained."

"Did you do anything to try and better the relationship?"

"For what? She already decided that I was the enemy. There isn't much you can do when a teenage girl makes up her mind."

"Is that how you feel about your daughter, Katie?"

"We are not here to talk about Katie. Please leave my relationship with my daughter out of it."

"Fair enough. Can you be a little more specific about your relationship with Gwen?"

"She didn't like me. What else is there to say?"

"How did she treat you?"

"She would try to be disrespectful to me and yell at me at times."

"What did you do when she behaved this way?"

"I got into her face and let her know that I was not going to tolerate that type of behavior in my house. I demand respect and I *will* receive it."

"I take it Gwen was not too pleased with your response."

"She got the message."

"You have a different take on situations then Evelyn."

"Evelyn is like my ex, Katie's mother. Believes if she tries to reason with her and walk on eggshells around her, she will eventually come around. That is garbage. Teenagers today have no respect for adults. In my day, I would have been slapped in the face before any words of disrespect could even make it to my lips. You did as you were told. No questions asked."

"Did you and Evelyn ever quarrel over how to discipline Gwen?"

"No. Her daughter, her choice. But I told her that I would not hold my tongue when Gwen got curt."

"Why do you think Gwen jumped from that tree?"

"Attention. Everything she did was for attention. She blew off the handle over every little thing. She would twist and turn your words to suit her next tantrum."

"You don't seem to think very highly of Gwen."

Keith's faced immediately reddened as he pointed his finger at Dr. Withers. "Don't try to put words in my mouth and don't try to blame me for this. I tried to be civil to her. I took her to the father daughter dance once when her father was too busy to do so. I am the one that used to take her to all of the different activities that she participated in. I am the one that was there when she got home from school. Did she appreciate any of this? No! She is a spoiled little brat that never cared about anything that I did for her. No matter how many hours I worked to give her a good life. No matter how much grief it caused me. Katie never cared about anyone but herself."

"Katie?"

"What?" Keith sounded confused.

"You just said Katie."

"No I didn't"

"You did."

"If I did then I must have misspoke."

"I don't think that you did. In fact, I think that a large part of the discord between you and Gwen can be attributed to her reminding you of Katie."

Keith lowered his tone. "I told you to leave her out of this."

Dr. Withers put both of her hands in the air. "Yes, I know, but please, as a professional courtesy, just indulge me. You don't have to respond if you don't want to."

Keith flicked his hand in the air.

"You had high hopes for Katie when she was born. You were successful in your career, you were married. The next logical step was to have a child to pass on your knowledge. Things probably went along smoothly when Katie was a baby and toddler. You read to her at night. Bought her anything she ever wanted and even things she didn't know she wanted: that baseball bat. She was enrolled in every class that you could think of: gymnastics, tap, taekwondo, ballet, horseback riding lessons, piano lessons, and soccer."

Keith smiled just a little.

"Please stop me if I'm wrong."

"That's pretty much it except it wasn't a baseball bat, it was a set of golf clubs and she didn't take piano lessons. It was guitar. She wanted to be able to rock out like Bruce Springsteen. She knew that he was one of my favorite musicians." Keith looked to the side as he briefly revisited his memories.

Dr. Withers continued, "You were happy. Katie was everything you could have hoped for and more."

"Then she turned twelve," Keith added.

"And she was no longer daddy's little girl."

"She didn't want me to walk her to class anymore. It used to be our thing. I worked a lot, but I always made time to take her to class. It hurt, but I brushed it aside. She was growing up and wanted her independence."

"What else changed?"

"Everything, it seemed. She never wanted to be around me. She stayed on her phone talking to her friends. Her grades started slipping. When I took away her privileges so she could focus on her studies, she started screaming at me and telling me that she hates me. Patricia, Katie's mother, told me to not take it personal. She said that it was just a phase that Katie was going through that all teenagers go through."

"Watching her go through this was hard on you."

"Yes. Every day she used to hug me and tell me that she loved me. It got to the point that I was lucky if she said more than two words to me. If she did, it was likely filled with animosity. Then came the drugs and alcohol. She was fourteen at the time. She called us one night from the police station. There was a party at one of her friend's house. When she asked us if she could go, she told us that the party was going to be supervised by the parents. Turns out they were on vacation in Wyoming. Bunch of teenagers trashed the place. A few were even caught having sex. I was livid. I was beyond livid. Katie turned on the charm. She said that she didn't know that the party was going to turn chaotic. She admitted knowing that the parents weren't going to be there, but didn't think we would let her go otherwise. She apologized profusely. She also swore up and down that she did not participate in any of the illicit activities. I looked into her large innocent eyes and I wanted to believe her. All I could see was my little girl again. But I knew it was crap. Her eyes were dilated, yet I told myself that it was because of the fear of everything or the lighting. I told myself whatever I needed to so that I could put it behind me and we could move on to being the family that I wanted us to be.

"Things were quiet around the house for a few months. Katie was back to being Katie. She didn't roll her eyes at me when she talked. Her grades were getting better. She even told me she loved me a couple of time. But fairy tales don't last forever. Katie was caught smoking marijuana on school grounds. She was suspended from school for a week. We grounded her at home. She wasn't allowed to talk on the phone or leave the house. This didn't deter her. She started sneaking out while I was at work. Patricia would

220

spend hours driving around town looking for her. Eventually she would find Katie drugged out somewhere. She would take her home where Katie would apologize and promise to never to it again. It didn't stop. Soon Katie became so brazen that she would just walk out the front door."

"How did you feel during all of this?"

"Helpless. My daughter was throwing her life away and there was nothing that I could do about it. Patricia maintained that we needed to keep supporting her. I felt that was crap. A judge got tired of seeing her and finally put his foot down. He told her that she had a choice: either go to rehab and get clean or go to juvenile detention. She picked rehab. Several times."

"Is she clean now?"

"Once an addict, always an addict. I can't trust her. She has figuratively spat in my face too many times. I have given her chance after chance after chance and she threw each and every one of them away."

"Addicts know that what they are doing is wrong, but they cannot control it. They lack the ability to control the impulse that makes them give into the urge."

"I understand addicts and how addiction works, but Katie, Katie had choices. She had other options. She didn't grow up without means or with parents who neglected her. She had everything she wanted, everything she needed and she still chose the underbelly."

"Did you feel that she chose this seedy life over you?"

"Essentially that is what she was doing isn't it?"

"And so you finally gave up on her?"

Keith shrugged. "You can say that. I mean I love her and I always will, but she stopped caring and I got tired of trying. She was hell bent on becoming a lackey; I mean she really put in effort to become nothing so why should I stand in her way. Why should I continue to stress myself out for someone who doesn't even care?"

"Did the on goings with Katie affect your marriage to Patricia?"

"Patricia and I had problems outside of the Katie debacle, but Katie's issues didn't help matters."

"How old was Gwen when you married Evelyn?"

"About ten."

"Katie was still your sweetheart at that age wasn't she? Your angelic daughter."

"Yep."

"Did you think, even subconsciously, that you were getting a second chance with Gwen?"

"Part of me considered that. Gwen's father wasn't in the picture much. I thought, well, if I can't pass on what I have to my daughter then maybe I could with Gwen."

"But it didn't work out that way?"

"She was a little snot right from the start. When I first met her, after her mother left the room, she turned to me and told me that I was wasting my time because her mother was still in love with her father and they were going to get back together soon. Evelyn tried to push me and Gwen into a relationship, and I complied for Evelyn's sake, but it was pointless. Gwen made up her mind about me before she met me. Nothing was going to change that. It is almost like Katie and Gwen were cut from the same cloth."

≈

"How long has she been here?" Keith asked Evelyn after kissing her on the cheek.

Evelyn turned around to look at Katie sitting in a chair next to Gwen. "Every day, all day. She rarely leaves her side. I think she is mostly here for me, but the reason doesn't matter much. I'm just glad she is here. It has helped a lot. Keeps my mind from wondering to the negative."

Keith rubbed Evelyn's arms affectionately. "I can stay here if you need me."

"No, you have to work. Katie's here. I'll be fine."

"Are you sure? It is no big deal. I can rearrange some of my surgeries."

"I'm sure."

"OK, but I'll come down to check on you whenever I have a break."

Evelyn smiled and hugged her husband. "How was your meeting with Dr. Withers?"

"Uneventful. She asked a few questions. I didn't have much to tell her though."

"You and Gwen didn't have the best relationship."

"And I told her this."

"Good." Evelyn's eyes drifted away.

"You don't think any of this has to do with me do you?"

Evelyn's eyes were full of tears when they returned to Keith. "No, of course not. I'm just…I'm just sad and scared."

Keith took Evelyn into his arms. "I know. This is a very trying time for you and I wish that you didn't have to endure it. Life can be cruel sometimes. Even to the most wonderful people." Keith moved back and grabbed Evelyn's hands. "You are wonderful person. The best thing that has ever happened to me. I want you to know this. I love you so much. I don't ever want to be without you. You make me a better person."

"Thank you," Evelyn said as she embraced Keith. "I needed that. I love you, too."

Keith noticed Katie standing behind Evelyn when the two separated. Her dirty blond hair was pinned back in a ponytail.

"Hey dad,"

"Evelyn tells me that you have been keeping her spirits up."

"I'm doing what I can."

"That's supposed to be my job, but I am grateful that you are here."

"You are all important to me. You are my family."

Keith was stunned, but smiled anyway. "Well, I have to head off. I'll be back down when I get a chance."

"Wait, dad," Katie said as Keith was about to leave. She walked up to him and wrapped her arms around him and squeezed. "I love you, dad."

It took Keith a second to react, but soon he returned the hug and told Katie that he loved her too.

≈

"I think you should tell your mother about the accident and the drinking," Katie said as she and Oliver ate dinner in the hospital's cafeteria.

"What?" Oliver said perplexed.

"You heard me."

"I don't think I heard you right."

"Why won't you tell her?"

"Because then she will worry over nothing. Besides, she has enough to deal with right now."

"I don't mean now. After."

"What good will that do? It was an *accident*. And I don't have a drinking problem."

"Who are you trying to kid? That mouthwash you gargled with before coming here isn't doing a great job of covering up the alcohol you drank."

"I didn't-"

"Don't lie and tell me that you didn't have anything to drink."

"I-I wasn't," Olivier said with a stutter. "I was just going to say that I didn't have that much. Just a little to take the edge off. What is wrong with that?"

"Everything."

Oliver put his fork down. "Don't tell me you are going to start nagging me over this. I'm fine."

"Who are you trying to kid, Oliver? This is me you are talking to. I know the game. I know the stories. "Oh, I only had one beer. Oh, no, I'm fine, my eyes are red because I'm tired." You keep repeating these lies until you start to believe them yourself."

"I thought you said you weren't an alcoholic."

"Same disease, different drug. Oliver, I'm not here to tell you what to do. I've been there. I know how sometimes everything can seem like too much and the pull of the numbness is calling you. It's so enticing to make it all go away, even if it is just for a little bit. You tell yourself that you will deal with it later. You will know what to do about it then. Right now, you just need to relax a bit. Then you find that you need to relax more often than you're used to. Before you know it, relaxing is all you can think about."

"I'm not you, Katie. Not everyone is an addict. Some people know how to control their consumption."

"No, you are not me. I made it out alive. I am sober now. If you don't get to where I am, there is no guarantee that you will make it out alive."

Oliver breathed out heavily. "Are you going to tell my mother?"

"I want you to."

Oliver chuckled. "Fat chance of that happening."

"I haven't decided yet, but I may tell her if you don't. Please don't make me have to do that. I am begging you to tell her yourself."

"Look, you do whatever you feel you have to do, but I'm not telling her anything."

"Gwen is not in the hospital because of you. I hope you know this."

"What is your point?"

"Don't beat yourself up over something that you had nothing to do with. I know it is hard to see your sister in a coma, but at the rate you're going, you are going to be in the room next to her." Katie stood up. "I don't want that to happen. I know your mother does not want that to happen. Do you?"

≈

"I'm glad you were able to make it," Dr. Withers said. "I know this is a very difficult time for you."

"You never expect to see your sister in a coma," Oliver said solemnly.

"No, you don't. How have you been coping?"

Oliver squinted at Dr. Withers. "What did Katie tell you?"

"Katie had her time to talk to me about what was on her mind. Now is your time. What do you want to talk about?"

Oliver considered her statement. "What do you need from me to make Gwen better once she wakes up?"

"How would you best describe Gwen?"

"What?"

"Tell me about Gwen. I want to know your impression of her. What words would you use to describe her?"

"She's my sister. She has a kind heart, good character. Her humor can be a bit dry, but that's subjective."

"How does she respond to unexpected events?"

"Like what?"

"Anything. Accidentally knocking over her drink or forgetting an appointment."

"She took it in stride like most people. None of that seemed to bother her much beyond the slight irritability factor."

"What about more important things like her personal life? How did she feel when she didn't make it onto any of the teams or clubs that she tried out for?"

"She was disappointed, but I talked to her. I told her that she was better off without them for now. She just needed to find her place and it didn't have to happen in her first year of high school. Give it time. They will come around. Soon they will be begging for her to join."

"Did she believe you?"

"She knew that I was giving her words of encouragement and it seemed to make her feel better. It was cool."

"Did any of the kids at the school mistreat her?"

"Naw, she is my sister and everyone knows that. No one would mess with her."

"No one?"

"Well, there is this one girl who messes with her a bit, but that could be because she likes me."

"And you don't like her?"

"She's not my type."

"Is Gwen overly sympathetic to you?"

"I don't know. Last year when I had the flu, she told me to suck it up, but then she made me soup and got me an extra blanket. She's thoughtful, but she does have a mean streak in her."

Dr. Withers slowly nodded her head. "How have you been feeling lately?"

Oliver looked suspiciously at Dr. Withers. "I knew it. Katie told you that I got kicked off the team didn't she?" Oliver didn't wait for a response. "Ugh! I knew it. You are going to tell my mother aren't you?"

"Katie only told me because she thought it might be related."

Oliver started to become agitated. "So she thinks this is my fault too?"

"No one is blaming you for anything, Oliver."

"Katie said something similar, but yet she told you. Apparently she felt otherwise."

"That is not how the information came out."

"Then how?"

"That's not relevant."

"It is to me." Oliver's tone was getting higher with each word.

"Oliver, I need you to calm down."

"I am calm."

"No, you are not."

"Look, I gotta go." But Oliver did not get up.

"I cannot make you stay, but I really wish that you will. This is important. I know Gwen is important to you."

"What is there to stay for? You have all made up your minds that this is all my fault. That Gwen tried to kill herself because she thinks I have a drinking problem."

"Do you?"

"Do I what?"

"Have a drinking problem."

"No, but I am guessing that Katie told you that I do."

"This is not about Katie. This is about you and Gwen. Does Gwen think that you have a drinking problem?"

He shrugged. "She was on the fence about it. She felt that something was wrong, but wasn't sure if I am officially an alcoholic. She got on my case a lot."

"She was concerned about you. Deeply."

"Yes and I understand. I would be concerned about her if the shoe was on the other foot. I'd probably react the same way she did. Heck, I'd probably even tell my mother." Oliver chuckled insincerely then put his face in his hands and started to cry.

"What is going through your mind right now?"

"I'm angry and I'm scared."

"About what?"

"Gwen. What if she doesn't make it through this? I don't want to be an only child. She can be a pain sometimes, but I love her and I want things to go back to the way they were."

"What else is bothering you?"

"I'm scared that this is all my fault. I tried to keep my issues to myself, but what if they spilled over to Gwen and that is why she did this?"

Dr. Withers spoke calmly. "I don't know why she did this. I don't know if her intention was to commit suicide. We won't know until she wakes up. However, statically, what you are claiming doesn't make sense."

"What do you mean?"

"People commit suicide for an assortment of reasons. Depression is usually a huge factor, coupled with particular events in that person's life. Events in another person's life, basically depression by proxy, isn't one that I have heard of. I'm not saying that it isn't possible, just not likely."

"I know it sounds crazy, but it is the only thing that I can think of. Nothing else makes sense."

"Tell me about the other relationships in her life. Start with your father."

"There isn't much tell. He comes around when it suits him. It's cool when he is around, but it is also cool when he isn't. Gwen sometimes puts him on a pedestal, but I think that is because it is easier to assume something is better when you don't have it. Her and

231

my mother get into it all of the time, but that is because they live in the same house. We see our dad once a month, if that. There is no room for conflict there. Unless you want to count the myriad of space he leaves by not being around."

"You don't seem to be bothered one way or the other."

"It used to bother me. I wanted my father around more, but I just had to accept that it wasn't going to happen."

"Did Gwen accept this?"

"I'm not sure. She didn't talk about him much except to hurt my mother. I don't know why she did that. Whenever he came around, it wasn't as if she really enjoyed herself. It got to the point that she just tolerated him. We used to joke sometimes whenever we knew our dad was coming around for a visit. We used to call him 'The Blast from the Past' because he always talked about when we were young. I guess that is where most of his memories of us are from. It's not like he is around much to make any new ones."

"Do you think that she secretly wanted your mother and father to get back together?"

"At first, yes. But I think she let it go after a while."

"Keith seems to feel differently."

Oliver showed his sparkling white teeth with his wide and infectious smile. "Those two are like polar opposites. If there were ever two people who should never be in the same room with each other, it is definitely those two."

"Do you feel as though Keith bullied Gwen?"

"Yes," he said while nodding his head. "But she gave it as good as she took it. He frustrated her, but she never backed down from him."

"How did your mother react to this?"

"I don't think she knew how to. There were two people in her life that she loved that could not stand one another. I think it got to the point where she was just biding her time, waiting until Gwen graduates from high school and leaves for college."

"That's dismal."

"What else do you expect her to do? Kick her daughter out? Divorce her husband? She loves them both. They just don't love each other. It's my mother's lot in life. Not everything works out the way we want it to. Sometimes you have to roll with the punches."

"You don't think that it is Keith's responsibility, as the adult, to take the high road? To be a better person?"

"He tried. I can't say he put his whole heart into it, but he tried. Can he do more? Probably, but I don't think it will make a difference. Gwen has made up her mind about him and she isn't one to change easily."

"Does Gwen have a boyfriend or a friend that she confided in?"

"She doesn't have a boyfriend, but she does have a friend that she has been hanging out with lately. I think her name is Marie."

"Have you met her?"

"I may have seen her at school. I'm not sure. She has been to the house, but we've never been formally introduced."

"It would be nice if I can get the opportunity to talk to her. She might know something that the rest of you are not privy to."

"I understand. I will look for her at school and she what she says. I'm sure it won't be a problem."

"Good. Tell me about Greg."

"My teammate?" Oliver realized his mistake and immediately corrected himself. "My ex-teammate."

"Yes. Gwen has a crush on him, correct?"

He snorted. "I thought she got over that."

"Apparently not. I was told that he kissed her."

Oliver repeatedly shook his head.

"You don't approve?"

"I told him to leave her alone. He isn't one for monogamy and I don't want anyone stringing her along. She deserves better than that."

"The heart wants what the heart wants."

"So I've heard. The brain needs to tell the heart to shut up sometimes."

Dr. Withers' laughed.

Oliver's facial expression changed. The corner of his lips dropped as all of the muscles in his face drooped.

"What's wrong?" Dr. Withers asked, noticing the change in Oliver.

Oliver closed his eyes and tilted his head back. "Damn!" He banged his fists against the couch.

"Oliver," Dr. Withers pressed.

"Greg."

"What about Greg?"

"He told me that he got Vivienne pregnant. Gwen must have found out."

≈

"How are you doing?" Evelyn asked as she hugged her son as he entered Gwen's hospital room.

"I'm fine. How are *you* doing?"

"Great. Doctor Gupta was just here. He said that Gwen has been doing very well and they are planning to wake her up from the coma as early as tomorrow."

"That is wonderful news," Richard said from the doorway.

"You made it." Evelyn said.

"I know that I'm late, but I had a lot of meetings to get to."

"I haven't seen much of you since the first day."

"Let's not do this Evelyn."

"I'm not doing anything. Just thought you would want to be here to support your daughter."

"Sitting here while she sleeps isn't helping anyone."

"I'm sorry that you see it that way."

"Hey dad," Oliver interjected. "Glad you are here."

Oliver hung around and chatted with his mother, father, and Katie for a bit. He was elusive when they asked about his meeting with Dr. Withers, offering not much beyond telling them that he answered all of her questions. He cut the visit short, saying that he needed to get back to school. It was a lie. The school day was almost over and the principal told him that he didn't have to return, but something was on his mind.

Oliver frantically searched the halls of the school. He pushed a few stragglers aside then apologized for his rudeness. He pressed further into the hall. His eyes rolled around, briefly scanned a face then moved onto the next.

"Hey, Oliver," said an unfamiliar voice.

Oliver looked at the rather tall skinny boy standing before him with an unruly head of brown curly hair. He opened his mouth to say something.

"You probably don't know me. I'm William. I know your sister. How is she?"

"You know Gwen?" Oliver asked unexpectedly.

"Yes, we ride the bus together and we have the same math class. How is she doing?"

"Um, fine." Oliver was distracted by his thoughts. "Do you by chance know her friend Marie? I'm trying to find her, but I don't know what she looks like."

"Sorry, I can't say that I know of anyone by that name."

236

"Have you seen Gwen hanging out with anyone? Maybe you can tell me what she looks like."

William searched his memory. "I've seen her talk to Izzy a few times and sometimes Ashley, but not lately. I haven't seen her with anyone lately."

Oliver peered over William's head as he spoke. "Thanks," Oliver said as he darted off leaving William standing alone. "Hey Greg, wait up."

Greg turned around to see Oliver running toward him. At 6 feet 3 inches and over 220 lbs., Greg overshadowed Oliver's 6ft 1 inch and 190 lb. frame.

"Hey, I'm sorry to hear about your sister. How is she doing?"

"Better," Oliver said without conviction. "I thought I made it clear that I didn't want you messing around with my sister?"

"Yeah, I stayed away from her."

"Are you sure about that?"

Greg analyzed Oliver's stern expression. His own face went from incredulous to apologetic. "It was one kiss. I was drunk, I'm sorry, but I didn't lead her on. I later told her that it was a mistake and that I didn't want to get with her."

Oliver's face grew gruesome.

Greg softened his tone upon seeing Oliver's manifestation. "I let her down gently. I told her that she is a great girl and any guy would be lucky to have her, but that I wasn't looking to be with anyone right now."

Oliver balled up his fist and clenched his teeth. The veins in his neck were on full display. Just when Greg thought Oliver was going to hit him - a move he was going to let happen once, just once, for Gwen's sake - Oliver opened his mouth wide and let out a scorching sound. Greg stepped back from the piercing noise. Oliver's body seemed to deflate when he finished screaming.

Everyone in the hall stopped to face the two of them when the screaming commenced. Some hurried off with worried looks on their faces when there was no follow up.

"Man, I'm sorry. I know that she is your sister, but you know how girls can get. I was wrong for what I did, but I did not lead her on. I promise you that."

"Does she know about Vivienne?" Oliver asked as he faced the wall. He could not bear to look at Greg.

A horrible realization swept through Greg and he lowered his head. "Vivienne said that she talked to Gwen in the bathroom that day. I wasn't really trying to hear what she was saying. I was still in shock over her being pregnant. Vivienne said that Gwen got upset and stormed out of the bathroom. She left the school. That must have been when she…"

Greg didn't finish his sentence. Not that Oliver waited around to see if he was going to. Oliver ran out of the building and hoped into his car. He sped away from the school and drove around aimlessly. He ended up in the parking lot of a seedy convenience store twenty miles away. After sitting in his car rocking silently for half an hour, Oliver went into the store. He first walked to the candy aisle. Nothing piqued his interest so he headed over to the chip aisle. His hand grazed over the Doritos and the Cheetos. He settled on a bag of Funyuns then walked to the back of the store. He was briefly stunned when he caught his reflection in the slightly frosted glass. This did not deter Oliver. He reached out and opened the door. With a six pack of beer in his hand, he headed confidently to the counter.

"ID," the cashier said reproachfully.

"I left it at home. Can you give me a pass this one time? I'm of age."

"Sorry, I need this job."

Oliver put an extra twenty on the counter. "I understand. I wasn't going to ask you without some type of payment for your extra effort."

The cashier eyed the money. He then made a slight gesture to the camera hanging over the door. "Show me some type of ID. Gotta make this look good in case the owner decides to review the tape," the cashier said in a low voice."

"No problem," Oliver said while flashing his license at the cashier.

Oliver tossed the Funyuns into the backseat and immediately opened a can of beer. It was empty in less than five seconds. Oliver laid his head back as he let the soothing alcohol consume his body. His eyes closed as he felt a dull numbness begin to wash away his anxiety and his fears. Instinctively, he reached over and grabbed another can of beer. Just as the cold metal of the can touched his lips, an image of Gwen flashed through his head. He relaxed his arm. He looked at the can and felt ashamed. Without a second thought, Oliver gathered the rest of the beer and tossed them into a large dumpster next to the store. Oliver walked back to his car, but he stopped short of opening the door. He glanced back at the dumpster. He closed his eyes and tried to open the door, but his hand betrayed him. Before he knew it, Oliver was climbing into the dumpster digging through discarded food and unwanted items before coming across the opened can he threw away. It was now half full. Oliver chucked it aside and picked up the four remaining cans from his original six pack.

With two cans of beer left, Oliver drove back to the hospital.

≈

"I suppose this is somehow all attributed to me?" Richard said gloomily.

"Why do you say that?" Dr. Withers asked.

"Evelyn told me what she said to Gwen. About the reason why we got divorced. She said that Gwen hasn't talked much to her since."

"When did you find out about it?"

"Evelyn called me later that day. She said that she was upset and that is why she blurted it out. We argued a bit. I was upset at her for saying such a thing to Gwen. She was upset for me not being there to properly support her with the kids. She was tired of always been seen as the bad parent while I got accolades for doing nothing."

"Did you talk to Gwen after you found out?"

"No."

"Why?"

"Busy, I guess."

"You were too busy to make a phone call to talk to your daughter about information that upset her? Information that directly concerned you?"

The room was quiet and thick with tension.

"I don't think that's true," Dr. Withers continued. "I think you had time to call her, but you made the conscious choice not to. Would you care to tell me why?"

"Since you have unilaterally decided that I am lying, why not continue with the reason?"

"I'd much rather hear it from you."

Richard flashed a spiteful smile. "It must be so easy for you. You probably go through life always doing the right thing, never making any mistakes along the way. That way at the end of the day you can perch yourself up high on your horse and point down at the rest of us."

Dr. Withers laughed unexpectedly. "That's hilarious. If only you knew my past, you would not say those words."

"Enlighten me. I want to laugh as well."

"All right then." Dr. Withers told of how she got off to a rough start after she graduated from college. She was just Angela then. Not wanting to settle down into an 'ordinary life' like her parents wanted, she took off with an older man. The two lived like bohemians in St. Paul, Minnesota. Neither could afford to move to New York City. They both did odd jobs for cash and she dabbled in drugs until one day she encountered a little girl. The little girl looked aghast at her and asked her mother what was wrong with that woman. She wanted to know why Angela looked so dirty and thin. The mother held her daughter close and said, "We are all destined for great things, but sometimes it takes people a little longer to get there." The little girl then walked up to Angela, gave her a dollar and said, "I hope you find your way soon. Good luck."

"Everything in my world looked so different after that. What was once chic and trendy, became trashy and disgusting. My friends, who I thought were hip because they treaded outside of the lines and snubbed their noses at being conventional, I saw as unbathed and pitiful. They wasted so much of their potential doing drugs and partying. Or just hanging out. Years of their lives went by and they had absolutely nothing to show for it. I decided that I didn't want that for myself."

"Bad girl turned good."

"I've never considered myself a bad girl. Although I did put my parents through a lot."

Richard smiled pleasantly. "Your story is not unusual. Many people have fallen off the road. Mine is a little different."

"They are all different. Even if it sounds the same, each person has his own life, his own choices. Your path is your own no matter how many other footprints are on it."

"I can respect that."

"I've told you my story. What is yours?"

Richard rolled his tongue in his mouth as he considered revealing himself to this stranger. For years he debated the issue in his head. At times he felt ashamed for even considering it, but mostly he felt as though he had no other choice. He was a determined man. He had expectations. Plans. What would become of them if he deviated too far from them? He made a choice and he stood by it. But now. What if he was wrong? He dared not consider the notion for too long.

"I regretted having a family," Richard blurted out.

"The kids?" Dr. Withers asked, seeking clarification.

"The wife, the kids, everything."

"Why?" Dr. Withers asked in a tone that did not judge.

"I wanted to be successful and I felt that having a family was getting in the way of that. When I was at home, all I could think about was work and when I was at work, I felt that I should feel sad that I was not with my family."

"Did you feel sad?"

"No, but I dreading going home. I knew that Evelyn was going to nag me about working so much so I worked more to avoid her."

"And the kids?"

"They were great kids. Are, great kids, but I wasn't ready to be a father. I wasn't ready for all of the responsibility. They required so much. I thought, OK, things would get better once the kids started walking and got out of diapers. But no. It doesn't end there. You have to help them brush their teeth. They never do what they are supposed to do. I don't know how many times I had to repeat myself. Bedtime is an event all in itself. Their rooms! Oh, their rooms! I could set off a bomb in a densely populated city and it would still have less destruction than they create. Homework, school, activities, playdates, it just never ends. I felt like I was going crazy. And when I pulled back, of course Evelyn was there busting my ass about slacking off. I just decided that I didn't want to do it anymore. I know that makes me a bad person, but I thought the kids would be better off not having a father that hated life."

"How did the kids respond to the divorce?"

243

"They seemed fine. I would pick them up and see them so it's not like I wasn't around at all. I know I could have been around more, but…"

"How would you describe your relationship with your kids?"

"Not perfect, but it's not horrible either. We don't scream and fight like Evelyn and Gwen."

"What do you talk about with Gwen?"

Richard opened and closed his mouth a few times before saying anything. "Not much. The weather and school. She has grown quieter over the years. I guess I can't blame her. I don't make myself available much."

"Are you satisfied with your current relationship with your children?"

Richard shook his head.

"What would you change about it?"

"I wouldn't know where to begin. It doesn't matter anyway. The past is the past. You can't change the choices you made. Best learn to live with them."

"Are you saying that you made a mistake concerning the relationship with your children?"

Forlorn filled Richard's words. "I was wrong. I should have never left. Or at least, I should have made an effort to do more. I missed out on so much of their lives. They are my children and I don't know that much about them. That hurts."

"Why not do something about it?"

"What? I've already set the pace. I can't turn around and act like the father that I should have been years ago. Sometimes Gwen will call me to complain about her mother. Even if she has a valid complaint, I can't help but to think, "Who am I to say anything to Eve about this? She is the one who has been in the trenches with them. She put in the time and the effort to raise them." And so I mumble something to her about waiting it out."

"So you just give up?"

"You can't give up something that you didn't start."

"To each their own. However, I hope you reconsider. That way, in the end, you at least know you tried. There can be no regret in that." Dr. Withers shifted in her chair. "Do you remember the last conversation you had with Gwen?"

"Yes. We were at a restaurant. One that we go to all of the time."

"Who chose the location?"

"I don't remember. We always go there."

"What did the two of you talk about?"

"The usual: school, weather, memories from when she grew up."

"Did she appear agitated or different in any way?"

"No."

Dr. Withers peppered Richard with questions about his relationship with Evelyn and Keith. Richard had the utmost respect for Eve although Eve probably would not describe it that way. While she is not as upset with him as she was around the time of the divorce, she still nags him from time to time about his relationship with his kids.

Richard echoed comments about Keith and Gwen. Keith wasn't high on his list of favorite people, but the two respected each other and Richard felt that Keith was a sufficient stepfather.

"You don't mind how Keith treats Gwen?"

"I don't condone his methods. He is an adult and he should know how to curb his tongue, but Gwen can be a bit high strung. Things are exacerbated when they go through her head."

Richard walked slowly to Gwen's room after his meeting with Dr. Withers. His mind raced over what he revealed to her. Part of him was glad to have finally told someone and another part of him wished that he could take it all back.

Dr. Gupta was in the room talking to Evelyn when Richard entered. Katie and Oliver were standing nearby listening intently. Keith was sitting on one of the chairs. Dr. Gupta stopped talking when he saw Richard.

Evelyn smiled at Richard. "She is recovering remarkably well. Dr. Gupta is ready to take her out of the coma."

"As I was telling Mrs. Jess-"

"Dr. Jess," Keith interrupted.

"Mrs. Jess is fine," Evelyn added.

Dr. Gupta smiled uncomfortably before resuming, "Gwen has shown great improvement. I feel that it is time to scale back the medication so that she can wake up."

"Is everything fine?"

"We won't know until she wakes up, but we are very optimistic. She is young and in general good health. Her body is healing remarkably well."

"How long will it take for her to wake up?"

"Once the drugs wear off. That can take several hours."

Dr. Gutpa answered a few other questions before sending in the nurse to begin the process. Evelyn stood next to Gwen and held her hand. Everyone else in the room sat in anticipated silence.

"Do you think Gwen will be committed when she wakes up?" Oliver asked, breaking the silence.

Evelyn turned awkwardly toward her son. "Why do you say that?"

"If she tried to commit suicide then they will have to commit her right?"

"*If* she tried to commit suicide then the psychologist will discuss a treatment plan. The treatment may include a stay at a facility." Evelyn scrutinized Oliver's face. "Do you now believe that she tried to commit suicide?"

Oliver filled his lungs with heavy air that pained him.

"Oliver?" Richard said impatiently.

"I just found out that Greg, my teammate who she has a crush on, kissed her."

"You think she did this over a kiss?" Evelyn said incredulously.

247

Oliver continued, "He turned her down. Told her that he wasn't looking to be in a relationship. Fast forward and he gets Vivienne pregnant."

"Who is Vivienne?" Evelyn and Richard asked simultaneously.

"A girl at school who has been bothering Gwen since forever."

"I thought that stopped," Evelyn said with guilt.

"Mom, please, let me finish. Gwen found out about the pregnancy on the day of the incident. She became enraged and stormed out of the school. Then she ran home."

"And she climbed that tree," Evelyn said finishing Oliver's story.

Everyone in the room looked at Gwen as they tried to imagine the anguish she felt as she bolted down the sidewalk, sans coat, her eyes rapidly filling up with despair. With no one at home to support her, she feverishly climbed the tree and with life looking so bleak and she feeling so raw with pain, she let go.

Chapter Seven
We're Not In Kansas Anymore

At around 3 am the next morning, Gwen's eyelashes fluttered. Then a hand moved.

Evelyn lifted her head from the side of Gwen's bed. Her hand was holding one of Gwen's. She thought she felt Gwen's hand move - that's what woke her up - but she wasn't sure. Gwen's eyes were closed and she wasn't moving. Evelyn looked around to see if anyone else noticed anything, but there was no one there. Everyone else left just after midnight with instructions for her to call when Gwen woke up.

Evelyn looked back at Gwen hoping to see some sign that she was waking up. Gwen's chest gently went up and down. Then her eyelids fluttered again. Evelyn leaned in closer to see if she was seeing things.

"Gwen," Evelyn called out. "Gwen."

Gwen did not respond.

Evelyn put an ear to Gwen's mouth. Nothing. She moved back feeling slightly discouraged, but then pulled back one of Gwen's eyelids. Gwen immediately snapped it shut and winced. Evelyn's body froze in excitement as she waited for more movement from Gwen.

Slowly Gwen's eyelids blinked open. Evelyn put her hands over her mouth to keep from screaming. Noticing Evelyn's actions, the nurse on duty hurried in.

"She's waking up." Evelyn said to the nurse.

The nurse checked Gwen's vitals then stood next to her and called her name. Gwen responded on the third repetition.

"What?" Gwen said groggily.

"Oh, my baby," Evelyn exclaimed.

The nurse smiled and continued to ask Gwen simple questions such as how old she is and when is her birthday. Gwen successfully answered all questions.

By morning, Gwen was fully awake and surrounded by all members of her family. Everyone was smiling and cautiously asking how she was feeling. No one dared mention the events that landed her in the hospital. At least not until Dr. Withers entered the room.

Dr. Gupta had given Dr. Withers the green light to move forward with her evaluation of Gwen after running through a series of tests and determining that Gwen did not suffer any lasting injuries that left her brain damaged. By evening, Dr. Withers was ready to begin. The room was cleared.

The family ate nervously in the hospital's cafeteria while they waited for Dr. Withers to evaluate Gwen.

"Everything will be fine," Keith said to Evelyn while he rubbed her back. "Either way this goes, she has the support she needs."

"If that were true then she wouldn't be in this predicament in the first place," Evelyn snapped. She immediately apologized upon seeing Keith's stunned reaction. "I'm just tried and scared."

"I know," Keith said accepting Evelyn's apology.

"When are you going to tell Dr. Withers about this guy, Greg, and the girl he got pregnant?" Richard asked.

"As soon as she completes her examination of Gwen. I assume Gwen will tell her. But it will be a bigger problem if she doesn't"

"How is that?"

"Because that means that she is not ready to face the problem, which makes recovery that much more difficult."

"We will all be here for her no matter what," Katie added.

"I know. Thank you."

At that moment, Greg entered the cafeteria with a bouquet of flowers in his hand. He spotted Oliver then headed in his direction. Oliver stood up when he noticed Greg a few feet away.

"This is not a good time," Oliver said as he walked over to cut Greg off.

"I just wanted to do something. I can't help but to feel responsible for this."

"I'm sorry, who are you?" Evelyn asked with a twisted face.

"Ma'am, I'm a teammate of Oliver's. I just wanted to come down and show my support in this difficult time." Greg displayed the flowers in his hand. "I brought some flowers for Gwen."

"Thank you. That is very nice of you…"

"Greg."

Evelyn mouthed his named silently. "Oh, well, it is very thoughtful of you to come down here and bring these flowers."

"Yes, but now it is time for you to go," Keith said rudely.

"I'm sorry. Am I interrupting? I was hoping that I would get to see Gwen."

"I don't think that will be a good idea," Evelyn said before Keith could manage to say anything else. "I will give her the flowers and let her know that you stopped by."

Greg looked around at all the faces staring at him unpleasantly. He put the flowers on the table and was about to leave when he turned around. "I'm sorry for what happened to Gwen. I don't know what Oliver told you, but I did not lead her on. Yes, I was wrong for kissing her, but I let her down gently. I swear I did."

"Yeah, after you made sure to get your rocks off then you went off and impregnated some girl. I'm sure you are a stand up kind of guy," Keith said.

Evelyn interjected, "No one is blaming you, Greg, but this is all rather raw right now. Thank you for stopping by. The flowers are beautiful."

Greg appeared to want to say something else when Oliver put his hand on his back and flicked his head toward the door indicating that Greg should leave. Greg nodded solemnly and the two walked off.

"You were a bit harsh with him don't you think?" Richard said to Keith.

"That prick knew exactly what he was doing. I would think *you* would care more. But hey, that would upset the balance of your universe wouldn't it?"

"What the hell are you trying to say Keith?" Richard said in an angry tone.

"Maybe if you were the father you were supposed to be, Gwen wouldn't be in such a fragile state and none of us would be here. But I guess that would be asking too much of you though wouldn't it?"

"Don't you try to judge me. The hell do you think you are talking to me like your world is so perfect. How many times has your daughter been to rehab?"

"You're right, my life isn't perfect. My daughter has made mistakes. Plenty of them. But I was right there with her through each and every one of them. I never turned my back on her. I never made her feel unwanted."

By now Keith and Richard were standing up and yelling at each other. Other patrons in the cafeteria stopped eating their food and began gawking at the two grown men. Evelyn and Katie tried to calm them down, but nothing seemed to work. The two were escalating. Oliver returned and sternly ordered them both to stop.

"We are not doing this," Oliver said looking at Keith and Richard. "I'm sure that one can say we all played our part in what happened to Gwen. None of that matters. What matters now is moving forward and we can't do that if we are bickering at each other. Maybe if we were a better family, a more conclusive family, Gwen would not be in this situation. I'm about to go upstairs to see how my sister is doing and to find out what I can do to help. If neither of you is interested in that then you both need to stay down here."

Keith and Richard stood in embarrassed silence. Katie reached over and affectionately squeezed Oliver's arm. Evelyn hugged him and whispered, "Thank you," in his ear.

Dr. Withers was exiting Gwen's room as the family approached.

"Ah, just in time," Dr. Withers said as she closed the door.

"How did it go?" Evelyn asked.

"Interesting."

"Interesting good or interesting bad?"

"I think we should go into my office and talk."

Evelyn and Richard took a seat in Dr. Withers' office while the others headed back to Gwen's room. Dr. Withers waited until the two were situated before she started speaking.

"I'd be lying if I said I wasn't nervous," Evelyn said as she shifted.

Richard smiled at her and looked uneasily at Dr. Withers. Dr. Withers gave each of them a pleasant, yet undecipherable expression.

"Let me first start by saying that Gwen insists that she did not try to commit suicide. However, her word is not definitive and could merely indicate that she is not ready to face what she has done. I evaluated Gwen using several factors that we look at to determine the suicidal risk of a patient such as level of hostility, depression, and major life changes. It came up a few times through the interviews that Gwen has been expressing a higher than normal level of anger. She admitted this, but does not know why it is occurring. She has stated that it seems that, lately, a lot of things annoy her to the point of wanting to explode. While this is problematic, it alone is not indicative.

"Gwen has not experienced any recent life changing events that I am aware of." Dr. Withers looked at Evelyn and Richard. Both

254

shook their heads. "And based on my analysis, she isn't depressed. The next logical explanation would be the onset of a psychological disorder."

"Are you trying to say that she is crazy?" Richard asked bewildered.

"My daughter is not crazy," Evelyn added.

"I'm not making a diagnosis," Dr. Withers said calmly. "I am merely pointing to the fact that it needs to be considered. It is common for people who attempt suicide to have exhibited some symptoms of a psychiatric disorder prior to the incident."

"Gwen hasn't," Evelyn insisted.

"Not that anyone is aware of. And, again, I'm not saying that she has a psychiatric disorder. I am saying that it would be imprudent of me to not consider it. Your daughter ran out into the extreme cold without a coat, climbed a tree then jumped. Her story that she simply fell does not make since nor does it explain her actions leading up to it."

"What about Greg and the pregnancy?" Richard asked. "Doesn't that explain her actions?"

"What pregnancy?" Dr. Withers asked while shifting her eyes from Richard to Evelyn.

"I'm sorry," Evelyn said. "I meant to tell you as soon as I saw you. Oliver recently told us that Greg, a boy Gwen has a crush on, apparently a big crush on, kissed her some time ago. Nothing came out of it. He supposedly turned her down gently, telling her that he was not looking for a relationship. Fast forward to the day of the incident, Gwen found out that Greg got Vivienne, a girl who has been bullying her, pregnant. Gwen stormed out of the school, ran home, up the tree, and you know the rest."

Dr. Withers slightly tilted her head back while her mouth made an 'o' shape. "That changes things a bit. Such information can be devastating to a teenager. While suicide is not the usual course of action, it can be if there are underlying issues or if at that time the teenager feels extreme hopelessness. Their hormones are raging at this age and it is hard to get a grasp on things. Sometimes things become too consuming. I think it is best if I meet with Gwen on a daily basis until she is discharged. I can make a determination at that time as to how to proceed from there."

"Are you thinking of having her committed?"

"That is only done in extreme circumstances. As long as Gwen is not an immediate threat to herself then she will be allowed to go home. These consultations will enable me to more accurately determine her state of mind."

"You are all making more out of this than necessary," Gwen said when Evelyn and Richard made it back to her room. The conversation quickly turned to the events of 'That Day.' "I wasn't trying to kill myself."

Evelyn frowned. "We know that you had just found out about Greg getting Vivienne pregnant."

Gwen spoke slowly and clearly, "Yes, I can see how, based on that information and my actions thereafter, you might come to such a conclusion, but you have to believe me when I say that I was not trying to kill myself. Why on earth would I do that?"

"Because you really cared about him and he broke your heart."

"I did care about him and it did hurt when I found out, especially given who the person he impregnated is. I ran out of the school because I was frustrated and I wanted to release that feeling. I wanted to be unburdened."

"And you climbed the tree because…"

Gwen paused. "It made sense at the time."

They all knew that she wasn't telling them something. That she was holding back some vital piece of information.

"Mr. Fletcher said that he saw you hold your arms out before you jumped."

"Mr. Fletcher?" Gwen said incredulously. "Eight-one year old Mr. Fletcher? Did anyone even consider that maybe his eyesight is not that accurate?"

Everyone looked at each other with a bewildered countenance.

"Talk to Marie," Gwen continued. "Since none of you believe me, talk to her. She will tell you."

"I tried," Oliver said. "But I can't find her. I don't know what she looks like."

"Long black hair. She usually wears funky, bright clothes. She is missing the forearm of her left arm, but you may not notice because she frequently wears a cardigan over her shoulders. She ditches school a lot." Gwen sheepishly eyed her mother. "I know." Gwen returned her focus to Oliver. "If she is not at school then you might catch her at her house. She lives on Viola Avenue off Fillmore. I don't know the address, but there is a handcrafted wooden bench on the porch with a large plant in a red pot."

"Can't I just call her?"

257

Gwen frowned. "I can't remember her number. I'm sorry."

"That's fine," Oliver said sympathetically. "I'll check the school again then, if she isn't there, I'll go to her house."

"Try her house first. She will use any excuse to stay home. I'm in the hospital. That would be good enough for her. When you find her, let her know that I'm OK."

"I'll bring her by."

"Thanks," Gwen said with a smile.

Oliver made a right onto Deacon Avenue then another right onto Hill Street. The neighborhood was saturated with small two and three bedroom ranch homes, each decorated with siding that ranged from off white to electric blue. He drove about a half a mile then turned left onto Fillmore. The number of empty lots increased. By the time he reached Viola, the empty lots seemed to have won the battle, save for one sad, lonely house.

Oliver parked in front of the house and got out to survey the area. It was depressing. The branches on the trees were bare and hung limp. Even the grass - what was left of it and not over run with dandelions and weeds - was brown and patchy. Oliver tried to imagine Gwen walking down this street. He visualized her bouncing on the sidewalk, viewing this place as one of potential rather than noticing the neglect. But then he shook his head. Gwen can be optimistic, but not *that* optimistic.

Oliver looked back at the house. "This can't be the place," he thought to himself as he walked up the walkway which was marred by cracks and weeds. On the porch sat a wooden bench and red pot like Gwen said, but the bench was old and worn and far from being described as 'handcrafted.' Also, the plant that probably once thrived in the red pot was now reduced to a dried out stem that would crack

258

at the slightest touch. The front door and windows on the ranch house were covered with wooden planks. Oliver didn't think that anyone lived there, but he knocked on the plank that covered the front entrance anyway.

After about five minutes of knocking on the plank and checking the windows, Oliver went around back, braving the two feet tall brush. An old blue Chevrolet Cavalier sat atop concrete cinder blocks. Oliver sighed when he saw that a wooden plank covered the back entrance as well. However, upon closer inspection, part of it had been pulled off the doorway that it had previously been nailed to, allowing for passage. Oliver slid his hands through a small opening near the bottom edge and pulled back. Carefully, he squeezed inside.

The house was full of dust and spiders, and short on furniture. Oliver walked around, but did not see any indication that Gwen had visited.

Two voices startled Oliver. He turned to see two school aged boys – around nine or ten years old – staring back at him.

"What are you two doing here?" Oliver asked.

The boys looked at each other, then the taller one – by half an inch – spoke up. "You don't own this place," he said with a hint of uncertainty.

"How do you know?"

"Because we've never seen you before and we've been coming here for a long time," said the shorter one.

"Have you seen anyone else here before?"

"What's it to you?" said the taller boy.

"Either you have or you haven't?" Oliver said, sounding frustrated.

"Maybe we have and maybe we haven't. Do you have anything to jog my memory?"

"You want me to pay you?" Oliver said incredulously.

"Just five dollars," the boy said in a compromising way.

"I'm not paying either of you anything. But I will find your parents and let them know that the two of you have been spending your free time in an abandoned building doing really bad things."

"We haven't done anything bad," pleaded the shorter boy.

"That's not what I'll tell your parents."

"You can't do that."

"I can do whatever I want, but I may not if you answer my question."

"Just a girl," the shorter boy blurted out to the taller boy's discontentment.

Oliver stepped in between the two, cutting the taller one out of the shorter boy's line of sight. "What did she look like?"

The boy shrugged. "A girl."

"Did she have skin like me?"

"Yeah, she was black with curly hair."

"Was she alone or with anyone else?"

"Alone. Always alone."

"Always?"

"Yep. We saw her two or three times."

"What was she doing?"

"Nothing really. Walking around talking to herself. One day we saw her staring at the car out back for about five minutes then walk away."

"Are you sure?"

"Yes," the taller boy piped up from behind. "She is weird."

Oliver held his tongue and race out of the building without saying another word. He hopped into his car and raced to the high school – running stop signs, pushing it to make lights and narrowly missing a garbage truck.

The school buses were making their departure as Oliver pulled up and spread his car over two and a half parking spaces. He ran inside pushing his way through the near empty hall to the principal's office.

Mrs. Alvarez eyed Oliver suspiciously as he stood bent over trying to catch his breath. "What's wrong?" she asked.

Oliver's breathing was heavy and his words were incoherent.

Mrs. Alvarez called for her assistant, but Oliver raised a hand to indicate that he was fine. Mrs. Alvarez asked her assistance for a glass of water while Oliver sat down.

"Does this have anything to do with your sister?" Mrs. Alvarez asked.

Oliver nodded his head then took a big gulp of water. "I need to fine a friend of Gwen's. Her name is Marie. I don't know her last name, but she is in the 10th grade. I've tried to look for her myself, but I can't find her. School is out for the day so can you give me her number so that I can call her? Gwen can't remember the number."

"I'm sorry, but I can't give you another student's personal information."

"Please," he pleaded. "It's imperative."

Mrs. Alvarez looked into Oliver's solemn eyes. "I can call the parent and get permission from her."

Oliver flashed a smile of approval.

Mrs. Alvarez scooted toward her computer. "What is the student's name?"

"Marie something. I don't know her last name. I forgot to ask Gwen. I can call her if you need it."

"That's not necessary," Mrs. Alvarez said while typing away. "I can scan first names. She is in the 10th grade correct."

"Yes."

"I don't see her," she said after a few minutes.

"She is a new student. Maybe she isn't in the directory yet."

Mrs. Alvarez stood up to leave and returned with Mr. George who handles admissions. Mr. George stood in the middle of the room with a hand to his chin, "I don't remember a new student by that name. It is possible that we have one, but I am usually good with names. Marie right?"

"Yes, long black hair and she is missing her left forearm."

Mrs. Alvarez widened her eyes. "I maintain the list of all disabled students and there isn't one by the name of Marie."

"Maybe it's a nickname."

Mrs. Alvarez shook her head slowly. "We do not have a student here that has such a disability."

"Maybe she hid it. Gwen said that Marie wears a lot of cardigans to cover up her arm."

"I'm sorry Oliver, but that is just not likely. I don't know what else to tell you."

Oliver sat speechless, his mind racing.

Mrs. Alvarez continued, "We will be on the lookout for this young woman. We do not allow non-students on campus. Should we find her, I will be sure to notify the authorities and your parents."

Oliver wasn't listening anymore. He sat blankly trying to process all of this information.

Evelyn was the only person left in the room with Gwen when Oliver returned. Katie went home to rest and both Richard and Keith had work to do. Oliver walked through the door with an obvious burden weighing on him.

"What's wrong?" Evelyn asked Oliver as he stood by the bed stone faced.

Oliver glanced over at Gwen. She was asleep. "The school doesn't have a record of a Marie in the 10th grade."

"What do you mean? Is she in a different year?"

Oliver shook his head. "There is no record of a girl at school named Marie who is missing part of her arm."

"Maybe Marie is a nickname," Evelyn offered.

"There aren't any girls at the school at all with that disability."

"I-I don't understand. There must be a misunderstanding," Evelyn said, stuttering.

"There's more."

"What do you mean you can't find Marie?" Oliver and Evelyn turned toward Gwen who was wide awake. "She goes to our school. I've seen her. I've talked to her. We have lunch together."

"Do you have any classes with her?" Oliver asked.

"No, but-"

"Then she isn't actually enrolled in the school. She's just a kid hanging around the school," Evelyn said sounding somewhat relieved.

"That's not it," Oliver said.

Evelyn looked grimly at Oliver who peered toward Gwen, but would not catch her eyes. "I went to the house where you said she lives. It's boarded up."

"You must have gone to the wrong house," Gwen asserted.

"No," Oliver said calmly. "There was only one house on Viola near Fillmore. There was a wooden bench and a red pot on the porch like you said. But the place was in disarray." Gwen was shaking her head in disbelief. Evelyn looked horrified. "The doors and windows were all boarded up. There was an old, rusty car out back. I went inside through the back door and the place was empty except for two metal folding chairs."

"She must have moved recently," Gwen suggested. "I can't believe she left without saying anything."

"The place has not been inhabited in years," Oliver said sternly. "There was dust everywhere."

Gwen and Evelyn eyed each other with confusion.

Oliver continued, "I ran into two boys there. They said that they've seen you before. You were always alone."

"Gwen?" Evelyn said in a low quivering voice.

Gwen's mouth moved, but no sound could escape.

"You need to tell Dr. Withers," Oliver said to his mother.

"No, wait," Gwen said, her eyes pleading to Evelyn. "There must be an explanation. I-I…"

Oliver sighed heavily.

"Mom, please," Gwen continued. "I have something to show you." Oliver looked up. "Alone. It will explain my actions that day. It will explain everything. I have been hesitant to tell anyone for fear of how people will look at me, but it is too late for all of that now."

Evelyn's eyebrows reached toward each other on her forehead giving her an apprehensive countenance.

"Please, just listen to what I have to say."

Evelyn nodded then looked at Oliver. He pulled his lips back tightly then left the room.

Gwen began her monologue as soon as Oliver shut the door. "I know this is going to sound crazy, but I need you to just listen to me. Some time ago, I was lying on the floor in my room staring at my lamp. I envisioned the lamp moving. I wanted it to move and so I put all of my energy into making that lamp move. Suddenly it shook and then rose into the air."

Evelyn looked at Gwen with wide, disbelieving eyes.

"I know it sounds crazy, but it is true and I can prove it. I can move something in this room. Like those flowers," Gwen pointed to the bouquet of flowers that were previously in Greg's hands. "Just watch."

Evelyn looked oddly at Gwen as she slightly turned her body to face the flowers that rested on the window sill. Gwen lowered her head a little and bore her eyes deep into the vase. Evelyn nervously watched as Gwen silently stared at the vase for over two minutes. Part of her worried that nothing would happen. A smaller part of her hoped that something would.

Gwen turned to face her mother. Her lips were spread apart in a substantial smile. "Did you see that?"

Evelyn crumbled internally. She clenched her teeth and smiled hard to keep the tears at bay. "That was wonderful sweetie. Absolutely wonderful."

Gwen continued to beam. "I told you."

Evelyn swallowed hard. "How does this relate to you climbing the tree and jumping?"

Gwen sighed. "I was trying to fly. I thought for sure that I could. I was so upset with the baby thing and I just wanted to feel free. I'd tried to fly before, but it never worked. I figured that I had to do what the little birds do and go higher. They don't fly from a safe distance. It is all or nothing with them. Marie agrees with me. We talked about it a lot. It made sense that I should be able to fly. I guess that I can't. But I can move things with my mind. You saw that for yourself."

Evelyn looked into her daughter's bright eyes. They sparkled with glee. It had been a long time since Evelyn saw that look in Gwen's eyes. "Yes, it's all very clear now." Evelyn looked around uneasily. "Well, it's getting late and I want to make sure that you get your rest."

"Do you have to leave?"

"I'll be back bright and early tomorrow. I promise. I love you so much." Evelyn stood up and kissed Gwen on the cheek. "So, so much. I hope you know this."

"I do," Gwen said with an innocent smile.

Evelyn made a b-line for Gwen's room as soon as she arrived home. Oliver called after her when he walked through the door behind her, but she did not respond. Evelyn threw open Gwen's closet. One by one, she pulled down her clothes, boxes and anything else that was on the shelf or hanging up. Then she got on her knees and started digging around in the containers that lined the closet floor. Evelyn stopped when she came across two beer cans attached to plastic rings. She held the beer up. It was the same brand that Keith drinks. Keith complained that someone was drinking his beer. She assumed that it was Katie or maybe even Oliver, but not Gwen. She put the beer aside and continued scouring the closet. When she was finished, she went to Gwen's nightstand.

"What are you doing?" Oliver asked from the doorway. The room was a mess from Evelyn's frantic searching.

"I'm looking for drugs." Evelyn said as she flung open the top drawer and began digging through it.

"Drugs? Why are you looking for drugs in Gwen's room?"

"What else explains what is going on with her?" Evelyn did not look up while talking.

"She's sick, mom. She's not on drugs."

Evelyn did not respond. Oliver walked closer to his mother whose head was darting about with her eyes inspecting every item in the drawer.

"Mom," Oliver said in a louder tone. He kneeled down and grabbed her hands when she didn't answer him. There were two containers of eye shadow in one of her hands: one purple and one green. Tears streamed down her face.

"I don't know what to do," Evelyn cried. "My baby is sick and I don't know how to make her better. How did this happen? Did I do something wrong?"

Oliver grabbed his mother in a tight embrace as she cried. "This isn't anyone's fault. We will get through this together."

≈

Dr. Withers listened intently as Evelyn recited the events from the previous day. She told Dr. Withers of how Gwen's friend Marie was nothing more than a figment of her imagination, how she believes that she has telekinetic abilities, and how when she climbed the tree that day, it wasn't to commit suicide; she was trying to fly like a baby bird.

268

"What's wrong with my daughter?" Evelyn asked.

"She is experiencing hallucinations and grand delusions. Her extreme moods might also be a symptom. It is possible that she is exhibiting symptoms of schizophrenia."

"Are you just throwing that term out there? Or…"

"I will have to evaluate her further, but so far that is what it looks like. I'm sorry, but don't feel like this is a death sentence. With the proper treatment, Gwen can go on to live a near normal life."

"What is near normal?"

"Schizophrenia is not something that can be cured, rather it is managed."

Evelyn rubbed her face fiercely with her hands. "It is going to be OK," Keith said.

"How?" Evelyn snapped "How is it going to be OK?"

"Because we will get through it together."

"Get through what? There is no cure for this. There is no light at the end of the tunnel. It is forever!"

"You are not in this alone," Richard said. "I know it is frustrating, but you are not in this alone."

"Oh, so now you want to join in? She is damn near old enough to move out of the house and now you want to step in and play the caring father? Screw you Richard. You shit. Where were you when she was sitting by the door waiting for you to take her to the father daughter dance? Where were you when she would cry herself in her room because she was upset over something stupid? Huh? Damn it! Where were you?" Evelyn's voice reverberated off the walls.

Keith squeezed her arm, "Calm down."

Evelyn snatched her arm away. "I don't want to! I just found out that my daughter *most likely* has schizophrenia. I think I am entitled to a meltdown." Tears formed in her eyes. "All these years of hard work. Scraping to succeed in my career. Fighting to raise my kids the best way I know how and now I have to deal with this. What kind of cruel world is this? What did I do that was so wrong that made me deserve this? Tell me?" Evelyn screamed at the room, her breathing intense. "Tell me!"

Dr. Withers stood up and walked over to Evelyn. She gently put a hand on Evelyn's shoulder and knelt down next to her. "Receiving news like this is devastating. Your reaction is nothing less than I would expect from a parent, especially one that has devoted so much of herself to her children. Our children require more from us than we could ever imagine. Their pain is our pain. Their triumphs are our triumphs. Their 'I just feel like being grumpy today, so deal with it' are ours as well. We want what is best for our kids and we will do everything possible to help them, to protect them. And if it is something that we can't do, we will find someone who can. But when the problem is not one that can be easily mended, it is understandable to become frustrated. This is a very trying time for you, but you will get through this. I have a support group for parents with children in similar situations. I think that it will be beneficial for you to join. We meet once a week on Thursday evenings."

"I don't want to sit in a circle and hold hands with people while we all cry over our woes."

Dr. Withers was amused. "Not quite the environment we have, but I wish you would think about it. It can be very therapeutic to talk to other people who are going through the same experiences. Some of them can offer advice on different things. And I promise you, we don't sing Kumbaya."

Evelyn laughed unexpectedly. Then her laughter returned to tears. "How is Gwen going to get through this?"

"I'm glad you asked. I have found that a two part treatment has the most success rate for people in Gwen's situation. One part consists of antipsychotic medication. There are a variety of medications we have at our disposal, each with its own side effects. I will work with you and Gwen to find the right prescription that works best for her."

"What kind of side effects are we talking about here?" Richard asked.

"Drowsiness, dizziness, blurred vision, rapid heartbeat, headaches, sensitivity to the sun, changes to muscle movement. There are more, but the side effect we are most concerned with is weight gain because of the threat of diabetes. So her weight will need to be strictly monitored."

Richard furrowed his eyebrows. "I don't understand why you are talking about giving her these powerful drugs when you haven't even diagnosed her yet."

"While I have yet to render a final diagnosis on Gwen's condition, it is clear that she is suffering from psychosis. These medications are used to manage psychosis."

The room was quiet while Dr. Withers waited to for any follow-up questions from Richard. His face went through a variety of positions, but he settled on silent concern.

"It will take some time," Dr. Withers continued, "but soon Gwen's delusions and hallucinations will subside."

"What is the second part of the treatment?" Evelyn asked.

"Psychosocial treatment."

"What is that? I've never heard of it."

"It is a type of talk therapy used to help the patient understand her illness, her behavior, her thought process. She learns about herself and what her triggers are. Most importantly, she learns problems solving skills, coping strategies, and better life management. Due to the adverse effects of the antipsychotics, many patients stop taking them, which puts them on a very dangerous path. Psychosocial treatment helps curb that. Patients learn the importance of taking their medications and get the support they need to continue with treatment."

"Why use the antipsychotics if the side effects are so bad that people stop taking them?"

"The side effects of using the antipsychotics outweigh the effects of not using them at all. I am not a proponent of pumping patients up with pills, especially the younger ones. However, they are important and frequently unavoidable. No one wants to deal with the side effects that come along with medications, but I assure you that it is in Gwen's best interest. She will continue deteriorate without any medication. Also, there are patients that decide to stop taking the antipsychotics because the medicine helps them like it is supposed to, but then they feel as though they don't need it anymore. This causes their symptoms to return. We don't want this to happen to her either." Dr. Withers gave the room time to digest her words before continuing. "My plan is to start her off on a higher dosage in the beginning then wean her down once all of the symptoms of psychosis have subsided. She will be able to stay on a low dosage as long as the symptoms do not reappear. During this time, I would like to see Gwen twice a week."

"So she will be coming home after she is discharged?"

"I don't see any reason why she can't."

"Will she be a danger to herself?"

"As long as the medication takes, she should be fine. Always call if you have any problems. You can have my service page me after hours."

"Will she go onto college? Get a job? Get married and have kids?"

"There is no reason why she can't. As long as she stays on her meds and continues psychosocial treatment, she can live a very fulfilling life."

"One problem," Keith added. "Your patient doesn't think anything's wrong."

Evelyn sat next to Gwen trying to repeat the words in her head. Dr. Withers felt that it was best if the information came from a family member. Someone Gwen is close to. Someone that loves her unconditionally. Someone that Gwen knows will walk through fire for her.

The words floated in her head like a wayward child; defiant and unencumbered by rules. She could not focus properly because every time she looked at Gwen, she saw her beautiful daughter for whom she had so many hopes and dreams. Even though Dr. Withers said that Gwen would be able to live a near normal life, Evelyn could not help but to see it as shattered; soiled by an unwanted mental illness. Her eyes burned. She tried to blink away the stinging pain, but every glimpse of Gwen made it return. Evelyn furtively wiped her nose on her sleeve so as to not alert Gwen to the mood she was trying to mask.

"Why is everyone so gloomy?" Gwen asked.

Evelyn forced out a smile. "I have to talk to you about something sweetie. I don't want you to get upset."

Gwen's expression turned serious. "Upset about what?"

Evelyn took a deep breath and pushed the words out. "You have schizophrenia."

Gwen smile uneasily. "Is this a joke?"

"No, sweetie. You have schizophrenia. You seeing and talking to Marie and thinking that you have telekinetic abilities, those are all symptoms of psychosis."

"I'm not crazy. I think I would know the difference between what's real and what's a hallucination." Gwen looked around the room for support. "I'm not crazy." She eyed Keith. "This is all your doing. You never liked me. You want me committed so that I can be out of *your* house." She turned toward Evelyn. "Mom, please. I'm not crazy. Keith, Keith is making this all up. He is evil. That day, that day in the driveway, when we were all arguing, I saw his eyes. Did you see his eyes? They went white. He is evil. He has the devil in him and he wants to do away with me because I know the truth."

"No, Gwen," Evelyn said, tears breaking free. "None of that is real. Don't you hear yourself? You are sick."

"Dad, please? You believe me don't you? I need you to protect me. Keith has mom under his spell. She will believe anything that he says. He has even convinced her to stay with him even though he has cheated on her. She knows not what she is doing. Be sensible. Help me. Stop him."

"No one is trying to hurt you, Gwen. We all love you and we are here to help you."

"Katie, Oliver, you know me. You know I am not crazy. Tell them."

"Calm down, Gwen," Evelyn said as she tried to hug Gwen. This feat was made impossible by Gwen's flailing arms.

"No. I will not let you send me away. No! No! No!"

Gwen continued to scream and fight anyone who got near her. It took five nurses to hold her down so that she could be given a sedative. Dr. Gupta and Dr. Withers were called in and both agreed to the immediate administration of antipsychotic medications.

Dr. Withers warned that the beginning is usually the hardest part.

Gwen remained unreceptive on her diagnosis. She did not wish to speak to anyone she deemed an enemy. She sat quietly and refused to acknowledge anyone that visited her. Dr. Withers put off Gwen's discharge.

Oliver sat across from Gwen during his visit. He was in the middle of one of his fail proof jokes that used to get Gwen roaring when he stopped short of the punch line and stood up. Gwen instinctively looked up at him.

"I stopped drinking," Oliver said. When Gwen didn't respond, he repeated his statement. "You told me that I had a problem. You were worried and you said that I needed help. I didn't believe you. I told you that I would know if I had a problem. I was wrong. I did have a problem and I didn't know it. I went into a dumpster to retrieve some beer. Even that didn't stop me from drinking. But you know what did? You did. Watching everyone rally around you to try and help you while you insisted that you did not have a problem. Those words burned through me. I heard myself declaring the same thing. But this time, I was on the other side of the fence.

Immediately I understood how you must have felt when you tried to help me.

Oliver walked closer to Gwen. "I wanted to help you, but I knew that I couldn't if I could not first accept that I too have a problem. That night, I went to my first AA meeting. I was nervous at first. I thought people would judge me, but I was wrong. This isn't going to be easy, but I am determined to stay clean. Today is day five of my sobriety. I am proud of myself and I know that you are too.

"Your path isn't going to be easy either, but I will always be there for you. Even if you are not talking to me. We can sit together while you listen to me drone on and on. I will never give up on you. Never." Oliver reached out and placed a small red and yellow diamond shaped pendant on the table attached to Gwen's bed. "Whenever you need me." Oliver turned to leave the room.

"I'm scared," Gwen said in a voice so low Oliver wasn't sure that she said anything at all. "I said I'm scared," Gwen said when Oliver didn't turn around.

"We all are."

"I've tried moving things with my mind, but I can't anymore. At first I was scared that the medication took my ability away, but now I am beginning to wonder if I ever had the ability."

"What does Dr. Withers say?"

"She doesn't know. I don't talk to her."

"You should."

"I know, but can we just talk right now?"

Oliver walked over to his sister and pulled up a chair next to her.

"I feel different since being on the medication."

"Different good or different bad?"

"A little of both. My memories of Marie are very vivid and so I have a hard time believing that she isn't real, but then the other day she showed up in my room. It was in the middle of the night and she was rambling on about some guy she met. A nurse walked by, but didn't seem to care that Marie was in my room at night. I just stared at Marie while she went on and on about this guy. Then she stopped talking and asked me why I was still in bed. She wanted to go out. It clicked at that point that maybe I do have a problem. Maybe she isn't real. This is very difficult to sort out."

"I know this isn't easy for you."

"The worst part is that I was so excited when I thought I had the ability to make things move with my mind. I so wanted to be special. I was tired of not having anything unique about me. Tired of being that boring girl that no one thinks about, the girl that blends in with the wall no matter the décor. Being telekinetic made me special."

"You are special."

"You're supposed to say that."

"No. Your parents are supposed to say that. I'm saying it because I mean it."

Gwen smiled lovingly at her brother then sighed. "So what's next? Do I go to the asylum?"

"You come home where you belong."

"Won't you all look at me differently?"

"Did you look at me differently when you believed I had an alcohol problem?"

"No, but that is not the same."

"Every day I struggle. Some days I wake up and the first thing on my mind is alcohol. I try to convince myself that it will be OK if I just have a sip or two. That is all I need to get through the day. It will help calm my nerves. There isn't anything wrong with that. Some people take medication, I just want a few sips. Just something to take the edge off. Then I have to remind myself that a few sips are never enough. It will lead to a full can then the entire pack. It is not easy."

"How do you manage?"

"One day at a time. I don't worry about tomorrow, I just work to make it through today."

"If I ask you something, do you promise to tell me the truth?"

Oliver tried to read Gwen's face for some clue as to what she was going to ask. "Sure," he said hesitantly.

"You knew that I liked Greg?"

"Yes," Oliver said sounding relieved.

"Did you tell him to stay away from me?"

A lump formed in Oliver's throat. "Why do you ask?"

"You said you would tell me the truth."

Oliver looked down. "Yes, but-"

Gwen sat back.

"Wait," Oliver said. "I had a good reason."

"You were trying to protect me."

"He would have used you. I've seen him go through so many girls and not give them a second thought. I did not want that to happen to you."

"I guess I should thank you. I could be in Vivienne's shoes. I was so wrapped up in the thought of him that I would have done anything he asked." Gwen chuckled. "You know he threw up in my mouth when he kissed me?"

Oliver was disgusted. "That's gross. I don't want to hear about that."

"What is worse is that I wasn't disgusted by it. I was in such awe that he kissed me that it didn't even bother me that I was covered in his vomit."

"That is sad."

"I guess that is what they call love struck."

"More like dumb struck. EW. You have just ruined my appetite for the rest of the day."

Gwen laughed loudly. "I think I ruined mine too!"

≈

"I'm glad you are feeling better," Dr. Withers said warmly. "You look happy and you are talking. That is excellent." It was the first time in a long time that Gwen did more than pick with her fingernails during her sessions with Dr. Withers. "Are you still experiencing the hallucinations?"

Gwen raised an eyebrow. "How am I to differentiate between a hallucination and reality?"

Dr. Withers nodded and wrote down a few notes. "Can you still fly?"

"I never could. I thought so, which is why I was in the tree, but I never actually took flight. Instead I hit the ground." Gwen lifted her left leg which was in a cast decorated with colorful doodles.

"Those are really nice. Did you do all of that by yourself?"

Gwen eyed the various designs on her cast. "No. I did most of it, but my family did some as well. And the nurses and Dr. Gupta. Plus a patient from across the hall. He just happened to be in the vicinity and I didn't want him to feel left out."

"That's lovely. Will I get the opportunity to add something to your cast as well?"

Gwen looked around the cast. "I think there is room near my calf."

"Dibs."

Gwen laughed. "It's always funny when an adult tries to be hip."

Dr. Withers joined in the laughter. "What is wrong with me saying dibs?"

"Only old people say that."

"Oh…well then."

"It's not your fault."

"Thank you. Now, what about side effects from the medication? Have you been experiencing any?"

"I still have diarrhea and I am dizzy sometimes. Plus my right arm has been hurting. I don't know if that is related or not."

"Was it hurting before you started taking the medicine?"

"No. When can I go home?"

"Do you feel that you are ready?"

"Yes. I think so. Do you think so?"

"How do you feel most days?"

"I'm OK I guess."

"Are you happy? Sad?"

"Somewhat happy. But then I remember that I have schizophrenia and I get a little depressed."

"Why is that?"

"Wouldn't you?"

Dr. Withers shrugged. "What is it about having schizophrenia that makes you sad?"

"On TV, people with schizophrenia are always shown as crazy nutcases that run around with foil hats and rambling on about government spying. They are usually unkempt and violent. No one ever wants to be around them. They are shunned by society. Pushed away into a dark slum area where no one has to interact with them else they are herded up like cattle and put into an asylum where they remain in a drug inducted, catatonic state."

"Do you fit that description?"

"No," Gwen said quickly.

"Then why are you allowing it to define you?"

"I'm not, but is that what I will become? Is that what I have to look forward to?"

"As long as you stay on your medications and continue to attend your sessions, everything should be fine."

"But that is no guarantee."

"Nothing in life is guaranteed. You focus on what you can control."

"And the rest?"

"Pray, meditate, leave it to fate, roll dice, do some jumping jacks. Do whatever you need to do to let it go. It is not in your hands. And as long as it is not an impending issue, it need not be on your mind. I can lie in my bed and worry about getting hit by a bus, but what is the point? I'm not even outside."

"But at some point you are going to go outside."

"The point is: spend your energy on things that you can control. Focus on what is within your means. What might happen tomorrow is not within your control. It is nothing more than a possibility. A chance."

"Aren't we supposed to work today to prepare ourselves for tomorrow?"

"You are not going to make this easy are you?"

"Am I supposed to?"

"No, no you are not. I'm glad that you are concerned and you have so many questions. This is a very good sign."

"What would you say if I didn't ask you these questions?"

"Let's not overdo it with the scenarios."

"What about other people's perception of me. Can I worry about that?"

"You shouldn't, but it is human nature to do so. People are always going to make assumptions about you no matter what. All you can do is be true to yourself. Maybe you will prove their assumptions right and maybe you will prove them wrong. Either way, it is not your concern. You cannot control people or their thoughts."

"People will treat me differently because I have schizophrenia."

"Have people been treating you differently?"

"No, but that is here. What happens once I go back home? Back to school? I don't even like to think about it."

"You are nervous that the kids at your school are going to make fun of you?"

"I'm worried that they are going to avoid me because they are scared of me or treat me like I am an exhibit or look at me differently…like my mom does."

"How does she look at you?"

"She looks at me like she is searching for something in my eyes, in my facial expression that will jump out at her. Like she is looking for proof of schizophrenia: a telltale sign. I don't want to be a freak."

"Do you think your mother sees you as a freak?"

"No, but I'm not the same."

"Well, events have taken place. Life isn't what it used to be. Do you think it is fair to expect your mother to revert to the way things were as though nothing ever happened?"

Gwen frowned. "I suppose not, but part of me wishes she could. Part of me wishes that I could rewind time."

"You and the rest of us, but we can't and so the world pushes forward whether we want it to or not. Your mother is worried. She came very close to losing her daughter. That does something to a parent."

"But I am here. I did not die. She doesn't have to treat me like I am so fragile. I won't break."

"It will take time, but your mother will come around. You need to give her time. This affects her as well. It affects your entire family."

"Marie came to my room last night." Gwen spat out the words quickly.

"She did."

"I know she isn't real, but she looks and sounds like everyone else. And right now, she is the only friend I have. Is it so bad that I don't want her to leave?"

"No. Humans need to socialize. It is a major part of how we learn. But you need to socialize with another human and not an illusion."

"Kids have imaginary friends. What is so wrong with me having Marie?"

"Having an imaginary friend can interfere with your personal relationships. Do you want to spend the rest of your life alone talking to yourself?"

"No."

"Then you need to interact with other people. You cannot spend all of your time with a friend who is a figment of your imagination. You are essentially spending time with yourself. There is nothing wrong with that occasionally, but you have to be careful not to let it consume you."

"One day at a time?"

"One day at a time."

EPILOGUE
Sometimes You Have to Stop to Smell the Flowers

It has been six months since I the day I decided to climb a tree in hopes that I could fly. My journey to be free has left me with scars that are not visible to the eye, and yet just as memorable and everlasting. I was in the hospital for just over two weeks before I was allowed to go home. Leaving the hospital and its sanitized, germ-ridden, structured shelters was both liberating and frightening. I was happy at thought of sleeping in my own bed, but was weary of what awaited me there.

My room was a cold replica of how I remembered it when I returned to it for the first time since leaving the hospital. A draft seemed to swim through the air giving me a chill. Everything was the same, but nothing looked or felt the same. I slowly spun around my room wondering if it was always going to be like this.

"It will take time," my mother said as though reading my thoughts. She placed my suitcase on the floor near the door and told me to come downstairs for lunch.

The entire family was at the dining room table when I emerged from my room. The inquiring eyes that I worried about at the hospital looked back at me tenfold. I ate in silence as my mother droned on about how happy she was that I was finally home where I belonged. The subject changed to school and I immediately suggested that I was ready to go back. I wasn't really, but I figured I'd fare better there as I slipped into the background rather than pitied upon as I was at home.

On the morning of my first day back, my mother followed me around the house constantly asking if I was sure that I was ready and reminding me that I did not have to go. I calmly told her that I had missed enough school and did not want to have to go to summer school just to get promoted to the next grade. Besides, Dr. Withers felt that it would be good for me to get back into my normal routine. My mother relented, but not before insisting that Oliver give me a ride.

Most of the students at school didn't take much notice of me as usual. A few took extra glances of me from the corners of their eyes. Some cupped their hands around ears to spread partial information that they stretched and colored. But for the most part it was business as usual and not much was unexpected. Except for when I ran into Comic Book Billy.

I was at my locker when Comic Book Billy tapped me on my shoulder.

"Hey," I said as I turned around.

"William," he said reminding me.

"I remember."

He smiled. "I'm glad your back."

"Yeah, but I have to keep this cast on for a month," I said as I leaned on my crutches and raised my left leg.

"Looks painful."

"Not so much now."

"Mind if I sign it?"

"Sure."

William produced a sharpie out of his folder and bent down. He stood up after a few minutes of writing.

"I'm really glad you are back," he said again.

I smiled, not knowing what to say.

"I had a cousin in your situation."

I thought he was referring to my leg, but then he went on to talk about how his cousin started hearing voices and talking to himself. William was young at the time (8 or 9) and didn't know what was going on. Most of his family shunned his cousin, who was 19 at the time. William's mother would not let him play with his favorite cousin anymore even though they used to play together every day after school. William was devastated. No one would explain what was going on. No one would tell him why he could not play with his cousin anymore. Then one day, a few years later, his cousin was found dead near some trash cans in a gritty part of town. He was alone and destitute.

"He didn't have anyone," William said solemnly. "The people that were supposed to love and care about him the most turned their backs on him. I always worried that he believed that I turned my back on him too. It wasn't true though. I would never do that. But I never got the chance to tell him. You are lucky. You have a family that cares about you and is there to support you."

"Who told you about my situation?" I asked feeling a bit slighted by the invasion of privacy.

"No one. I used to see you talk to yourself at lunch. You would sit alone in the back so not many people noticed you, but I always notice you." William blushed. "I remember my cousin doing the same thing. I was concerned about you, but I didn't know what to say. I just want you to know that I am here for you as well. I know that you have your family, but I am here too."

"Thanks," I said feeling a little uncomfortable.

"Do you think Jeremy will be proud?"

"Your cousin?"

William nodded.

"Of course. Even though you weren't able to tell him yourself, I am sure that he always knew how you felt about him and that you did not turn your back on him."

After that day, William became a good friend of mine. He introduced me to the finer things about comic books. I must admit that I was a little apprehensive at first, but after a while they became as addictive as a daytime soap opera. You know that it is bad for you, but you just can't stop.

Greg resigned to merely waving at me ceremoniously. I assumed that our study sessions were permanently on hold; not that I was interested in resuming them. Vivienne no longer attacked me with her arsenal of words. She was forced to inform her parents of her delicate state. They immediately marched her to the clinic and had the issue eradicated. After the procedure, Vivienne still carried the same enviable qualities that she once flaunted, but she lacked the desire to carry out her attacks. She spent most of her time dutifully listening in class and taking notes. Occasionally, she would even flash a smile my way. We never spoke about what happened that day in the bathroom, but her anxieties about me seemed to have disappeared.

Every Tuesday after school I go to Dr. Withers' office to talk about my feelings. Dr. Withers always laughs when I summarize our meetings such a simplistic way.

My medications had to be altered several times due to the side effects; specifically because the induced diarrhea would not subside. Dr. Withers warned that it could take several attempts before she would be able to reach the correct dosage. I went through vomiting, muscle cramps, and blurred vision before finally settling on occasional dizziness and dry mouth.

Over time my temperament calmed. It made me realize how I was easily agitated before. Anything would set me off and I felt that I had good reason for being set off. Now I just felt silly and ashamed of my behavior.

On Saturday evenings, my mother and I attend a group session with other similarly situated families. My mother made me cry when she stood up in front of everyone and praised me for my bravery and the dignity with which I have carried myself throughout all of this. "You are an amazing person who is growing up to be an amazing woman. I couldn't ask for anything more in a daughter."

Other members of my family attend these meetings as well, just thankfully not as often. There is only so much crying a person can handle.

I've treaded carefully with my father since learning the truth about why he left my mother. And us. It hurts to know that my father saw me as a burden. Even though he now realizes his mistake and is trying to rectify things, I can't unlearn that information. I understand why my mother kept it from me and Oliver for so long and I wish that she was able to exercise more constraint that day. Dr. Withers said that I have to release these thoughts else they risk gnawing away at my progress. Work on what you can control and let the rest go.

Two months after I came home from the hospital, my father called and asked me out to dinner. We tossed around a few restaurants, but somehow ended up at Mancino's. I decided to not to make a big deal out of it, but I stopped my dad when he brought up a funny thing I did when I was five.

"I met a guy at school," I said interrupting my dad's trip down memory lane.

"Did you?" my dad said; his voice filled with worry.

"It's nothing serious. He is really cool and I like him. He is good for me, plus he understands what I am going through."

My dad gave me the typical speech about boys and girls and how he thought I should take my time and make sure he treats me right. I smiled the entire time because it was the first time we were actually having a conversation relevant to my current life and I felt like I had my dad's complete attention. He actually cared and was acting like a dad. I only wish that the little girl who waited patiently for her dad to take her to the school dance could see this.

Oliver came clean to everyone about his drinking, the accident, and getting kicked off the team. He told them that he was attending meetings and was committed to staying sober. My dad considered having a talk with the coach to see if he would give Oliver a second chance, but Oliver wouldn't let him. Oliver said that his actions required consequences else he risked sliding back to his old ways.

A few decent colleges offered Oliver a scholarship and a place on their football team. Oliver respectfully turned them all down. He decided to spend two years at a local community college before immersing himself at a university. But he wasn't going to be alone.

Soon after Katie completed her court ordered community service – for which I learned was for throwing a chair through a

291

dorm window while playing around at a party – Katie received a letter from her school. The board felt that it was in the best interest of the other students if Katie did not return to school. The remainder of her tuition would be reimbursed and her belongings shipped at the school's expense. Keith was livid when he found out. He called the Dean of the school and blasted him on his "inept ability to run a school." The Dean listened professionally to Keith's rant, before finally repeating his stance and hanging up the phone.

Katie wasn't depressed about getting kicked out. She had resolved to do something positive with her life and felt that being at our house would give her the support she needs to stay on track.

Things between my mother and Keith quickly soured. My mother grew increasingly frustrated by all things Keith. I talked to Dr. Withers about this strange phenomenon since, if anything, Keith behaved better than he did before I went to the hospital. He no longer berated me and even offered a few compliments. Dr. Withers said that sometimes when people go through a life changing event they reevaluate their life. What once was a minor inconvenience becomes a deal breaker. Occasionally they move past this period and others times they don't.

Keith moved into a temporary apartment while he and my mother decide how to move forward. I wasn't as ecstatic about it as I thought I would be. Much to my mother's delight, Katie chose to stay with us in the house.

I still see Marie, albeit not as often. No matter how hard I try, I can't stop my heart from jumping from excitement when she appears. I know that she isn't real and that I need to ignore her, but she was an important part of my life and I can't just throw those memories away no matter how fabricated they were. Dr. Withers told me that I am setting my recovery back every time I speak to her.

For weeks I let Marie drone on in the background while acting as if she wasn't there. But then William kissed me and I had to tell her. That was the type of information that she thrived on. Plus, she liked William and was the only one who wasn't warning me that now is not the time to get involved with a guy.

Being diagnosed with schizophrenia isn't the death sentence that I initially thought it was. The connotations attributed to schizophrenia are scary and based on some truth. But there is another side. While I will never be cured and will always be on medication, I know that with the proper care and support from my family, I can live a normal live. I am fortunate and I know this. I wake up every day thankful for what I have. Each day is a gift. While I may not have the ability to fly like the birds, my experiences have given me wings and they will carry me anywhere.

THE END

About The Author

Denise Okonkwo earned her B.S. in Computer Engineering then worked as a software engineer before going to law school. Having previously focused her writing on poems, Denise finally felt capable of composing a novel after acquiring her license to practice. Denise has written several novels. Beguiled is her first published novel.

Denise lives in Illinois with her husband and three active children. She works on her future novels when her family spares her the time.

6251614R00178

Printed in Great Britain
by Amazon.co.uk, Ltd.,
Marston Gate.